RIGHTFULLY

MINE

MORE BOOKS BY CHRISTINE YOUNG-ROBINSON

We Didn't See It Coming

Do What You Gotta Do

RIGHTFULLY MINE

CHRISTINE YOUNG-ROBINSON

More info: miraclewriter4u@aol.com

Dedication

This book is dedicated to my father, Mr. Celess Young. God called him home in the midst of me writing this book. It's been a struggle to complete it, but I did because I know this is what my father would have wanted me to do. Thanks, Daddy, for being one of my biggest inspirations and role models. It's not a day go by that I don't think of you. Love you, Daddy. Rest in Peace.

ACKNOWLEDGMENTS

First and foremost, I would like to thank God for making me a miraclewriter4u.

To my mom, Ruby Young, thanks for always being my other biggest inspiration and role model.

To my hubby, Joseph, thanks for being such a great husband, father, and grandfather.

To my children, Nishika and Rahim, you're my hearts. Thanks, daughter, for two wonderful and smart grandchildren.

To my siblings, Tynetta, Maxine and my twin, Christopher, you're my rock.

My heavenly siblings, Celess Young, Jr., Lonnie, and Charlene, I miss you so much, but I know you're smiling down on me.

To my mother-in-law, Ola Mae Smith, I'll always remember the last words you said to me. "I love you too." Rest In Peace.

To my angel, Mrs. Witherspoon, I miss you.

To the book cover designer, Dynasty's Visionary Designs (Angel Bearfield) Facebook: www.facebook.com/dynastys.coverme "Awesome job."

Thanks, Tynetta Cohen, graphic designer, for my promotional needs. Thanks, Eshana Young-Pierre, graphic designer, for my promotional needs.

Thanks, LaKeysha Thompson, for my book cover T-shirt and personalized tumbler.

Thanks to my beta readers, Kim Wells-Melikian, Mercy Thomas and Barbara Jones. To editors: Thanks, Lataryn Rainey-Perry (Penwork Publishing), for first edits.

Thanks, Charmaine Parker, for the final edits.

Thanks, Joan Dash (my bestie), for always being there for me.

Much love to Marvy Moore, Pamela Williams, Gaye Harper, Victoria McCornell, Minnie Dix, Tia Wright, Nadirah Muhammad, Theresa Lewis, Carol James, Zane, Dr. Maxine Thompson, Ricky Black, Linese Martin, Mary Trayham, JoAnn Howard, Robin Duncan, Vanessa Brown-Hall, Carmen Hampton-Julious, Minnie Dix, LaShanda Shuler, Chante Cole, Faverta Robinson Renetta Pearson, Sylvia Santiago, Jeanell Brown, Sandra Lambright, Gennara Mack, Sheina Garrison-Stewart, Cotasha Campbell, Beatria Moore, Rita and Paul Daniels, Jacqueline Bouvier Lee, Summiya Dash, and Michelle Branch-Howard.

To my family and friends, thanks for your love and support.

Thanks, Eleuthera Book Club, for the wonderful book recommendations and discussions.

To my author-friends, thanks for always showing me love.

Thanks to the bookstores, online vendors, media, and book reviewers.

I'm grateful for the readers whom I've met and look forward to meeting many more in the near future.

I know I may have missed someone, but it was not intentionally.

CHAPTER 1

*A*niyah Powell thought she had hit the jackpot when she had secretly married Jarvis Powell, son of Jarvis Powell, Sr., a well-off banker.

Her history of preying on wealthy men made her father-in-law suspicious of her. Powell, Sr. had labeled her a tramp and not good enough for his son. Even her being the mother of his grandson did not score any points with him.

Fed up with her father-in-law, Aniyah had sprung the news about her marriage to his son during his hospitalization while he was half-sedated on his sickbed. The frown on his face had showed her he was not happy about her news.

Once discharged, her father-in-law had separated himself from her and his own son. He'd cut off all personal contact with them.

With Powell, Sr. unable to no longer run his bank business, he'd retired, leaving his son in charge. He only trusted Jarvis when it came down to overseeing his banks. That was the only relationship that he'd kept with his son. And, it was by phone or email.

Aniyah did not like her father-in-law's decision to cut her off from living in the luxury world of marriage to a Powell—she yearned to live in Lake Murray, South Carolina at the Powell's family home.

Acting in revenge, she and Jarvis had denied him any contact with their two-year-old son, Jarvis III.

While Aniyah slipped on a pair of sandals, it baffled her that her father-in-law had summoned her to visit him. He had instructed her that a driver would wait for her at her home.

Aniyah peeped through the blinds. She spotted a driver standing outside a white limo. Tossing a bag over her shoulder, she dashed out of the house.

When she stepped out of her front door, the sun beamed on her forehead. The driver tilted his hat at her, and then opened the limo door.

Aniyah sat on the plush, beige leather seats. A bottle of white wine was at her disposal. In midday, she poured herself a drink into a crystal wineglass. She sipped it.

"Would you like to hear some music?" the driver asked, eyeing her through the rearview mirror.

"No, Sweetie. I'm relaxing with this drink."

The closer she got to Lake Murray, she sniffed the aroma of the water. Crossing over the dam, she took in the scenic view, miles of water with sunlight beaming onto it. Aniyah smiled. She hoped that meeting with her father-in-law would be a new beginning for her to live the life she yearned to live.

Any other time, she would have dressed in a fitted, shorts outfit, but to seal the deal of getting into the good grace of her father-in-law, she wore a simple sky-blue, A-lined linen dress. It fell a little below her kneecaps. Her eyes were covered with shades. Her lips popped with a soft-pink lip-gloss, in contrast from her usual popping red lipstick.

The driver drove up to a security gate. She watched the guard acknowledge him, and the black wrought-iron gate opened, leading them onto the Powell estate.

She admired the beauty of the palm trees and the carpet of green grass along with the landscaping of beautiful flowers, but when she eyed the enormous-sized brick home, it took her breath away. "This got to be my house. Papa Powell needs one room for his behind to stay in," she mumbled.

Once the driver parked in the paved driveway, he hopped out and opened the door for her.

Aniyah, holding her head up high, felt like a queen. She winked at him. "Thanks. Soon you'll be my personal driver."

The driver tilted his hat once again.

There was no need for her to ring the bell. A woman greeted her at the door, escorting her up a long flight of stairs and down a hallway into a master suite. Then the woman opened the suite door, and with a sway of her right hand, she gestured Aniyah to enter.

The smell of chicken noodle soup absorbed her nostrils. Aniyah's eyes darted at her father-in-law, sitting in a cranberry-colored leather recliner and slurping noodles. It had been two years since she had seen him. She noticed his tired face. His grayish hair had thinned.

Her eyes lit up when she noticed he wore a nasal cannula. The plastic tube was wrapped over his ears. Two prongs fitted into his nostrils. Her eyes were drawn to the oxygen tank on the floor.

Jarvis never mentioned his papa needed oxygen to breathe. Does he know about this? she wondered.

Powell, Sr. looked up at her. In a grumpy tone, he chuckled. "Trying to dress like a lady for once in your life?"

Aniyah puckered her lips to strike back at him. Instead, she squeezed her lips together, walked over to him, and hugged him.

Powell Sr. pushed her away. He ordered, "Get off me with that phoniness. Go sit your tail down."

Before Aniyah did as he'd asked, she strutted through the French doors that led to a private balcony and screened-in deck. She stared into the waters of the lake. Taking a deep breath, she turned around and went back inside. She took a seat in one of the curved-back swivel chairs at the foot of the king-sized, cherrywood bed.

With one leg crossed over the other, she asked, "Are you ready for my family and me to move in here with you? I see you might need our help."

"That will not happen. I've plenty of staff to take care of me."

When Aniyah heard there was no chance of her living in the Powell home, she barked, "What the hell you call me here for?"

"The nasty tramp has revealed herself." He coughed while he laughed.

Aniyah jumped up. "I don't have time for this."

"The only thing I need is for Jarvis to divorce you. He

and my grand-heir can come live here. How much will it cost for you to get lost? Go find another powerful man to sponsor your dreamy fancy lifestyle."

Aniyah stormed toward him. "Have you forgotten? He's not your son. His blood is a Houston."

"I raised him from a baby. His heart and soul will forever be a Powell—not a Houston."

Jarvis Powell, Sr. had never fathered a child. He wanted an heir to carry on the Powell name. When his friend, Rupert had impregnated one of his mistresses by the name of Sina, she delivered a baby boy. Rupert had manipulated her to sign over their son. He granted his friend's wish and gave Powell the baby. Powell gave the baby his name, and he raised him like a businessman. Jarvis, Jr. wore suits at a young age.

Aniyah tossed the tray from his lap onto the floor, spilling his soup. Snatching the nasal cannula from his nose, she argued, "See, I'm trying to change my ways. I don't understand why you won't let me. I served my time for that petty crime." Aniyah flung her arms. "It's called a past."

Aniyah was born Rosie Aniyah Sanchez. Her Mexican mother, Julia, raised her in Cancun, Mexico. The only thing she knew about her father was that he was African American. She was a product of a one-night stand of her mother and a tourist; she did not even know his name.

At the age of sixteen, like her mother, Aniyah had met a tourist named Danny who had charmed her by paying her to show him around Cancun. She'd thought this was a better way for her to make money than watching her mother and her mother's only sister, Tessa, work domestic jobs. Happy to be with Danny, Aniyah ran away from home with him to Atlanta, Georgia. She loved the attention he gave her and she'd hungered to live a better life. It would give her the opportunity to bank her money to make a better life for her and her Sanchez family.

When she arrived in Atlanta, all was great between her and Danny until he told her his job had laid him off. Then her life went downhill. Danny had introduced her to his so-called friends, whom turned out to be escort clients, forcing her to have sex with them for money to hand over to him. She worked for Danny until he met another girl to replace her and threw her out on the streets. Aniyah wanted to return home but was too embarrassed to face her family. Aniyah started her own escort business, going to nightclubs to entertain clients until a nightclub owner set her up with a major married client, Rupert Houston of Houston Commercial Construction Company based in South Carolina. She learned fast that Rupert was the man whom her mother's only sister, Tessa, had worked for years ago, impregnated her, fired her, and sent her back to Mexico, only for her to lose the baby.

Aniyah hungered for money. She became exclusive to Rupert. She left Georgia and made Lake Murray, South Carolina her home, living in one of his properties until like Danny, he became tired of her and forced her out on the streets. To get back at Rupert, Aniyah had convinced him she was his daughter from her Aunt Tessa, getting him to add her in his will. All worked in her favor. Rupert and his wife passed away on the same day. Aniyah inherited their estate until his youngest daughter, Kenley, discovered that Aniyah was a fraud. Kenley and her two sisters, Noelle and Milandra, got back their inheritance. Aniyah landed in prison for the crime.

Powell snatched the nasal cannula from her hand and placed it back into his nostrils. "You may have gotten your hands on my buddy, Rupert's money, but you won't get your paws on mine."

"I don't want your money," she lied. Then she spoke her truth. "I love your son."

She wondered, if he would ever forgive her for trying to manipulate funds from his friend.

"Never will I claim you. Now pick up the mess you've made."

Aniyah kicked the tray under the bed, "I'm not the one to play with." She snatched the cannula again from his nostrils. "This house will soon belong to me and my family."

Losing his breath, her father-in-law coughed. Aniyah saw him gasp and she jammed the cannula up his nostrils.

"Never call me again," she said.

Powell, Sr. hit a button on a device, contacting his staff.

"Yes, Mr. Powell," the woman answered over an intercom.

"Come throw this tramp out of my house."

"You're going in a nursing home sooner than you think." Aniyah headed out of the room, bumping shoulders with the woman.

Powell, Sr. roared, "Throw that tramp out in the road."

Aniyah walked out of the Powell home and headed to the limo. She presumed the driver would get out of the limo and open the door, as he'd done earlier, but that did not happen. She noticed that he was busy talking on his phone and banged on the window.

"Open this darn door for me." She tried to open the door for herself. It was locked. "Take me the hell home."

The driver put his call on hold. He rolled down the passenger front window just enough for her to hear him. "Sorry, but Mr. Powell told me to not move this limo."

"That jerk got me here. He's gonna see to it I get back home."

"Sorry, Ma'am, I wish I could take you. Boss' orders. I'm to stay parked right here." The driver rolled the window up.

Aniyah banged her fist against the pane. "You'll be the first one I'll fire when I move in here."

She headed back to the front door, turning the knob. She discovered it also was locked.

Pressing the bell, she yelled. "Open this doggone door. You creep. Tell your driver to take me home."

After several attempts, and no answer, she gave up on any response from her father-in-law. She pulled out her cell phone to call for help. She had not shared with her husband of his father's request for her to visit him. Not to disrupt his day, she counted on her girlfriend to come to her aid.

"Hey, Nellie, I need a ride. I'm in Lake Murray. Papa Powell's house. Come pick me up."

"You're in luck. Roy and I decided not to go shopping today," Nellie said, speaking of her boyfriend. "Aniyah, I thought you couldn't go there?"

"It's a long story. Please come for me."

"That man will not let me in the gates."

"I'll meet you there."

Aniyah took off her low-heeled pump sandals. The hot pavement heated her bare feet. She skipped on the grass. To keep from getting angrier, she focused on the beauty of the landscaping. When she reached halfway to the entrance, the sprinkler heads popped up. The water soaked her dress, yet it cooled her off. She ran onto the paved road.

She bellowed, "You old fart. You did this on purpose."

Aniyah heard laughter. The security guards, inside the entrance booth, got a kick out of watching her.

With her hair stringy in her face, she fussed at them, "I'm getting rid of all of you. Just wait and see."

One guard responded, "You wish."

The other guard opened the gates. Aniyah slipped on her sandals and strutted through them. The gates closed once she made her way out. She turned, looking back at her father-in-law's castle.

"Papa Powell, it's just a matter of time before you have no choice but to bow down to me.

CHAPTER 2

*R*upert and Alana Houston had raised their three daughters in a loving luxury home. They saw to it that Kenley, Noelle and Milandra had all the finest things. The sisters had enjoyed spending time with their mother. Their father was different. He was the breadwinner of the family. He stayed working or having ex-marital affairs. However, Rupert was protective of his wife and daughters. No man was good enough for his girls.

The sisters had never dated until after their parents' death. Kenley never married. The men, the other two sisters married, would never have been their father's choice for them. Noelle married Sid, their limo driver, and Milandra married Nolan, the owner of a moving company.

Curiosity brought two of the Houston sisters to the home of Powell, Sr.

Kenley and Noelle did not understand what Powell, Sr. wanted with them. However, the oldest sister, Milandra, who joined them, was quite aware of why he had summoned she and her sisters to his home. She had kept them in the dark.

With Milandra leading the way, the sisters strolled in one by one taking a seat in the curved-back swivel chairs, covered in gold-leathered fabric, resembling a set of identical triplets. The room was lit up from the sunrays that beamed through the opened French doors.

Milandra, dressed in a white linen sundress, patted the sweat from around her neck with a white handkerchief, "Let's get down to business."

"It's Friday. No brain work for me," Kenley said, once she finished reading a text message from her boyfriend. "I have things to do."

After attending college for graphic design, Kenley worked for the Houston Commercial Construction Company in the advertising department, while her sister, Milandra had educated herself to take over as CEO with Noelle as her vice president.

"Hush, Kenley. Give Mr. Powell time to speak," Milandra said.

Powell, Sr. propped up on two pillows, coughed, letting an unlit cigar fall from his mouth onto the bed. The nasal prongs tickled his nostril. He yanked it from his nose.

"You can't be still smoking cigars with breathing problems?" Noelle wondered.

"Nah. It soothes me." Mr. Powell chuckled.

Noelle fanned herself. "You scared me for a moment."

"Please get to the point, why am I here?" Kenley blabbed.

"Aniyah was here earlier," he said.

"What does that have to do with us?" Noelle wondered. "She's no concern of ours."

"She thinks she has the right to live in my home. I

worked hard for this place. We need to get rid of her for good," he said, referring to his daughter-in-law.

"Speak for yourself. She's not in my life," Kenley said.

"The tramp tried to get your daddy's money after he died," Powell, Sr. argued.

"Aniyah served her time for it," Noelle said.

Throughout the state of South Carolina, Aniyah had a bad reputation of a woman who preyed on the wealth of powerful men.

"I agree. She needs to vanish," Milandra said.

"As long as she's not bothering me, I'm good," Kenley added.

"She has done nothing else to bring harm to us or our half-brother. Or has she?" Noelle wondered.

Powell, Sr.'s face turned red. "Jarvis is my son. I raised him. He's a Powell," he barked.

"I agree, Mr. Powell. I'll never claim him as a Houston," Milandra said.

"I'm with Noelle. No matter what, Jarvis is my brother," Kenley said.

Milandra changed the subject. "Back to Aniyah. She's parading around town like she's a part of the elite society."

"Yes, she is. Jarvis' weak self had to marry her. I wish he were here. I'd slap him with this oxygen tube." Coughing several times, Powell, Sr. took a sip of cold water.

"He loves her," Noelle said.

"She doesn't love him. Greed is what she loves," Milandra retorted.

"Maybe she does. She has Jarvis' baby. Maybe this has

helped her to change her ways," Noelle said.

Milandra argued, "I can't believe she has gotten to your brain."

"I'm not saying I want to be friends with her, but people can change," Noelle responded.

Kenley jumped up out of the seat. "I'm not wasting my time on Aniyah. I'm outta here. I have a life besides trying to dissect a villain."

"Sit down," Powell, Sr. roared. "I have a plan to get rid of her."

Kenley placed her hands over her ears. "Sorry, Mr. Powell, no disrespect, but I don't want to hear it. I'm out." Kenley scurried out of the room.

"Kenley Houston. Get your rear back here," Milandra demanded.

Noelle stood up, brushing her linen white pants. "I'm leaving too. I want no parts of this mess."

"Go ahead," Milandra said, "Turn your back on being a real Houston."

"Bye, Sister," Noelle said.

No longer than it took for Powell, Sr. to clear his scratchy throat, they left Milandra alone with him.

"I don't understand my sisters. It's the men in their lives that have turned them from being a Houston into someone else."

"You're still your father's daughter. You're the chosen one. You wanted to add them in. I see it won't work."

"I'm glad you revealed nothing. They might've spoiled your plans."

"Rupert would be proud, you let no one walk over you."

Milandra stood by his bedside. She grabbed his hand.

"I'm grateful we can do business."

"I'm getting weaker and weaker each day. Your strength has put me at peace."

With watery eyes, it broke Milandra's heart about the hurt the old man felt of not having a daughter-in-law he could be proud of.

Months ago he had summoned her to his home. He lectured her with words of revenge that took things to another level.

In a squeaky tone of voice, Milandra said, "Are you certain this is what you want?"

"The Powells are like the Houstons. We stand strong to the love of what's ours."

Milandra tossed her arms around his neck, showing him love. Then she placed the nasal cannula into his nostrils.

"You can rest. I'll handle things from here on." She chuckled. "Here's your cigar." Milandra placed the unlit smoke between his lips.

With watery eyes, Powell, Sr. said, "Get on it quick. That tramp can't move in on the money I self-made."

She kissed him on the forehead. "No worries. Your plans are in good hands.

CHAPTER 3

*R*eturning from a business trip, Jarvis Powell Jr. drove up to the entrance of his childhood home. It was time he made another effort to visit his father. They had not had one-on-one or face-to-face time with each other in a long time. They communicated by text messages and phone calls only for the family business. Jarvis understood his father was a man that held grudges.

A security guard greeted him at the gate. "Hello, Jarvis. Long time no see."

Jarvis smiled, enhancing the deepness of his childhood scar that was on the left side of his face. It went from his chin to his lip. He was accidentally cut during an argument between his parents. "Good to see you too. Could you let my dad know I'm here?"

Jarvis watched as the guard did as he requested. Once he hung up, he said, "Mr. Powell asked that you call him from your own phone."

"Thanks." Jarvis sat still while he contacted his father. He saw the guard waited to get the okay whether to open the gates.

Powell Sr. answered, "Jarvis, are you here to give me

good news?"

"Dad, I haven't seen you in months. Can we please come to some kind of agreement with our father-and-son relationship?"

Powell, Sr. took a deep breath. "The only way you'll step back into this house is if you're here to tell me you're done with that tramp."

"Dad, you're taking this too far. Aniyah wants nothing from you."

"You're as crazy as her and your mother."

"Please don't mention my mom. Respect the dead."

Jarvis thought of his single mother, Sina. He cherished the last days he'd had with her. He had been by her bedside at the retirement community where she had resided in a two-bedroom garden home. Sina passed away with Jarvis not being on good terms with his father. She had considered Powell, Sr. an evil jerk.

Out of respect for his mother and her wishes, Jarvis never shared with his father or Aniyah that she had given him ownership of her old two-story home and her garden home. They presumed that his mother's property had gone to the state. Sina wanted him to have the joy of having something of his own.

Powell, Sr. blasted in his ears, "Are you here to tell me you're divorcing the tramp?"

Jarvis sternly said, "Dad, no name calling. Aniyah and I are solid."

The call ended.

The security guard never received orders to open the gates. It left Jarvis no choice but to put his vehicle in reverse and leave.

***

Jarvis sold the penthouse that was once his and Aniyah's love nest before marriage. He moved their family into a 2,500-square-foot, two-story home.

From a long day of work, he could not wait to see his wife and son. He opened the door from the garage to enter his home. Jarvis locked eyes with his wife's sparkling brown pupils. She was dressed in a midriff spandex top, with her tummy exposed to show off her diamond navel ring. He admired the low-hipster, spandex shorts that exposed her tanned cheekbones.

His eyes lit up when she fell into his arms. They wetted each other's lips with a juicy kiss.

"Aniyah, you're my world." He looked over her shoulder, ready to hear the giggles and paddling feet of his son. Instead, Jarvis III was nowhere in sight. "Now where's that kid of ours?"

"He's already asleep."

"Lot of running around at school."

"Plenty of alone time for us. That's if you're not too tired."

Aniyah brushed her hand against his crotch. Instead of going into the house, he pulled her down the two steps into the garage, leaning her against the front bumper of his vehicle. He watched his wife take off her top and slip out of her bottoms.

His member hardened.

While he kicked off his shoes and freed himself of his clothing, Aniyah hopped on top of the hood, resting her back on the windshield and summoned for Jarvis to join her.

Jarvis crawled on top of the hood. He rested his muscular body on top of hers. He smothered her lips, while he entered her passage, stroking her with force. They both moaned from the pleasure of each other's body. It did not take long before they came to a mutual explosion of satisfaction.

Off of his wife, with sweat dripping down his face, Jarvis rested next to her. "So how was your day, Mrs. Powell?"

Aniyah laughed. "It started crazy. But you, Mr. Powell, made it steamy."

Jarvis felt her tongue glide up the side of his face.

She whispered, "How was your day?"

"Great, until I tried to visit my dad."

"How did it go?"

"He didn't let me through the gates. I didn't comply to his wishes."

"Let me guess. To get rid of me. He's a creep."

"No name-calling," Jarvis told her. "So you say your day started out crazy. Anything I should be concerned with?"

She stroked his member. "It's perfect now. Take care of me one more time."

Jarvis rolled back over on top of his wife, giving her another round of passionate lovemaking

CHAPTER 4

*T*he Houston Estate, one of two family properties of the Houston sisters, was remodeled after their parents' tragic death. Their parents had died a few years ago from a heart attack on the same day. The quarters where workers once lived no longer existed. The workers traveled daily to the estate premises. Unless the Houstons hosted a family event, it was the only time Milandra opened the doors to the quarters for their overnight stay. Kenley and her long-time boyfriend, Pete, made residence in one. Milandra lived in the main house, while Noelle settled to live in the family's second property, the Houston Villa.

On the grounds of the Houston Estate, spending time on the tennis court, Milandra stood across the net from Noelle. With her legs spread apart, Milandra held her tennis racket up in the air, ready to receive a serve from her sister. As soon as the ball came to her, she swung her racket hitting it back to the other side of the court. Noelle slammed the ball back at her. It took a few seconds before Noelle missed it on Milandra's return to her.

"I told you I'm the best player in the family," Milandra bragged.

Noelle clapped back, "You only got lucky. We'll see who gets the next point." She wiped her forehead with the back of her hand.

Kenley argued, "I don't care which one of ya'll win. It's too hot to be out here. I'm being tortured. Why am I here?" She sat on the ground on the sideline of the court, dressed in the same white skirt and cami tank top as her sisters.

Milandra called to her, "It's our sister's time."

Milandra took hold of the ball. It was her turn to serve. Tossing the ball up in the air, ready to hit it, she heard her phone ringer go off. She caught the ball.

"Wait, I have to answer my phone," she said.

"You brought your phone on this court?" Noelle noticed.

"Yeah, Milandra, you made the rule. No cell phones on the tennis court," Kenley said.

"This is an exception. I've been waiting on this call." Milandra answered it. "Hold on," she said to the party on the other line.

Milandra muted the phone. Her voice escalated, "Kenley, get over here. Make yourself useful. Play for me until I finish my conversation."

"Oh I see. I'm a fill-in for you," Kenley responded. She ran over and snatched the racket from her sister's hand. "Make it quick."

While her sisters played, Milandra walked off the court, through the gates and took a seat on a nearby bench.

"I'm back," she said, but all she heard was a barking cough from her caller. "Mr. Powell, are you able to speak? Drink water. Are you using your oxygen?"

Powell Sr. cleared his throat. "I don't want any slip-ups. I'm counting on you."

"Haven't I already handled things according to plan?"

"I want Aniyah gone for good."

"Trust me, I despise her. I'll handle that trash for the both of us with pleasure."

He choked.

"Hang up, Mr. Powell, and ring for your caregiver. I'll call you tomorrow." Milandra ended their conversation. She put her cell phone into the pocket of her skort and ran back on the court where her sisters chatted while they played.

When Kenley spotted her, she ran to hand Milandra back her racket.

"Here, finish your own game," she said.

Once Milandra took hold of the racket, her cell phone buzzed again. Her eyes dotted at the incoming call. She shoved the racket back into Kenley's hand.

"Keep playing."

"Nah. You're supposed to be playing with Noelle."

On the other end of the court, Noelle was annoyed and twirled her racket. "Will one of you please play? I'm tired of waiting."

Milandra held up her finger as if to tell her sister to wait one more minute. She turned her back to them and took the call.

"Hello," she said, and then responded. "This is Milandra Houston." She took in every word the caller said to her. Once she hung up, she turned to her sisters. "I have to run an errand. Kenley will finish playing with you."

"If you're leaving, so am I." Kenley tossed the racket

into Milandra's hand.

Noelle fussed, "I thought this was supposed to be our sister's time. Now you both are leaving."

Kenley explained her point to Noelle, "It was Milandra's idea to have sister time today. I didn't want to come. Let it had been me leaving first, she would've been yelling at me."

As Milandra packed her racket in its carrying case, she called, "I hear you, Kenley. You would leave earlier for foolishness. I have business to attend to."

Noelle headed toward them. "Is there something wrong on a construction site that we should be concerned about?"

Milandra tossed her carrying case over her shoulders. "This is personal business. Nothing you or baby sister should be worried about."

Kenley sighed. "Thank the Lord. I'm outta here."

It was like a race. Kenley and Milandra made their way out of the tennis court, leaving Noelle alone to finish gathering her tennis gear.

CHAPTER 5

*L*ess than a year had gone by. The hot weather and freezing weather had vanished. The April showers were gone and the lilies bloomed in May. It was the first Tuesday in the month, opening day for the outdoor farmers market and the only day for business. Unlike other women, who carried baskets or grocery totes for their purchases, Aniyah wore a crossbody bag. She strutted across the grassy field in flats, wearing a pair of jeans with holes in them. She sported a lightweight jean jacket with a powder-blue tank top underneath. Jarvis loved for her to buy produce from local farmers.

She looked across the field and noticed a few women gathered around one particular vendor's stand. Curiosity caused her to work her way over to them. Pushing to the front, her eyes landed on the top of the farmer's head. He bagged a basket of peaches for one of his customers. She noticed his sandy hair was cut slightly close to his head, but long enough for her to admire the waves. He wore a long-sleeved, fitted T-shirt, which exposed his bulging muscles. His shirt was pushed in his dark blue jeans. When he lifted his head up, his face looked to her like he had moisturized more than any of his female customers. His smile exposed a dimple in the left cheek. He had the dreamiest slanted eyes. Aniyah browsed his stand. She took her time to decide what she wanted to buy—any excuse to admire his good looks.

"What can I get you, Beauty?" he asked, once he finished clearing the other women from his stand.

"I'll have four lemons, a basket of string beans, red potatoes, and two bunches of broccoli."

While he bagged her items, he made conversation. "What's your name?"

"Aniyah Powell." She bragged, "My family owns Powell Banks. I'm married to Jarvis Powell."

Not fazed by her family status, he responded, "I'm Brant Logan. Everyone calls me Logan. Jarvis is a lucky man."

Aniyah blushed. "Yes, he is... and so am I." Watching his dimple disappear, she believed she had disappointed him.

"Enjoy the rest of the day," he said.

When she took the last bag from him, he caressed her hand. His sexy eyes made her heart flutter. She hurried and took hold of the handle. She could feel his eyes on her as she walked away. Looking back, she locked eyes with him, causing her to turn back around and sway her hips. It was nothing wrong with her teasing him. She dared not think of cheating on her husband. Her future was golden as long as she stayed a good wife.

Aniyah got into the Chrysler, gifted to her by Jarvis. Her ringtone from her cell phone announced: 'It's your hubby.'

"Hello, Honey," she answered, placing him on speaker-phone.

"I got bad news."

She wondered did her father-in-law go too far and fired Jarvis from the bank.

"Dad passed away."

By the sound of his raspy voice, Aniyah realized her husband was crying. "Really? I'm so sorry."

"I got a call from the housekeeper."

Still in shock, Aniyah blurted, "Gone to hel... heaven."

"Yes," he wept. "I feel terrible. I haven't spoken to Dad in a long time—being on the road off and on for the bank. Ever since he found out we were married, our relationship never mended."

Listening to Jarvis talk about his father made her think about her last visit with Powell Sr., which was months ago. A visit she had never shared with her husband. It was no need for her to reveal it now.

"It's not your fault that he didn't believe that I really do love you."

"I'm on my way back from Rock Hill. I'm headed to the family home."

Aniyah sniffled. "I can get there faster."

"I don't think that's a good idea. Dad wouldn't want you there."

"Jarvis, he's gone. It's my duty as your wife."

"It doesn't feel right for you to go there. Not yet."

"Jarvis, drive safe." Aniyah ended the call and then celebrated. "Hallelujah." She bounced in the seat. "Is this really happening? Finally, I'll get my wish."

She married a Powell and wanted all the trimmings that came with it. Aniyah made a sharp U-turn. She sped to Lake Murray to claim her new residence.

The road to the Powell domain was filled with blooming assorted flowers and beautiful palm trees.

"What can I do for you?" the guard asked, once Aniyah arrived. He was one of the workers that had laughed at her the last time she'd visited the home.

"You know who I am. Open this doggone gate. I need to get in."

"Sorry, Miss Aniyah. Strict rules to not let you in."

"My papa-in-law is dead. Open the damn gate. My husband and I are in charge from this day forward. You're fired."

The guard stood his ground. "You don't have any authority to fire me. So hot mama, I suggest you back your car up and leave."

Aniyah placed her vehicle in park. She swung the car door open. Stepping to him, she flung her flowing dark hair and pointed her finger at him. "I'm not in the mood for bull. Hit that button to let me in."

"Ain't happening. Get in your car and leave or else. You're trespassing."

Aniyah came to the conclusion that she would have to wait for the arrival of her other half. "When Jarvis gets here, I'll see to it he fires you."

The guard laughed. "Gold digger, get outta here."

She moved her vehicle far away from the entrance to avoid any other problems with security. She waited for her husband.

***

It did not take long before Aniyah, looking into the rearview mirror, eyed the front bumper of her husband's royal-blue convertible Mercedes-Benz. To get his attention, she blew the horn.

Jarvis drove up beside her, letting his passenger window down. "Baby, I told you not to come here."

"I'm your wife. I should be here."

"Go pick up J.P." He identified their son who was at preschool by his nickname.

"I have plenty of time to get him," Aniyah switched the conversation on him. "That crazy guard wouldn't let me enter the gates. Jarvis Powell, Jr., you will not get rid of me too. I'm going with you inside. Lead the way."

To not get into a domestic verbal altercation with his wife, Jarvis rolled the window up. Aniyah watched him shake his head in disbelief. He led the way with her close up on his bumper.

When they reached the security station, Aniyah blabbed at the guard. "My husband is here. Now open the doggone gates."

The guard directed his attention to Jarvis. "May I help you?"

Jarvis did not recognize the security guard on duty. "Hello. I'm Jarvis Powell, Jr." He pulled out his identification and handed it to him. "I got word that my dad has passed away."

"Sorry, Sir, no one is allowed inside," the guard said.

"This is my family's home. Powell property. Open the gates."

"Sir, I can't."

Aniyah's eyes widened when she watched her husband jump out of his vehicle, confronting the guard.

"Fire his behind," she said.

"Who gave you these orders?" Jarvis asked.

"I'm only doing my job. I do have something to give you." The guard went into his office booth and returned with a white envelope. He handed it to Jarvis. "I suggest you read it."

Jarvis snatched the envelope from his hand. Aniyah hopped out of her vehicle. Hurrying over, she stretched her neck to read the document.

Jarvis looked up at her. "Baby, get back in your car."

"What's in the envelope?"

"It says to go to Dad's office."

Aniyah pouted. "We can't go in the home. Now a stupid paper tells you to go to your job."

Overheated, Jarvis loosened his tie. "This is some of dad's craziness. It's his handwriting. It also says for you to be there." Jarvis' heart rate lowered. "I believe Dad is playing games. It's sad to say, but maybe Dad is faking his own death."

"He wants to see if you'll come running to his office. Why in the hell does he want me there?"

He sighed. "Who knows what Dad is up to? I'm a fool for his games. I'm headed to the bank. Maybe you shouldn't go. I'll handle this situation."

"I want to see what the old fart is up to. He's a turkey that needs to be roasted."

"Go pick up J.P.," Jarvis suggested. "I'll call you later. Back your car out, so we can leave."

Aniyah stormed to her vehicle. She did not listen to a

word Jarvis had said. When he swerved around her, she was right on his bumper. She followed him to Powell's Bank.

CHAPTER 6

*T*he anticipation of seeing Powell, Sr. still alive made Aniyah's stomach growl. She patted it to settle her nerve. Along with her husband, she got off the elevator on the eighth floor of Powell Bank. Once through the doors, the receptionist greeted them, recognizing the couple.

"Hello, Mr. and Mrs. Powell."

"Hi," Jarvis responded. Aniyah did not bother to speak.

"You can go ahead into the office," the receptionist said.

"Is my dad present?" Jarvis asked. He hoped the news of his father's death was false. He wanted to confront him for the sick trick he was playing with him.

"You can go ahead into his office," the receptionist repeated.

Jarvis walked ahead, while Aniyah leaned over the desk.

"Next time my husband asks you a question, you better answer him or you'll have to answer to me." Aniyah flipped over her pencil can.

Startled, the receptionist pushed back from the desk. Aniyah strutted away, catching up to Jarvis.

They entered the room decorated with photography. A

self-portrait of Jarvis Powell, Sr. hung on one wall, and two walls had a photo of golfers and a beautiful oil painting of the waters of Lake Murray, South Carolina.

Two men were conversing, and Aniyah recognized one immediately. The other was a stranger to her.

"Look who's here, the puppet lawyer?" Aniyah locked eyes with Baron Chavis, her Aunt Tessa's husband, the aunt whom she had not spoken to since her son was born. The family relationship had been destroyed because of Aniyah's history of having her way with men, to include dealings with her own aunt's husband. Her manipulative ways and wrongdoings had led her aunt to disown her.

During her Aunt Tessa's younger days, she had worked for the Houstons. She and Baron had liked each other, but her employer, Rupert, had forbidden them to date. He had made it clear to his attorney to cease contact with her. Rupert wanted her for himself until he'd sent her back home to Mexico.

During Aniyah's scheme to get Rupert's assets, she needed all the ammunition to get to his money. Aniyah met Baron Chavis. She made him believe she was Tessa's daughter, since she favored her. Aniyah learned he loved her Aunt Tessa. Aniyah used the information to her advantage. She got Baron drunk and seduced him. Then she snapped photos of them in a compromised position. She cropped the photos, replacing her image with Rupert's middle daughter, Noelle. Rupert knew about the photos as she had sent him a copy. Once he had passed away from a heart attack, she would use the image against his lawyer, but things worked in her favor, if only for a short time. Her Aunt Tessa returned to South Carolina from Mexico. She was not happy how her runaway niece was living her life. Aniyah had no love for her aunt. She thought her aunt showed more love to others than her own blood relative. Tessa rekindled her relationship with Baron. Once Aniyah was released from a two-year prison sentence, her aunt attempted to help her. Not satisfied with her aunt's help, Aniyah attempted to destroy her marriage. Tessa cut off all contact with her.

Jarvis spoke, "What's going on here, Mr. Chavis?"

"Hello, Jarvis." Baron ignored Aniyah's comment. He shook his hand. Then he introduced his colleague. "This is Attorney Marion Bloomberg."

"Hello there," Mr. Bloomberg said. He shook Jarvis' hand. Then he bowed his head at Aniyah.

Kenley and Noelle interrupted them when they walked into the office. The room became fuller.

"Hello, everyone. I see Kenley and I are not the only ones summoned to be here," Noelle said. She walked past Aniyah and hugged Jarvis. "Sorry for your loss."

Kenley embraced Jarvis too.

Hearing Noelle acknowledge that Powell, Sr. was deceased, Aniyah mumbled beneath her breath, "Hallelujah."

"I got a feeling some mess is going down in here," Kenley said.

"It sure is. What are you and your sister doing here? You're no relative of my papa-in-law," Aniyah responded.

Kenley rolled her eyes at Aniyah. "Like you're his blood. I don't think so. Jarvis is our brother."

"Enough, ladies," Baron said.

Aniyah turned up her nose. "It's great your stink attitude

sister isn't here. It's stuffy enough in here."

Like others, Aniyah noticed the high-back chair behind the desk was backward. She ran and spun the chair around. To her surprise, the seat was empty.

"Move away from the chair," a voice said. Milandra Houston entered the room, making her way to the desk.

Everyone's eyes, except the legal representatives, widened when she scooped around Aniyah and took her seat.

Aniyah ordered Milandra, "Get up. The only two people that get to sit in that chair is my papa-in-law and my husband."

Jarvis spoke, "Milandra?"

She smirked. "Surprise."

Jarvis made his way to the desk. "What kind of games is my dad playing here?"

"Have a seat, Jarvis." Milandra pointed to an empty chair.

Aniyah argued, "You don't tell my man to have a seat in his own place of business. You're the guest, not him. Get it straight."

Milandra pointed at Aniyah. "You can leave," she said with a stoned face.

"Make me!" Aniyah did not budge.

"I don't think you want to go there." Kenley defended her oldest sister.

"I want some answers like Jarvis," Noelle said.

"Take the floor, Mr. Bloomberg," Baron suggested.

"I'm Mr. Jarvis Powell, Sr.'s attorney. I'm sorry to say, he's deceased and cremated. His ashes discarded in the designated place where Mr. Powell requested."

With watery eyes, Noelle said, "That's terrible." She

dropped down into another chair.

Aniyah shouted, "That old fart is a jerk to do that to my husband."

Tears watered Jarvis' eyes. "Dad is really dead and put to rest. He hated me that much to not want me to oversee his last wishes?"

Jarvis dropped down to his knees, bursting into tears.

Kenley cut her eyes at Aniyah. "It's this gold-digger wife of yours, he hated. It's her fault."

"You're correct, sister," Milandra said. "Mr. Chavis is here as my attorney, and Mr. Powell's attorney is here to verify what I'm about to reveal."

Aniyah went up to the desk. "I don't want to hear nothing you have to say. Get lost. From here on out, I'll help my husband handle his papa's business."

Milandra laughed but not once did she bat an eye. "See your way out of my... bank."

Flinging her hair, Aniyah rolled her eyes. "Excuse me, what did you say?"

Jarvis lifted his head up. "Say what?"

"That's right. I'm the new owner of Powell Bank. It'll be almost a year since Mr. Powell signed it over to me."

"Nah. He wouldn't do that," Jarvis argued.

Mr. Bloomberg confirmed Milandra's words. "Yes, he did. Not only that, the former Powell Estate belongs to Milandra."

"Now that's some shady bull," Aniyah said.

Noelle jumped in. "Milandra, it's not right you keeping Jarvis' rightful property. He's Mr. Powell's heir."

"I'm not a beneficiary. I purchased it fair and square."

"We'll take all of my papa-in-law's money and transfer

it to another bank," Aniyah said.

Milandra burst into laughter. "Will you please, Attorney Bloomberg, enlighten the empty-headed tramp of Mr. Jarvis Powell's finances at the time of death?"

"Again, I'm sorry. Mr. Powell had zero dollars. He disbursed his funds, assets, gave to numerous charities, and cancelled any life insurances policies he had. His final arrangements were paid in full before his death."

"That can't be," Aniyah said. "That old fart was in love with his money."

Jarvis Jr. was confused. "Dad would never give away his assets."

Milandra smiled. "Watch this for confirmation."

Aniyah and everyone watched Milandra straighten the loose strands in her French roll. Up out of the seat, Milandra went over to a laptop computer and clicked a video file. It streamed on a nineteen-inch television screen. Everyone darted eyes at Old Man Powell, who sat up in a recliner chair. By his side were two men.

With the oxygen tube in his nostrils and a big smirk on his face, Powell Sr. spoke, "Hello there. My name is Jarvis Powell, Sr. I got more sense than my damn son, Jarvis, Jr. Tell them, docs."

Moving his head, Powell acknowledged the men in the video who stood next to him.

The first doctor, who stood on his left, spoke, "My name is Dr. Fester McLord. I'm a licensed board certified psychiatrist in the State of South Carolina. I've confirmed that Mr. Jarvis Powell, Sr. is of sound mind and is able to decide on his health and assets."

The second doctor spoke, "My name is Dr. Kaleem

Ethan. I'm a licensed board certified psychiatrist in the State of South Carolina. I also confirmed that Mr. Jarvis Powell, Sr., is one hundred percent able to make any decisions pertaining to his health and assets. This man has a brain like a teenager."

Once the doctors finished speaking, they exited the video. Powell, Sr. coughed to clear his throat. He took a sip of cold water before he spoke.

"Jarvis, it was I that groomed you to take charge and be the man to carry on the Powell legacy. I thought I raised you well." Powell Sr. waved an unlit cigar as if he were pointing at his son. "Somehow you lost track of what was important... and that's loyalty to me. You allowed that tramp, you call a wife, to break up the father and son bond we've built."

Aniyah yelled at the television. "I never liked you either."

"Girl, respect the dead," Kenley said.

"Be quiet," Milandra ordered them.

Jarvis kept his head down while he listened to his father voice his feelings.

Powell, Sr. continued, "Aniyah Sanchez, you're the reason my son gets zero. He'll see how much you really love him. I have no assets to leave him. How do you like that, tramp? The Powell fortune died when I left this earth. The new owner of my home and cars is Milandra Houston. My bank accounts have been depleted. I canceled my insurance policies. I was able to live the rest of my sick days peacefully. Milandra saw to it funds were used on me and only me. Aniyah, you thought my grand-heir would seal the deal. You should've turned him over to me. Let me raise him."

Aniyah was quite aware that Powell had wanted to raise Jarvis III. He hoped she would have made him his guardian.

Powell, Sr. continued to speak, "Well, I'm taking my rest. Son, I love you enough not to leave my possessions with you for your gold-digging wife to get her paws on it." Powell burst into laughter. He pointed an unlit cigar at the camera. "Aniyah, you should've taken the money I offered you and run."

The video ended.

"Aniyah, I wish Mr. Powell could see your face." Milandra laughed.

Lowering her widened eyes, Aniyah said, "Shut up. I smell your stink breath from here, Milandra."

"This is some deep stuff," Kenley said.

Noelle added, "I'm so sorry, Jarvis." She went and placed her hand on his shoulder. "This must be devastating to you."

"I'll be going," Bloomberg said. He headed to the door.

"Me too," Baron said. He made his way to Jarvis. "Sorry man. I'm not a fan of what your father has done to you. Yet, you know I'm not a fan of your wife as well. I pray she does love you for you. Time will tell."

"I do love my husband. I don't care what you or anyone else in this room thinks of me. That includes the old dead fart. Go home to your weak wife," Aniyah said.

"I'm happy Tessa didn't come with me. It disappoints her that you've made a bad name for her family."

Jarvis held his head up. Barely able to talk, tears flooded his face. He wiped them and said, "This is my Dad's wish. I have no choice but to accept it."

Noelle went to her oldest sister. She begged, "Milandra, please do the right thing? Give it back to Jarvis."

"I won't." Milandra stood. "Jarvis may keep his job. That, I'll do for him."

"Gee, so nice of you. Give my man back his business," Aniyah demanded.

"Stop, Aniyah," Jarvis said. He pulled her by the arm, keeping her from going after Milandra. "I need time to think. I'll let you know whether I want to stay on here, Milandra."

"Don't leave your job. I'll get Milandra to change her mind," Noelle said. She then questioned her sister. "Does Nolan realize what you have done?"

"What my husband knows or don't know is our business. Discussion closed," Milandra said. She headed to the door. Then held it opened. "Meeting is adjourned."

"You can be mean, big sister," Kenley said.

Noelle walked past Milandra. "You're the worst."

"Grow up, Noelle, and be a Houston," Milandra said.

Mixed feelings traveled through Jarvis' head. He stormed out of his seat, running to the framed photo of his father on the wall. He tossed it on the ground and stomped it until his father's photo was unrecognizable. He ranted. "Damn you, Dad!"

Aniyah ran to join her husband. She dug her heels into the photo. "This is for doing my honey wrong."

"Jarvis, you and your crazy wife, stop it," Milandra called to him.

Aniyah ran to her, pushing her out the doorway. "Back off!"

Kenley leaped at Aniyah and pulled her by the arm. "Keep your hands off my sister."

Noelle blasted, "This is not the way to handle things. Stop it, Kenley and Milandra."

When Jarvis saw that his wife was about to have an altercation, he seized from releasing his frustration.

Aniyah felt his hand around her arm.

"Baby, let's go," Jarvis ordered.

Aniyah moved toward her husband. With his arms around her waist, they exited the room. She argued back, "This isn't over, Miss Uppity."

CHAPTER 7

*W*ith Jarvis III up in her arms, Aniyah strolled through the beveled glass mahogany door of her home, the place she had thought would be up for sale once she ever got word that her father-in-law had died. Now she was stuck living in a four-bedroom home. It was a great size, but it was nothing compared to the enormous Powell family home. *That old-fart papa-in-law has ruined everything for me. Jerk!* she thought.

Resting her son's two feet on the floor, she held his hand, and they made their way to the kitchen.

"Honey," she called when she spotted her husband scooping a mouth full of ice cream in his mouth.

Jarvis III's eyes lit up once he saw his father. "Papa-Dad."

He caught Jarvis' attention. Jarvis dropped the spoon into the bowl. He dashed to his son. "Hey, lil' fella." He picked him up and snuck a kiss on the cheek. "Love you, man. You and your mom."

"We love you, too." Aniyah threw herself into her husband's arms and pressed her lips against his. Next, she gave Jarvis III a kiss on the cheek.

She watched her husband snuggle their son into his arms, giving him plenty of affection. Her mind went to the man at the market. *Farmer has nothing on my man. I've got the best hubby in the world.*

Jarvis may not have had the looks of the farmer, but his heart of gold captured her heart. She loved every bit of her husband's muscular bronzed body. She watched Jarvis put his son down on the floor.

Jarvis III ran to a small table that sat in the corner of the spacious kitchen. He sat down ready for his snack. "Cookie." He hit his hand on the table.

While Aniyah prepared chocolate chip cookies on a napkin and a small glass of milk for her son, she said, "Honey, I can't believe your papa would treat you so cold."

"He left here the way he wanted to. Dad has always been headstrong. I didn't think he'd make me pay for marrying you in this cold-hearted way."

"It's my fault," she said.

After Aniyah handed Jarvis III his snack, she found her way to a nearby stool at the kitchen island. She rested her head on the granite stone. Jarvis placed his arms around her. She cried, "I hope you don't hate me. I visited your papa not too long ago. He offered me money to leave you and our son."

"You should've told me."

"I didn't want to upset you."

"I told Dad over and over I love you. He didn't want to hear it. Money doesn't control me. As long as I have you and our son, that's all that matters."

"Will you continue working at the bank now that the

witch owns it?"

"I've decided I'm not leaving. I have invested too much of my time and expertise into Powell Bank. I have to keep a roof over our family's head."

Aniyah whined. "It's not right. Uppity should give it back to you. She's like your dad. She loves being in control."

"I'm hurting, but I'm not defeated. I pray you're with me through this change in my life."

Aniyah rested in her husband's arms. They kissed until Jarvis III called, "More cookies."

They laughed.

The water ran down Aniyah's back. She wiped away the last of sudsy shower gel that coated her body. Turning off the water, she stepped out of the shower and heard her husband's footsteps entering their master suite. Soak and dripping wet, she walked into the bedroom and handed him the towel. She stood there with her legs spread apart. He dried her body. When Jarvis stopped, Aniyah eyed him sniffing the towel, absorbing her body scent. This was something that they enjoyed doing to each other. It turned them on. Jarvis dropped the towel and pulled her into his arms. She felt his luscious lips against hers. Before long, he led her to the bed.

Easing her body down, Jarvis rested on top of her. "Help me forget this horrible day." With no other words said, he got lost into the softness of her body.

Aniyah moaned from his touch. When he entered her, she cried in pleasure. Their bodies were sweaty from their own body heat. She loved every bit of their lovemaking.

They exploded.

Jarvis rolled off of her. "I forgot to tell you. I have to leave in the morning."

"Where to?"

"I'm scheduled to attend a three-day conference in Jacksonville, Florida."

"Your papa gave his company to 'Uppity.' Let her go."

"Aniyah, it's my job."

She lay on her left side. "Jarvis, your papa is gone. Left you broke. Stop letting him have control over you."

"There are many employees that I'm thinking of. They need not be a part of my dad's mad decisions. Nor Milandra's. I hope you understand."

"Good night, Jarvis." She turned her back to him and pulled the comforter over her body.

Aniyah lay awake. Once she heard her husband snoring, she eased from under the cover. She wrapped her bare body in a lightweight robe. With her cell phone in her hand, she peeked inside her son's room. Jarvis III rested in his bed with his face hidden halfway under the covers. Aniyah vanished to the kitchen.

She contacted her friend. "Nellie."

"Aniyah, you're up late. Is everything okay?"

"My papa-in-law died. He's cremated and his ashes are God knows where. That fool set it up so Jarvis wouldn't be called until after everything was over with."

"That's crazy. Why would Mr. Powell do that? May he rest in peace."

"Restless in hell."

"He loved the lake. Maybe they sprinkled his ashes in

the water."

"If they did, his butt has muddied it. Poor fish."

"Aniyah, that isn't nice to speak of the dead that way."

"I don't care. The old fart left Jarvis nothing. Zero."

Aniyah rummaged through the refrigerator. She grabbed a bag of boiled peanuts. "He got rid of his house, money and bank. The fool handed it over to Milandra Houston."

"Nothing surprised me about Mr. Powell."

Aniyah popped one peanut in her mouth. "I should live like royalty. Milandra's greedy self already has a business, money and a mansion. She's got her nasty fingers on the place I should move into. I'm not having that."

"You live in a nice home. Blessed with a wonderful husband and great son."

"I'm happy for the family I have. Not this house. I'm here until I figure out another way to get the Powell property from that uppity Milandra Houston."

Again, Aniyah cracked a peanut open between her teeth, then sucked the juices out of the salty shell.

"Be careful. You don't want to do anything stupid."

"Let's talk more tomorrow. Meet me for lunch. Twelve o'clock at the chicken and waffle place."

"Okay. Get a good night's sleep."

"Not until my hubby gets what's rightfully his."

CHAPTER 8

*W*ith her pumps in her hand, Milandra dashed inside her master closet, filled with designer clothes and shelves of shoes. She placed her white slingback pumps into one of the slots.

"Milandra?"

She heard her name called. "I'm in the closet."

"Hey, I couldn't wait to get home to you." Her husband, Nolan, entered their room. Nolan was a self-made businessman, owner of Rice Moving Company.

Nolan rushed up behind his wife, wrapping his arms around her waist. He gave her a peck on the neck, turned her around and unzipped the linen dress she wore.

"I need to share some important information with you."

"Not right now. I want my wife."

He slipped the dress off her shoulders. It dropped to the floor. He led her to a chaise lounge. She rested her back on it while he undressed.

Nolan crawled on top of her. Their lips became one. She eased her fingertips down his muscular arms, traveling to his back, down to his rear. She squeezed his firm behind. Moisture built up between her legs. Nolan spread them apart and entered her. She moaned. Another stroke and they reached another powerful marriage of great sex.

Nolan rolled off of her and stood to his feet. "Just what a man needs after a day of hard work." He picked his clothing up from the floor. "Give me the important news."

Milandra hoped her revelation would not spoil their romantic moment.

"Mr. Powell has died."

"That's sad. Poor Jarvis."

"Mr. Powell has been cremated without Jarvis' knowledge."

Milandra passed by her husband and went into the bathroom.

"That's foul." Nolan followed her. "Why would he do that?"

"Mr. Powell didn't want Aniyah anywhere near him, much less, his property or business. He left Jarvis penniless. I own everything."

Nolan's eyes lit up. "You're his beneficiary?"

"He didn't will it to me."

"Then how did it become yours?"

"I purchased it for a little to nothing. Mr. Powell wanted to get rid of his assets before he passed away. He was sick and had limited time to live. Jarvis had no knowledge of this information."

While he shook his head, Nolan wiped his lips. "Jarvis is a hard worker. He gives his all to the bank. Hell, he was raised in that home. Why would you do that to him? He's your half-brother."

Milandra faced her husband. She did not bat one eyelash. "He's a Powell. I got it fair and square. It's a business deal."

He gripped her by the arms. "You also, underhandedly, played me. I didn't get a say-so on your major shopping deal."

Milandra jerked away from him. She argued back, "I use my family fortune whatever way I choose. Deal with it."

She watched Nolan storm out of the bathroom. It did not take long before he returned to her. She noticed that he was fully dressed.

"Give it back to Jarvis or else."

"I will not. Deal with it," Milandra said.

Nolan's bottom lip fluttered. "I want a divorce. Now you deal with that."

"I'm not surprised. My world is over your head. It wasn't appropriate for me to marry someone of your status—no real wealth," she admitted.

With raging eyes, Nolan slapped her across the face. "I've never hit a woman before, but damn, you gave me no choice."

Milandra held back the tears. "Leave or I'll have you arrested." She grabbed a washcloth and drenched it in cold water, then placed it on the left cheek.

"I'm leaving. Keep your money. It doesn't make me. My freedom away from you is enough for me. Hell, if Aniyah was free, I'd date her."

Milandra threw a bar of soap at him. Nolan ducked. The soap missed his head.

"If my father was alive, he'd kill you for hurting one of his daughters."

Once Nolan exited, Milandra slammed the bathroom door shut.

A good night's sleep was what Milandra needed to help forget her hectic and distressful day. She covered her eyes with a mask.

Flipping over on her side, she was alarmed by the sound of her cell phone. She lifted the eye mask to rest on her forehead.

Once she saw her sister's number displayed on the screen, she answered the call. "Hello, Noelle."

"Are you and Nolan divorcing?"

"He had to call you. Did he also tell you he slapped me?"

"Yes. He regrets it. Milandra, what has gotten into you?"

"I should ask you the same question. You and Kenley have abandoned the integrity of being a Houston."

"No we haven't. We still love our family. We're not letting our money and power rule us. We're doing what's right."

"I've done what our father would've done if he were alive. He'd never let go of the chance to own more assets if he had the opportunity to acquire them."

"Mother wouldn't be happy."

"That's the reason why father took control of the business in the family."

"Please give Jarvis back what's his, and work on saving your marriage."

"Noelle Houston, stop meddling in my business ventures and marriage, or I'll have no choice but to cut my sister off."

"I pray you see the wrong you're doing before it's too late."

"Noelle, I need to get my beauty sleep. This conversation is over."

CHAPTER 9

*D*ressed in a black top and skinny jeans with a light-colored jean jacket, Aniyah took a seat in the far corner of the restaurant. The fresh strawberries atop a nearby customer's waffle invaded her senses.

When the waiter took her drink order, her phone rang. Nellie's name displayed on the screen.

"Where are you? I'm ready to eat," Aniyah said.

"I'm so sorry. I have to run errands for a client."

"Take a break. Come meet me."

"I can't. She wants me to come straight back to her."

"You're working for sick people that are pushy."

"My client is nice. I don't mind being here for her."

"You will stand your best friend up?"

Aniyah watched the waiter set a glass of iced tea and a saucer of lemons in front of her.

"Gotta make that money," Nellie said.

"Bye, Girl." Aniyah ended the call.

Ready to eat, she studied the menu.

"Beauty shouldn't be eating by herself."

Aniyah looked up once she heard the masculine voice. She nearly jumped out of her skin, when she locked eyes with the farmer.

"Didn't mean to scare you. I noticed you sitting here alone. Are you waiting on your other half?" he wondered.

"I'm not expecting anyone. Hubby is out of town. My girlfriend stood me up."

"This must be my lucky day. I'll keep you company." Brant eased into the chair across from her. "That's if you don't mind."

Aniyah did not see any harm in having a bite with the farmer.

"You can stay. I can use the company."

"Lunch is on me."

"You don't have to do that."

"Take it as a customer appreciation lunch." Brant slid her glass of tea to the corner of the table. He called to a waiter that walked past them. "Hey, can you get us two glasses of wine?"

The waiter nodded his head, yes.

"My Jarvis loves wine." Aniyah purposely mentioned her husband's name.

"It's about you, right now."

Brant attempted to take her by the hand. Aniyah snatched her hand away from him.

"No flirting. I'm married."

He feasted his eyes on her as if he could see through her. "You're lonely and not happy."

"Lonely? Heck no. My papa-in-law passed away."

Aniyah did not volunteer to expose any more of her family issues.

"Sorry for your loss."

When the waiter returned, Aniyah did not give him time

to put her glass down on the table; she grabbed it and took a big gulp of the drink.

They placed their orders.

The waiter served Aniyah a plate of buttermilk waffles, topped with strawberries and whip cream. The farmer dined on wheat waffles, topped with blueberries and lite whipped cream.

Aniyah reached for her fork and knife, but Brant got to the utensils first. He cut her waffles into bite-sized pieces. When he placed the fork to her lips, Aniyah opened her mouth and devoured her food. She tasted the sweetness of the strawberries mixed with the waffles. Once again, he attempted to feed her.

"My hand works." Aniyah took hold of the fork. He winked his eye at her. "You're a flirt."

"I like feeding, Beauty. You love the attention." He ate his waffles.

"What makes you think that?"

"You haven't run away from this table yet."

Aniyah continued to eat. What he'd said was true. Any other woman would have cursed him out. It was his gorgeous looks that kept her seated. His face was a magnet. She watched other women, who came into the restaurant, snicker over his good looks. She was not about to leave. It made her feel special that she was the one who sat across from Brant. After their meal, he covered the bill. Brant walked her outside to her vehicle. Aniyah noticed he had a limp to his walk.

"Thanks so much for paying," she said. Aniyah unlocked the car door and got in.

Brant stood inside the door, keeping her from closing it.

He removed a cell phone from his pocket and placed it in her hand. "Give me a call. My number is programmed in it."

Aniyah could not believe the farmer was making a quick move on her. "I can't take this. I'm happily married. Sorry if I gave you mixed signals."

When she attempted to place the phone back in his hand, Brant pushed it back into hers. He leaned his head over into the vehicle and gave her a lustful kiss. Aniyah pushed him away, shutting the door closed. Her heart palpitated, but her nipples blossomed. She felt a tingling sensation between her legs—something she only was to experience with Jarvis.

As Aniyah sped off, she looked into the rearview mirror. Brant stood at the curb, staring at her vehicle. She headed home.

When she parked in her driveway, Aniyah saw the phone that Brant had given her and the charger that had fallen into the passenger's seat. She turned it on and discovered it was fully charged. She checked the contact list, and there was his last name—Logan. She dropped the phone on the seat. It rang.

"You better not answer it...Okay, only this one time," she mumbled.

In a soft tone, she said, "Hello."

"I knew you'd answer me."

"Logan." She called him by the name he requested her to use.

"See you at the same place tomorrow for lunch." Brant abruptly ended the call.

Aniyah turned the phone completely off. She went straight to the trashcan and dumped the phone in it carefully, not to let it crack.

CHAPTER 10

*A*fter Aniyah settled her son in bed, she went into the kitchen and heated herself a warm glass of milk. She wondered if the farmer had tried to contact her again. Merely thinking of him, she hurried and called her husband, but it went straight to voicemail. "Jarvis, I miss you so much." She hung up and texted the words she had spoken.

Aniyah turned off the kitchen light. Walking through the darkness, she made it to the staircase that led up to the bedrooms. The porch light, emitting through the door, caught her attention. With the cup in her hand, she turned around and opened the front door. Aniyah went over to the trashcan and retrieved the phone. When she turned it on, she saw a text message from the farmer.

Logan: Beauty is what I need. See you at lunch.

Instead of discarding the phone back into the trashcan, Aniyah carried it inside the house. She contacted Brant.

"I can't throw a good phone away. I'll meet you tomorrow, only to give it back to you."

"If that's your excuse to see me again, it works for me," Brant said. "By the way, I can still taste the sugar from your lips."

"Good night."

Aniyah headed to her master suite. Just as she got comfortable under the gray and mint-green comforter, her cell phone rang.

"Jarvis?" she called his name after seeing it display on the screen. She snuggled under the covers relieved to hear her husband's voice. "I miss you."

"I saw you left me a voicemail and a message."

"I need you home."

"Aniyah, what's wrong?"

There was no way she would tell him that she had a hot man chasing after her.

"I feel lonely when you're away."

"It's quiet in this hotel room. I wish you were here with me."

"Do you have to stay the extra day?"

Aniyah did not want to fall back to her old ways, nor did she want to make a disaster of their marriage. Jarvis being home would cure her appetite for drooling after Brant. After all, Milandra had temporarily destroyed her future riches. In due time, she would figure out how to fix that.

"I'm training on some cool new software for the bank."

"Jarvis, face reality. It's not your bank."

"It's a part of me. I'm not letting Milandra, my dead dad or anyone put me out of working there."

Aniyah raised her voice. "Forget working there as help. You need to own it. Fight back!"

"Money and things, don't make me. I hope now you're done with letting it rule you."

Aniyah lowered her voice. "I have you and our son. That's enough."

"I love you, Aniyah Sanchez-Powell."

"I love you, too."

Aniyah turned on her side. Burying her face into the pillow, she closed her eyes. All she saw was a vision of the farmer. "Pretty boy, get out of my head. I can't be with you."

The next day, doing her daily routine, Aniyah dropped her son off to preschool. Next, she carried her husband's shirts to the cleaners to have fresh ones for work. When she returned home, she baked lasagna in the oven, and then changed out of the lightweight jogging suit she wore and into a dress. She looked as if she were going out for a special dinner. She checked her hair to make sure she had no loose strands and made her face up, smoothing a coat of a deep-reddish lipstick on her lips. She wanted to look her best to show off, to another man, that Jarvis was the chosen one to have her as his wife.

Out the door, she got in her vehicle. Aniyah turned on the cell phone that Brant had given her. She noticed he had left her another message.

Logan: I hope Beauty will be in my presence today.

Aniyah did not respond to his text.

Walking inside the chicken and waffle restaurant, she saw no signs of Brant. Instead of taking the same seat that she sat in the day before, she went to the other far corner and sat in the back.

She flagged over a waiter. "Water, please."

"Will someone be joining you?" the waiter asked.

"Can't let Beauty eat all by herself," Brant said. He took a seat across from Aniyah.

The waiter took his drink order.

"Wow. You don't look like you're here to give me my phone back." Brant studied her sexy attire.

"Well, I am."

Aniyah slid the phone across the table. Never once did she make eye contact with his dreamy eyes.

When the cell phone landed on his end of the table, Brant did not pick it up. "I think you're afraid of me. You can't even look straight at me."

Aniyah held her head up. "I have no problem looking at you. Remember I'm a married woman."

Brant chuckled. "That's something you should remember—not me."

Aniyah took a gulp of her glass of cold water. She felt like she was having a private summer moment. Brant was right; Jarvis crossed her mind every second she entertained him. Once the waiter returned, they ordered their meals.

Brant sipped on his glass of wine, while Aniyah cooled down with her glass of water. He fed her a lot of sweet words. Aniyah ignored his flirtatiousness.

She became as red as a ripe strawberry when her friend tapped her on the shoulder.

"Hi, Nellie."

"Do we need to have girl talk?" Nellie dotted her eyes at Brant.

He laughed.

"It's nothing like that. I'm a professional trainer," he

lied. "Sometimes I meet potential clients at restaurants to go over ways to make smart choices on the menu."

"Fried chicken?" Nellie looked at her friend's plate. Then she dotted her eyes at Aniyah, not buying Brant's story. "Really?"

"He's telling the truth. It was my choice to eat greasy food. So, please don't say anything to Jarvis. I do want to drop a few pounds for him." Aniyah felt as if she were about to faint.

"You don't need to lose weight. You have a slamming body."

"Thanks, Nellie," Aniyah said. "This body can always be tightened."

"Join us?" Brant said, pointing to an empty seat.

"Can't do. I'm here to pick up a to-go plate for my client. I'm a personal caregiver," Nellie explained.

He teased her. "Like I'm your friend's personal trainer."

Aniyah cut her eyes at Brant before she stood up. She gave her friend a hug. "Love you, girl. Talk to you later."

"Bye, girl," Nellie said. She waved at Brant. "Bye, personal trainer."

Aniyah watched her friend leave the place with her takeout bag in her hand.

She sat back down. "I need to get out of here," she called to their waiter, who was at another table placing drinks in front of a customer.

The waiter came over.

"May I have a to-go-box?"

"Relax." Brant grabbed her hand. "We're only eating, and your friend believes I'm a trainer."

Aniyah watched him bend his left arm and flex his muscle. She wanted to touch him. No longer hungry, she scraped her food into the box.

Brant paid for the meal. "Keep the change," he said to the waiter.

Aniyah got up out of the seat and scurried toward the door. Once outside, she hurried to her vehicle.

"Slow down." He caught up to her as she opened her car door. He snatched the keys from her. "I will not let you drive nervous."

"Hand me my keys." She stared at him, wishing he had an ugly mask to cover up his good looks.

"Get in the car and relax for a second. Then I'll hand them to you."

As she sat in the driver's seat, Aniyah looked over to the passenger seat, where Brant had hopped into her ride and parked himself.

She fussed. "Give me my keys. Get out of my car."

He pulled her into his arms in broad daylight in the back of the restaurant. "This is how you relax."

Pressing his lips against hers, Aniyah tried to push him off her. When the touch of his hand crawled up her thigh, she slapped his hand away.

Brant backed away from her. "Stop playing games. You love the attention."

With teary eyes, she responded, "I love my husband."

In reality, she wanted to tell him, she had changed her ways since she had married Jarvis.

Brant tossed the phone and keys at her. He exited the vehicle, never looking back. Aniyah froze in her seat. She could not move for a few minutes. Tears flowed down her face. She would not let her old ways ruin her marriage.

She pulled her dress down and sped off.

Aniyah kicked her shoes into the closet. She slipped off her dress, changed into an olive-green short set and slid her feet into a pair of flats. She could hear a phone ringing from the inside of her handbag. Aniyah fished the phone out and answered it.

"Jarvis," she called her husband's name, needing to hear his voice.

"It's Logan," Brant said in his strong masculine voice.

Aniyah double-checked, looking at the phone, and it hit her that the call was not from her personal line.

She puckered her lips and sat on the bed. "You were wrong to get inside of my car. I didn't give you permission."

He twitched his lips. "Thanks for letting me kiss you again."

"I didn't give you permission the first time or the second time."

"You loved it, Beauty."

"It's totally wrong, and, you were supposed to take this phone back. My husband wouldn't approve of it," she admitted.

When she mentioned Jarvis, Brant frowned into the phone. It was bad news to his ears. He spilled his findings of her family business.

"Your husband is broke."

Aniyah became irritated. "You don't know what my husband has."

"News gets around. He lost his inheritance. And you thrive on a man with lots of money and honey."

"Like you got cash. You're a small-time farmer."

"That's where you're wrong. Farming is my hobby. I have millions. When I lived in California, I hit the lottery for one hundred million dollars. I'm not a flasher. I lay low with my cash. Now, never speak of your husband again when you're talking to me."

Aniyah's eyes lit up. She tried not to fall out from the dollar signs that fluttered through her mind. A man with one hundred million dollars and pursuing a married woman doesn't want to hear her talk about her husband. It was the perfect time for her to convert to her wicked old ways. Two could now play that game. Brant would be the man that would give her the opportunity to embezzle funds, for the sake of helping her husband to get his assets back or build his own wealth.

"I won't throw it away."

He grinned. "I thought you wouldn't."

"It's a good phone."

"Meet me again for lunch. Read my text tomorrow for the location."

"Tomorrow it is."

Aniyah ended the conversation. Falling back on the bed, she felt a throbbing headache coming on—she was in a sticky situation.

Staring at the phone, she said, "This will be an easy job to do. This fine-looking man is sexy and into me. I'm doing this for you, Jarvis Powell, Jr."

CHAPTER 11

Aniyah went through her closet, deciding what to wear for the day. Brant's good-looking face flashed across her mind, and she flung the pants back on the hanger. She found herself in a brand-new, hot-pink dress that hugged her curves. She brushed her long locks. Jarvis III was dressed in his navy pants and white shirt. He slipped his arms through the straps of his tiny schoolbag and carried it on his back.

He smiled. "Mama-Mom, go." He pulled Aniyah by the hand.

"My handsome little boy." Aniyah embraced her child, then held his hand as they left to start their day.

After dropping Jarvis III off, Aniyah went through the Starbucks drive-thru, picked up a yogurt before she pampered herself with a full pedicure from the Alicia B Nail Bar. She shopped at Target for toiletries.

Entering her vehicle, she heard both cell phones with different ringtones go off. She pulled the phones out. One was a call from Jarvis and the other was a text message from Brant.

She responded to her husband first. "Hi, Honey."

"Hey, my love," Jarvis said. "How are you and my son managing without me?"

"We need you home." She yearned for some affection from her spouse.

"I'll hit the road tomorrow night around seven."

Aniyah felt a weight lift off of her shoulders. Once Jarvis returned home, it would help her to get out the crazy idea to use Brant. "Drive safe. No speeding."

"That's what I love about my wife. She looks out for me."

"And, my hubby takes good care of me and our kid."

"That's what a man does, when he loves his wife and son so much."

Aniyah listened to the kisses Jarvis blew into the phone at her.

"See you soon." She ended their conversation.

The ringtone from the other cell phone went off again, indicating that she had another text. She looked at the first message.

Logan: Join me if you dare.

Logan: 212, Holiday Inn.

"A hotel room? I can get what I want out of you without going that far."

Aniyah: Logan, you don't know me that well. I thought we were meeting for lunch.

She awaited his response. It did not take long for him to text back.

Logan: I've prepared a private lunch for my Beauty.

Aniyah chattered to herself. "Dang, I want to beat you out of your cash. But going in a hotel room with you might be dangerous."

While she turned the ignition on, the room number flashed in her brain. "Go away. This is so wrong," she uttered. Then the thought of everything Jarvis had lost baffled her.

Traveling on the opposite side of the street, Aniyah landed on the block of the hotel.

After a quick U-turn, she swung into the parking lot, parking in the rear.

Aniyah flipped the overhead mirror down. As she stared at herself, she spoke, "Back this car out of here. Right now!"

She dropped her head on the steering wheel.

"Only this once. After this, no more of your old ways, Aniyah." She held back her tears. "You're doing it to help your husband."

Strutting down the long corridor, Aniyah passed a housekeeper that busily snatched towels off a cart while preparing to clean a room. She turned her head, not to show her face, as if the housekeeper was someone that could identify her.

Instead of taking the elevator, she took the stairs to the second floor. Aniyah approached room 212 and knocked twice. Brant swung open the door and stood before her in a pair of jeans with no shirt on, exposing a well-chiseled chest. He looked good; Aniyah felt tempted. She thought he would sneak her with another kiss like he had done before. To her surprise, Brant stepped aside, giving her permission to enter. Her eyes landed on the desk in the room. He had set it up for a lunch for two.

It differed from the romantic lunches prepared for her by her husband. Jarvis' delight for her was two glasses of chilled wine, lobster, a medley of vegetables and a stuffed baked potato. Brant's idea for a romantic lunch was a bowl of tossed salad greens—cucumbers, tomatoes, carrots, boiled eggs, and red onions, topped with strips of grilled, blackened chicken on top.

"Lunch looks mighty healthy," she said.

"My usual way of eating," he bragged. "Everything from my organic garden, even the eggs and chickens are from my farm."

"I can't wait to eat." She tried not to be distracted by his sexy body. Aniyah stood in the middle of the room, waiting for his next move.

"Have a seat, Beauty." He pointed to a wing chair near the window.

Aniyah followed his instructions.

"What type of dressing do you like? I have Italian and an olive oil vinaigrette."

"Italian is good."

She watched him pick up one bowl of salad. He drizzled the dressing on it. Taking the chair that was closer to the desk, Brant set it in front of her.

Instead of handing her the bowl, he put salad on the fork. "Open wide." He held the fork to her mouth.

Aniyah parted her lips. She devoured the food, crunching the fresh garden veggies.

"Beauty needs her nutrition."

His stares weakened Aniyah. She got lost into his world, while he fed her.

"Aren't you're going to eat?"

"Later. Beauty first."

He spoon-fed her the salad. Something about the way he served her was sensual. She felt moisture build between her legs. Something she was not supposed to feel. It took will power for her not to throw herself at him. She would let him stay in charge until the right time for her to make her move.

Brant placed a cold glass of fresh lemonade to her mouth, and like a small child drinking out of a cup for the first time, Aniyah sipped on the drink.

"I'm full," she said.

"Good, then we can go on to the next thing."

She wondered if he was about to show her the rest of his assets. Instead, Brant put the bowl and the drink on the desk. He helped her out of one chair, and sat her in a square-back one. The one he had got up from.

He whispered in her ears. "Close your eyes."

Aniyah, intrigued by him, did as she was told.

With her eyes shut, she felt the tip of his fingers on the temple of her head. He massaged her down to her neck, rubbing the muscles in her shoulders with his strong hands, but gently enough not to hurt her or leave any marks on her. She felt as if she was about to be put to sleep.

Once Brant was convinced her upper-body muscles were loosened, he said, "Stand up."

Aniyah followed his orders.

Brant pulled her into his arms. He kissed her on the lips. She kissed him back. Their tongues did a slow sensual dance, until Brant broke away to come up for air. Aniyah was shocked that he did not want her to respond to his attempt to be with her.

"Relax, Beauty, I'm in control. See, you need a man like me to take care of you."

He stroked her long locks of hair, and then wrapped his arms around her.

He whispered, "Suit-wearing men want you to run errands for them, wash their clothes, get their shirts cleaned and take care of the house, while they work long hours and go on business trips. They have other women at their disposal while they're away. With me, all you have to do is relax and let me take care of you."

Brant locked lips with hers before she could say a word. He placed her hand on his hardened member. It was like she was in another world. She attempted to stroke him, but he moved her hands.

Brant stepped away from her.

Aniyah watched him disappear into the bathroom, presuming he would get a rubber to cover himself for protection.

He called to her. "Relax, Beauty, I'll be there in a second."

Contemplating if she should allow herself to go further with him, Aniyah crossed her legs and tried to stop the tingling sensation she felt. When Brant returned, she locked her eyes on the crotch of his pants as he made his way over to her. A T-shirt was now covering his once-bare chest.

He tapped his middle finger on her lips. "I hope I made you feel a little more relaxed." He grabbed his keys. "I have to leave. See you here tomorrow at the same time?"

"I'll have to think about it."

"You'll be here." He gave her a wink. "You can leave whenever you're ready to."

Aniyah watched him vanish. She felt confused. What kind of game was he playing with her? No man refused her. *This can't be for real*, she thought.

She saw that it was more she had to learn about Brant's mysterious ways.

CHAPTER 12

*T*ucked under the bedcovers in his room, Aniyah would have no worries of her son interrupting his parents. He slept through the night after the active day that he'd had. Placing unlit candles around the master suite, she prepared for the return of her husband. She was in need of lovemaking after Brant had aroused her. It was for the best. Jarvis was the person she was supposed to give herself to only. Aniyah slipped on a low-cut, sheer, white-laced nightgown, and her breasts peeked through the lace. It was her husband's favorite nightwear for her to wear for him.

Aniyah crawled into the bed hoping Jarvis would arrive home soon. She had dozed off while awaiting him and woke up to him planting a kiss on her forehead.

She smiled. "Hey, Honey, you're home."

"Missed my wife and son so much."

Throwing her arms around her husband's neck, Aniyah pulled him down into the bed with her. The smell of his cleansed skin turned her on even more. Aniyah pushed him on his back and crawled on top of him, giving him kisses on his head, face, neck and his masculine body.

With her teeth, she pulled at the drawstring of his sweat-pants until it loosened.

"I have a hot woman on me tonight." He loved that his wife had missed him.

"I love you so much, Jarvis."

"I love you more, Aniyah; you're my world."

Jarvis flipped her over. She landed on top of him. He palmed her breasts, admiring their roundness. Aniyah moaned when the wetness of his tongue came in contact with her hardened nipples, while his hands caressed her body.

Thoughts of Brant invaded her mind. His muscular body and gray eyes. Aniyah shook those thoughts out of her head and focused her attention on her husband. She gripped his member and massaged him.

Jarvis eased himself inside of her. She loved the way he made love to her. He never was lax in that department, but even with his great lovemaking skills, her body yearned to experience Brant.

Aniyah had no doubt that Jarvis had no interest in other women. He always reached his peak quicker after going a few days without sex.

Breathing heavy, she complained, "Honey, is that it?"

"Baby, this is what happens when a man is away from his wife too long."

Aniyah tickled him under his right arm. "You owe me."

Jarvis laughed. "Hey, the night is not over yet. Don't count me out." Giving her a kiss, he got out of the bed, and came back with a small box in his hand. "I got you a little something."

Aniyah sat up, placing the pillow behind her back to

give her support. She opened the box wrapped in red ribbon. Inside, she pulled out a sterling-silver necklace with three princess-diamond stones, representing the past, present, and future. "This is so sweet of you." Aniyah gave her husband a peck on the lips. She turned around, and he hooked the necklace around her neck.

"Jarvis, can we afford this?"

The gift was one of many he had picked up for her while he was away.

"No need to worry about our finances."

"I do love it." She touched the necklace.

"Looks great on my lady."

Jarvis crawled on top of her. Again, they made out. She tried to bury Brant's face from her mind. The vision of his glared stares and lustful body made the sex from her husband take her to a place where she wanted to do a hallelujah dance. This was not how she wanted to feel—having another man in her thoughts while her attention should have been focused on the joy of lovemaking with her husband. At that moment, she was ready to give Brant back his cell phone. She was happy she did not go any further with him. It was a big risk for her to ruin her marriage over swindling Brant out of his money.

CHAPTER 13

*W*ith Jarvis home, Aniyah felt secure. Caught up in a handsome man and dollar signs was a moment of stupidity. She was eager to end her ties with Brant.

When Jarvis left for work, she did not dress in a fancy dress. Instead, she slipped on a Nike lightweight sweat suit and a pair of sneakers. Once inside her vehicle, Aniyah turned on the phone from Brant and saw that he had left her another text.

Logan: Rm. 214

He had gotten a room next to the one where they had met the previous day. Time came soon enough, and she was at the door. She knocked once and Brant opened it. When she entered, she noticed there were no lunches prepared for them. Instead, she eyed a tray of fruits and chilled water bottles.

"You look relaxed today."

"Brant… Logan," she hesitated. "You need someone that you can have for yourself. I'm taken. This is wrong."

He laughed. "Broke businessman must be back at the crib."

"Yes, my husband has returned home." She pulled out

the cell phone and held it out for him to take. "I don't need this anymore."

Brant smirked. He folded his arms and took a seat on the edge of the desk. "Yesterday you were ready to give yourself to me." He cut his eyes at her. "He must have given you, last night, what you really wanted from me."

"I'm not discussing with you, what me and my husband do in our bedroom." Since Brant did not take the phone, Aniyah set it on the bed. "I'm outta here."

When she started for the door, he snatched her into his arms and pushed his tongue into her mouth. Aniyah gasped for air, trying to speak. She attempted to pull away from him, but Brant held a tight grip on her. He stuck his hand underneath her top and fondled her breasts.

Aniyah found her way closer to the desk with the bowl of fruits. Brant picked up a handful of strawberries. With her top up, he crushed the fruit, and let the juices trickle onto her breasts.

He licked her flesh. "I have what you love... plenty of cash."

Before Aniyah could answer, he shoved his tongue in her mouth again. She gasped. He let up merely enough for her to still breathe. While he fondled her nipples, he kissed her on the earlobe, and then whispered in her ear. "I want to show you the mansion I'm building at the lake. Would you like to see where you could visit and have your own personal key?" Brant pulled her top down. He picked up two strawberries, gave one to her and then popped the other into his mouth.

She demanded, "I want more than a key. I like money in

my purse. A private personal bank account and an open line credit card. Pamper me with nice things, that's what I want."

"I can take care of that." He squeezed her cheek. "My place will be ready in two months."

"I need to see it. Tell me exactly where it's located."

Access to a home on the lake was one of the things she aimed for. With the cell phone back in her hand, Aniyah watched him head to the door.

He placed his hand on the knob. "Not today. I'll text you when I'm ready to show it off. You can go."

"First, you didn't want me to leave. Now you're throwing me out. What's up with you?"

"When you stop playing with me, I'll stop playing with you."

Aniyah stood next to him at the door. "I used to run rings around men like you. I've given up that lifestyle, thanks to my husband. Yet, I'm here putting my marriage on the line. I don't want to hurt Jarvis. He's been good to me."

As soon as she mentioned her husband's name, Brant forced his tongue in her mouth, kissing her before he rambled his bitter words. "I don't want to hear his name. I'm what you need."

Aniyah's personal phone rang. She had forgotten to shut it off.

He demanded, "Don't answer it."

However she did. He walked away, popping another strawberry in his mouth.

Aniyah perked up her voice as she spoke to her friend. "Hey, Nellie."

"Girl, are you all right?"

Aniyah took a deep breath when she felt Brant stroke her neck with his tongue. After another deep breath, she said, "I'm good."

"You don't sound okay."

"I'm moving fast."

"Girl, slow down. You're breathing mighty heavy."

"I'm fast-walking around Sandhill Village. Trying to get some exercise in," Aniyah told her, hoping that she would buy that story.

"That personal trainer got you moving?"

"Yes," Aniyah replied, remembering the lie that Brant had fed to Nellie when she saw them out having lunch together.

"Jarvis will see your new sexy figure soon enough. Not that you needed to do anything about your weight. Well, be safe. Chat later."

When Aniyah hung up, Brant snatched the phone from her.

"From now on, never speak to him while you're with me."

"It was my friend. The one you met." She took her phone back. "We're not in a relationship, so cut the jealousy act."

Brant twirled a lock of her hair around his finger. He stroked her face with his hand, kissed her on the lips. Then he opened the door. "Keep that phone safe. I don't want to have to go toe-to-toe with you know who."

Aniyah saw the seriousness in his eyes. If Jarvis ever learned of their communication, Brant would not back down from him.

Again with mixed emotions, she felt uneasy. She repeated, "Maybe you should find someone else to be with."

Her eyes watered. One minute Brant was comforting and the next he turned into a jerk. To empty the farmer's pockets for the good of her man without dishing out would be fine with her, but if Jarvis ever found out about her cheating on him, it would be hell for her to pay.

CHAPTER 14

*T*he moment Jarvis stood in front of the bank, his eyes flashed to the new name on the building, *Milandra Houston Bank.* "Unbelievable," he uttered. He never thought that he would not be the next in line to be the CEO of his family's bank. Shaking his head, he hurried inside, making his way to his office on the sixth floor.

Jarvis unfastened his suit jacket and took a seat at his desk. He looked toward the door, hoping his situation was a joke, expecting his father to burst through the door. Instead, he dropped his head, bursting into tears. Ever since he could remember, he had been told that he would be the next heir to the family business. Aniyah as his wife had estranged his relationship with his father. But never did he think it would flow over into his father's last wishes—disinheriting him.

He raised his head when he heard someone burst into his office. Wiping his tears, Jarvis retrieved his shades from the inside of his suit jacket and placed them over his eyes. "This is my office. Please knock the next time," he said.

"This is my establishment." Milandra struck back at

him, dressed in a sky-blue two-piece, quarter-sleeved skirt suit, with a matching handbag on her arms. She strutted straight to an empty chair near the desk.

"You don't waste time. I see you could not wait to put your name up for the town to see."

Milandra giggled. "It would've been your name hadn't you fallen for Aniyah. So don't complain."

"I'm busy. What do you want?"

"I have an offer for you."

"Like what I need to do to get back this company? You can keep the home."

"That's not up for discussion."

"Get to the point. I'm busy." Jarvis clicked an ink pen.

"You can continue to run the banks. You can relocate your office upstairs into your father's old office."

"You need me."

"Never do I need anyone. I can offer the job to someone else. That person can become your boss. You'll have to answer to them. Is that what you want? Because, I'll arrange it."

Milandra stood to her feet. She headed toward the door.

"Wait," Jarvis called to her. "I want no parts of my dad's old office. I'll stay put here."

Milandra smiled. "I'll remodel it. Give it a feminine touch. I'll make it my private office whenever I'm needed here."

Before she grabbed the handle of the door to exit, Jarvis received a knock at the door. There was no need for him to invite the party inside. Milandra pulled the door opened. She came face-to-face with her husband.

"Nolan?"

"I'm here to see Jarvis," her husband said.

"What business do you have with my employee?"

Nolan walked beyond her. "Hey, Jarvis. I need to talk to you in private." He dotted his eyes back at his wife.

Milandra did not budge. She closed the door shut. "This is *my* bank. I should be in on any discussion you have with Jarvis."

"Trust me, this is not bank business," Nolan said.

"See you later, Milandra." Jarvis dismissed her. "Have a seat, Nolan."

"I'm not leaving," she said, standing firm.

"Hell, stay," Nolan said. He went to Jarvis, giving him a handshake. "I want to apologize, on behalf of my wife, for taking what's rightfully yours. This bank and your dad's house belong to you, not her. I had no knowledge of what transpired before. I don't agree with what Milandra has done. I've pleaded with her to give everything back to you."

"Yes, you did. However, I purchased it fair and square. It's business. Admit it, Nolan, you can't handle a smart and powerful woman," Milandra said.

"I can't stand a self-righteous and manipulative woman. One who thinks that family doesn't come before money," Nolan said.

Jarvis listened to their marital disagreement. "Nolan, it's fine. My dad didn't want me to have it. It's his way of having control. I'm not sweating it. If I do, my dad will continue to have power over me even in his death."

"See, it doesn't bother Jarvis. So leave. You're disturbing my employee," Milandra said.

"You're a real character," Nolan said. "Divorce can't

come through fast enough."

"Nolan, don't let this end your marriage. You guys do love each other," Jarvis said.

Milandra chimed in. "Sometimes love isn't enough."

Nolan dotted his eyes at his wife and then back at Jarvis. "Talk to you later, man. Again, sorry for the way things went down."

A heated Nolan exited the room.

Milandra waited to hear backlash from Jarvis. He held his head down and dived into his work. He never looked up until after she exited his office.

"This isn't the end of it," he grumbled.

Jarvis got Noelle on the line.

"Hey, I would like to take you and Sid out for dinner tonight. You were nice to come to my defense when I learned of my dad's wishes."

"I believe in what's right. No supper necessary."

"I know you don't like my wife. But please, this one time, come and dine with us?"

Noelle hesitated. "Jarvis, I'll be cordial and go. What time?"

Jarvis made the dinner arrangements. He just needed to share the news with Aniyah.

CHAPTER 15

*A*fter leaving Brant, Aniyah received a call from her hubby. He told her about the arranged double date with Noelle Houston and her husband. This was not an evening she was looking forward to. She had no desire to be in a room with anyone named Houston. It was Jarvis' quest to show his gratitude to Noelle. Nonetheless, Aniyah arranged for a babysitter for their son.

That evening, she slipped into a black dress with a peek-a-boo cut-out, showing off her cleavage. She dazzled her long locks with washable gold streak highlights. Next, she did her makeup, setting it off with a glossy ruby-red lipstick. Hanging from her ears were long silver chain-link earrings. When she paraded down the staircase, Aniyah held her head up high, and swayed her hips with every step she took.

At the foot of the steps, Jarvis awaited her. His eyes widened in admiration when he saw Aniyah. "You look gorgeous." He gave her a peck on the cheek.

Turning in a circle, Aniyah showed off her curves. Jarvis patted her on the behind. "Let's get out of here, before I call Noelle and cancel the evening."

In her head, she wished Jarvis would do that. She locked arms with him, and they went out for a deserved date away from their son. Also, it gave her the chance to be free of the spell Brant had on her.

When they arrived at the restaurant, Noelle and Sid sat in the lobby. Noelle wore a black scallop-hem lace dress that complemented her mid-sized silhouette. Sid was dressed in a black suit.

Aniyah admired Noelle's hairdo, brushed to the side, hanging long enough to lie on her bosom. She did not utter a word to compliment her.

Jarvis went over to Noelle. "You look like Hollywood." He gave her a hug.

"It's a little something I ordered from online," Noelle said.

Sid praised Aniyah as he embraced her. "That's a hot number you have on."

"Thanks. It's specially made," Aniyah said, cutting her eyes at Noelle.

With Jarvis' arms around her waist, Aniyah felt him pinch her. They led the way into the restaurant, with their guests following behind them. As they took their seats, the sound of soft jazz serenaded them. Aniyah noticed a live band.

Sid spoke louder over the noise, "Cocktails?"

"Yeah man and some food. I'm hungry," Jarvis said.

Once the waiter arrived, Sid ordered. "We need two bottles of chilled wine."

To escape conversation, Aniyah snatched up a menu to read. So did Noelle. The waiter brought over the wine, popped the cork and filled each of their glasses halfway.

"Let's toast," Sid said. He dotted his eyes at the women at the table. "Jarvis, we're blessed men."

"Here's to our beautiful wives. They're the most valuable assets in our lives," Jarvis said, with his glass held high.

"Aww," Aniyah said. "That's so sweet." She kissed Jarvis on the cheek.

Hearing her husband's confession of his feelings for her, she felt guilty talking to another man. Brant had flashed across Aniyah's mind. "Cheers," she said. Aniyah took a swallow of her drink.

"Tap glasses first," Jarvis reminded her.

They toasted again and this time Aniyah clinked glasses with her husband and his guests.

Browsing the menu, Aniyah ordered a whole fried red snapper, and for her sides, garlic mashed potatoes and asparagus. Jarvis joined in and ordered the same dish, but Noelle and Sid went for the lobster, which they picked out from a large aquarium tank.

The men chatted over dinner. Aniyah focused her attention on reading data on her cell phone, as did Noelle. The men noticed their wives' dislike for each other.

"Aniyah and Noelle, you ladies haven't exchanged words," Jarvis said.

Sid voiced his opinion, "Not even a hello?"

"Put the bad blood aside," Jarvis said.

Sid nodded. "I agree."

Noelle sighed. "I can be cordial. Aniyah, I hope you're enjoying your food."

Aniyah cut her eyes at Jarvis. She looked back at Noelle. "The food is delicious. I hope yours tastes good, too." It was like a block of ice had been cracked in half.

When it was time for dessert, Aniyah shared a chocolate strawberry cheesecake with her husband. With their own forks, they dived into the cheesecake. On the last bite of the dessert, Aniyah put the fork up to her mouth. Looking straight ahead at the front of the restaurant, Brant's magnetic gray eyes caught her attention. She spat the cheesecake out.

"Honey, are you okay?" Jarvis asked, patting her on the back.

Aniyah reached for the bottle of wine, filling her glass up to the rim. She gulped it down in one shot. Not to be obvious, as she drank out of the glass, she glanced again over at the door, but Brant had disappeared.

Relieved, she took a deep breath. "The cake went down the wrong pipe."

"Your face is red," Noelle said.

"I need to go to the bathroom," Aniyah said, excusing herself from the table.

"Noelle, maybe you should go with her," Sid said, concerned.

"No. I'm fine to go alone. Once I splash some cold water on my face, I'll be good," Aniyah assured him.

On her way to the bathroom, Aniyah searched for any sign of Brant. He was nowhere to be found; it was as if he had never been there. She located the ladies room on the far right of the restaurant's entrance and went inside.

With a weakened bladder, Aniyah hurried and used the toilet. She washed her hands and splashed cold water on her face. She did a once-over in the mirror and started for the door. When she swung it open, Brant stood before her.

Startled, she said, "What are you doing here? I can't be seen talking to you. I'm here with Jarvis."

Annoyed, Brant said, "I told you never to mention his name around me."

Aniyah tried to push past him, but Brant pulled her into his arms, snuck a kiss, and then fled. Back inside the bathroom, Aniyah splashed more water on her face from the elevated temperature of her body.

She smacked her lips to smooth out her lipstick and returned to the table.

"Feeling better?" Jarvis asked.

"Perfect." She gave him a kiss on his lips to wash away Brant's kiss.

By the end of dinner, Aniyah had drunk several glasses of wine. When it was time to leave, her body weighed like a ton of cement blocks. She barely stood up.

"Aniyah, I believe you're drunk," Jarvis said feeling embarrassed.

Her speech slurred, she responded, "I'm sick."

"Take her outside," Sid suggested.

Jarvis escorted his wife out of the restaurant.

About the time they arrived at their vehicle, she had brought up her full meal and dessert.

"Yuck," Noelle said, squeezing her nose. "No class."

"Honey, be quiet," Sid said, "It helped her to feel better."

Aniyah wiped her mouth with Jarvis' handkerchief.

"Let's get you home," Jarvis said, and helped her into the vehicle.

With an aching stomach, Aniyah lay back in the seat and closed her eyes. She heard Noelle and Sid say their good nights to Jarvis. She was in no shape to speak to them.

Somewhere between the restaurant and home, she dozed off.

When Aniyah woke up, it was the next morning.

Her head ached as she saw Jarvis was dressed for work.

"I'm sorry. I embarrassed you last night."

Jarvis put his arms around her and held her. "Yes you did. You need to not drink so much when we're out in public. You couldn't walk. I had to help you."

"I didn't mean to drink so much," she lied. "I had a good evening being with you. Not Noelle. Her husband is nice."

"You threw up on the ground. Thank God you didn't do it in the car."

She mumbled to herself, "It's Brant's fault."

"I'm sorry, Jarvis."

"Aniyah, watch your intake of drinks."

"Please don't ask me to go out on another double-date with Noelle and her hubby."

"Bye, Baby."

CHAPTER 16

*W*hen Jarvis pulled out of the driveway, Aniyah wrapped herself in a bathrobe and ran down the stairs. She went to her vehicle and searched the trunk for Brant's cell phone. It was under the spare tire.

She contacted Brant. He answered after the first ring.

"You've gone too far. Who told you I was out with my husband?"

She received no answer—only the sound of the dial tone humming in her right ear. Aniyah sucked her teeth. Annoyed, she called him once again. "Did we get disconnected or did you hang up on me?"

Brant dismissed her question and instead said, "Come see me."

"Not today. I don't feel good. Last night, I had too much to drink. Thanks to you."

Aniyah hurried into the house.

He blurted, "I'm taking you today to see my new house."

Aniyah attempted to perk up, but her head throbbed. "My little boy is home. I didn't take him to school today. That's how terrible I feel. He's still asleep."

"I'll massage your head. Get a babysitter. I want to spoil you today."

"You're becoming too possessive and demanding. I'm not the one for that. I say we end this foolishness. I'll dump this phone in the recycle bin."

His showing up at the restaurant made her feel like he was stalking her.

"You either bring the phone to me or I'll come get it."

Aniyah panicked. "Do you have my address?"

She flopped down on the bed, worried that Brant had her investigated, or better yet, Googled her on the Internet.

"I'll bring you the doggone phone. Please do not come to my house."

"See you when you get here. I'll text you the room number."

Out of the bed, headache and all, Aniyah contacted her friend.

"Nellie, please tell me you're off today."

"I am, why?"

"Bestie, I need your help. J.P. is at home today. I need you to watch him. I have an emergency."

"Is everything okay?"

"J.P. is fine. He's sleeping. For me, I promised Jarvis I'd run errands for him. He thinks it's been taken care of. But I haven't done a thing."

"Because I love that little boy so much, I'll come," Nellie said.

"Oh, to hell with me, huh?"

The ladies giggled before they hung up.

Aniyah hurried and got dressed.

***

As soon as Brant opened the door, Aniyah stepped inside and shoved the phone in his hand.

"You crossed the line showing up at places where Jarvis and I attend."

Aniyah placed her hand over her mouth, realizing she had mistakenly mentioned her husband's name. It was like she had triggered Brant's brain cells. He became out of control. He snatched her into his arms and smothered her lips. Aniyah felt like she was being suffocated. She pushed him away.

"I see you don't want no more parts of me." He pointed at the door. "Bye."

Aniyah shed fake tears. "I do want to be with you. You're not making it easy."

She hated she had allowed herself to go back to some of her old ways, but this was what she had to do to help out her husband.

Calming down, Brant consoled her. He wiped her dampened face with his T-shirt.

"Give me another chance. I'll do better," she begged.

Brant took her by the hand, leading her to the bed. He sat down bringing Aniyah to his lap. While he rubbed her forehead, and stared into her eyes, he rocked her.

His grayish eyes mesmerized Aniyah. The longer she stared at him, the more her body became relaxed. Being in his arms was comforting.

To her surprise, he did not strip her of her clothes. That afternoon, she dozed off in his arms. About an hour or two passed before he woke her up. Aniyah could not believe she had fallen asleep in his lap, cuddled in his arms.

Her stomach no longer ached, and the throbbing feeling in her head had gone away.

He smiled at her. "How do you feel?"

"Better."

"I have the power to uplift you."

"You're such a mystery man."

"Mysteries are to be solved. And, I'm the only solver."

Brant urged her to get up off his lap, patting the bed for her to take a seat while he went and gathered up a bowl of grapes and fed them to her.

Aniyah chewed the sweet, seedless grapes. She watched him look down her blouse, while pouring water in between her cleavage, simply to watch her nipples perk up. He fed her more ripe grapes, while every so often trickling water on her breasts.

His teasing had Aniyah feeling aroused. One touch of his hands on her flesh and she would have no choice but to give in to him. It would give her power to seal the deal in landing him into her wicked world. Once the last drop of water flowed down on her breasts, Brant placed the cup on the desk.

"What's the verdict? Do you want to keep the phone?"

Her eyes aimed at the crotch of his pants. She noticed his bulge. Her body reacted to what he had to offer her. She surrendered.

"Yes."

Brant pulled her up off of the bed, and then smothered her into his arms. When he rubbed against her, she felt his manhood. She waited and waited for him to have his way with her. It did not happen. Instead curiosity got to her. She attempted to make a move on him. Aniyah eased her hands down in his boxers, but he stopped her.

"I like that you're going for what you want. You didn't come here for that. Remember you came here to return me my phone. Maybe I'll share my goods the next time, only if you say you're here for me."

"You're contagious."

He returned the phone to her.

"You need to go. Call me when you're really ready for me. That's when I'll take you to see my house at the lake."

Brant headed to the door and opened it.

"You said you were taking me today. What about my presents?" Aniyah pleaded.

"Another day." He pointed the way out of the door.

Aniyah swung her handbag on her arms. She rolled her eyes. "Bye, Brant Logan."

The air-conditioned hallway of the hotel helped to cool her off when she exited the room.

Brant was a piece of work. It would take longer than she thought for her to be in full control. He was the most difficult man she had ever met.

Over the next few weeks, Aniyah never heard from Brant. She checked the phone constantly. She acted like a high school student with a crush on a football player. Aniyah stopped by the farmers market, but he was not there. He was blocking her goals to help her husband. In reality she missed Brant.

It took another one of Jarvis' business trips, thanks to Milandra, to get her to make the call.

"Hi, Logan."

"It took long enough for me to hear from you."

His jolly tone of voice led her to believe he was happy she had contacted him.

"I would like to see you," she said.

"Your businessman is out of town… another overnight trip?"

"How do you know that?"

"He's in Charlotte."

"Stop tracking my husband."

"I don't want to talk about him. I like the way you're talking today. I'll come and get you. We'll go and see my new house."

With Jarvis III in preschool, Aniyah was ready to jump in her vehicle. "I'll come to you," she said.

He paused when his phone beeped indicating he had another caller. "Looks like you and me got to meet up at another time. Got another call."

"Ditching me for a girlfriend?"

He chuckled. "Hit you back later."

Aniyah mumbled, "Men."

She went ahead and dressed. She did not put on her usual runaround clothing. Instead, she slipped into a green T-shirt dress, something she could easily remove if necessary. She did not bother to wear makeup; she applied a cocoa-colored lip-gloss onto her lips.

When she didn't hear back from Brant, she called him several times. There was no answer.

CHAPTER 17

*T*he morning after Jarvis returned home, Aniyah went to her vehicle in search of her cell phone charger. She checked her secret phone for any messages from Brant. When she turned it on, the phone's notifications went off. Then it rang. She looked toward the front door of the house, to make sure that Jarvis did not catch her with it.

She bent down on the floor, pretending to search for something. "You pick a fine time to call. Where have you been?"

"You miss me?"

Aniyah did not respond to his question. Instead, she muttered, "I can't talk like I want to right now."

"Is your suit jacket man around?"

"Yes. He's getting ready for work."

"Call me when he leaves. Today I'll take you to see my house."

"I've heard that before."

"I promise. I'll even pick you up at your door."

"Not happening. I'll meet you in front of the hotel."

"If you say so."

Aniyah dropped the phone on the floor, when she heard

her name called.

"Coming, Jarvis."

She turned the cell phone off and stuck it under the driver's seat.

Aniyah rolled up the legs of her lightweight jogging pants over her knees. Then, she did the same to the sleeves of her matching pink top.

Jarvis entered, dressed in a gray-and-black tweed suit jacket over a pair of black slacks. He walked over and pulled her into his arms. "Happy Anniversary to the love of my life."

"Back at you," she responded.

Jarvis attempted to lift off her top. Aniyah tapped him on the hand. "You'll be late for work."

"With a beautiful wife like you, it'll be worth it." He twirled her hair around his finger.

Before long, he thrust his tongue into her mouth. Aniyah accepted his passionate kiss. Once she felt his hands easing between her legs, she gently shoved him away.

"Our son is waking up soon, and you need to get going."

"You win this round." He tapped her on the tip of her nose.

Together, they left out of the room. Instead of going down the stairs, she watched Jarvis go into their son's room. She followed behind him. She watched as her husband's lips spread into a wide smile. His skin glowed.

"That boy must be boxing in his sleep."

They laughed. They saw their son had kicked the covers off of him.

"He's a busybody. Now, you better get to work."

They headed to the ground floor. As they walked down the stairs, he asked, "When will you reframe the pictures of us and J.P.? It's been only two days and I miss having them displayed on my desk."

"I'll do it today. You can take them to the office with you tomorrow."

Going along with their normal routine, Aniyah walked her husband to the door. He turned around to face her, and she stared into his eyes, which sparkled on his moisturized face. She landed one last goodbye kiss on his thick lips.

"Today is our third anniversary," he reminded her. "No cooking tonight. I have the perfect night planned. I'm a blessed man to have a gorgeous wife and handsome son. I love you."

Tears welled in her eyes, and she muttered back to him, "I love you, too."

Standing in the doorway, she watched Jarvis hop inside his Mercedes-Benz with royal-blue leather seats.

As he eased out of the double-garage driveway, he rolled down the driver's-side window and called to her, "I'm the luckiest man in the world. I love you, Mrs. Aniyah Powell."

"I love you, too."

Aniyah shut the door, once he drove off.

When she headed toward the stairs, the doorbell chimed.

"Jarvis?" she curiously called her husband's name, since she had seen him leave the driveway.

She opened the door. Her eyes lit up. She looked down

the road, thankful there was no sign of Jarvis returning. "Logan, you shouldn't be here. I told you that I would meet you outside the hotel."

"I told you I'd pick you up."

"Wait in your truck. I have to get my son dressed."

"I need to use your toilet."

"No you don't."

"I'm a man. I can go right here on your front lawn."

Aniyah stepped out of the way. "Hurry up."

She escorted him to the half-bath on the first floor.

He chuckled. "Nice place, but no comparison to my home."

Under her breath, she said, "Only for you, Jarvis, am I putting up with this fine creep."

She stood on guard outside the door until Brant came out. Aniyah escorted him to the front door. Once he rested his shoes on the concrete, she deadbolted it.

Her hands trembled. "This is all for you, Jarvis," she repeated to herself.

"Wake up, J.P." She gently shook her son.

Her son rubbed his eye. "Sleepy."

He stretched his arms and turned over on his other side.

"Oh no you don't. It's time for school."

Aniyah scooped her son up out of the bed. She stood him on his two feet, and he awakened. She led him toward his private bathroom to use the potty. Once Jarvis III finished, Aniyah washed his face and helped him brush his teeth. She had bathed him the night before. Aniyah dressed her son in a pair of beige pants and a navy shirt. She slipped a pair of socks on his feet. He pushed his little feet into a black pair of string-up shoes.

When they made it to the first floor, Aniyah went into the kitchen. She warmed an apple-flavored Pop-Tart in the toaster for her boy, while she filled his Sippy cup with orange juice.

Jarvis III took a sip. He cried, "I want Papa-Dad take me to school."

"He's at work." She placed the warm Pop-Tart in foil and slipped his arm through the straps of his little backpack. "Time for school."

"I want Papa-Dad," he repeated.

"He's working. Let's go."

With Jarvis III by her side, Aniyah hurried down the driveway. She looked down the road and hoped that her retired neighbor, Mrs. Stewart, was not out taking her daily walk. Their homes were spaces apart. She got her wish; Mrs. Stewart was nowhere in sight.

"Come on. I don't have all day," Brant hollered.

Aniyah walked up to the Ford truck, parked in front of her mailbox at the end of the driveway. Opening the rear-passenger door, she placed her son's carseat inside and strapped him in.

"No, stranger," Jarvis III cried once he saw the driver.

Aniyah consoled her son. "That's Mister. He's a nice man. Mama is getting in the truck with you."

"Hey there, Kid, if you stop crying, I'll give you a sucker," Brant said, with his hat turned backward on his head. When Brant held up the cherry-flavored lollipop, Jarvis III settled down. He attempted to hand it to the child. Aniyah snatched it from his hand.

"No candy for my son. It's too early," she said. Instead,

she handed Jarvis III his Pop-Tart. He nibbled on his morning breakfast.

When Aniyah settled into the seat, she strapped herself into the seatbelt. "I need you to take me to drop my son off at school first. I need to be home early enough to get my car. I don't want to be late from picking him up. I can drive my own car and leave it closer to his school," Aniyah suggested.

"Nah, I'll have you back home in plenty of time. You're safe with me, Beauty."

Aniyah looked out of the window. She continued to search for any sign of Mrs. Stewart. "Let's go before my neighbor sees you."

Brant pulled off from the preschool. When he stopped at the red light, he unlatched the seatbelt and leaned over to give Aniyah a kiss.

She smiled. "I'm ready to see this fabulous home you're building on the lake."

"I want you to wear this." He handed Aniyah a sleeping mask.

Her eyes widened. "What the hell for?"

He drove off once the light turned green. "I want you to be surprised when you see it."

"We're nowhere near there. I'm not riding with this thing over my eyes."

Brant cut his eyes at her. "Put it on when we get closer to the lake."

He drove until he came in the vicinity of the waters. He pulled over on the side of the road. "Now put it on."

Aniyah slipped the mask over her eyes. In darkness, she

felt his lips touch hers. He bit her as they kissed, letting off a slight pain, but yet it stimulated her body. She figured he would have his way with her in his vehicle, but he did not.

"Now, that's better." Brant turned on the ignition. With her eyes covered, Aniyah sniffed the aroma of the lake. She yearned to live near the water.

She felt the vehicle come to a stop. "Are we there?"

"Yes." Brant removed the mask.

Aniyah adjusted her eyes to the sunlight. Her eyes widened when she saw the familiar place.

"Is this some kind of joke? This is my father-in-law's old home. Powell Property."

"Not anymore. I own it now."

"I thought you were building a house."

"I lied."

"That uppity snob, Milandra, sold it to you?"

Brant laughed. "Yeap. I closed the deal. Money talks."

He pulled Aniyah into his arms. "You'll have free access to come and go as you please. Our secret."

When Aniyah grabbed the truck door to open it, Brant hit a button and locked them inside.

"I want to get out. Open this door."

As if she had the power, Aniyah was eager to go and fire the security staff because of the way they had treated her the last time she had visited the home.

"I'm having it renovated. It's not ready for showing. I do have another surprise for you."

"What? You're keeping your promise; we're going shopping?"

"Put the mask back on. This surprise is bigger than this

one."

"I'm still in shock over Milandra. She's a piece of work."

Brant turned the ignition on and drove off.

Aniyah sat with a smirk on her face. It would be easy as ever to get back her husband's property. *Wrong move, Milandra,* she thought.

CHAPTER 18

*T*oo curious about the next surprise, Aniyah opened her eyes behind the mask. She strained her eyes to see through the black silk fabric, but still she was in darkness. She had reared the seat back to lie down, hiding from other people on the road. Soon enough, her body jiggled from the bumpy road. The crunching sounds led her to believe she was on a graveled road.

Sniffing the odor of hay, she asked, "It smells like we're on a farm. Where are we?"

"You'll find out shortly, Beauty... relax."

Aniyah had never visited his home. She wondered if he were taking her to where he lived. As Brant continued to drive, she smelled the pine trees that lined the road. A short while later, Brant turned off of the main road and the vehicle came to a stop.

"Don't take off the blindfold yet," he warned her. He jumped out of the vehicle and went to the passenger side, opening the door for her.

With his help, Aniyah got out, and he led the way. She walked up two steps. It felt to her like she had climbed up a stepstool. When her feet touched the inside of the unfamiliar place, she heard the click of a latch. Aniyah assumed Brant had locked a door. He took her by the hand and led her three more steps before he helped her to sit on a thirty-inch-deep loveseat.

Aniyah reached for the blindfold, but Brant grabbed her hand.

"Play along with me a little longer. It'll be worth it."

Aniyah put her hand down. "You're running out of time."

Brant did not respond to her. He rested her back on the cushioned seat.

Aniyah touched the sides of the loveseat. It felt to her like a bed cot.

Brant flopped on top of her, forcing his tongue into her mouth. He stirred his tongue around the walls of her jaws. There was no turning back for Aniyah. She had passed the danger zone unless Brant pulled another one of his tricks and dismissed himself.

It had been a long time since she had made love to another man besides her husband. As wetness of sweat puddled between her breasts, turned on, Aniyah reached at his rugged plaid shirt and unbuttoned it. She eased if off his arms. Brant removed his shirt. Aniyah felt him take her by both hands and lift them over her head to slip off her top to expose her black bra. To assist him, she slipped out of her pants and laced black underwear, letting him get an eye full of her lowered body.

Brant unlatched her bra, and her breasts bounced right out. He took each one for his liking. Next, he squeezed them as hard as he could. Aniyah screamed. The excruciating pain ceased once Brant released his hand.

Brant kissed her on the belly button. He played with her long locks. Then stroked her face, and before long, he was stroking the rest of her body. Aniyah moaned, desiring for him to enter her. Instead he grabbed her by her hands and lifted her to her feet.

"It's almost time for me to remove your mask. Give you your grand prize."

"I hope it's a bank and credit card account."

"Something more than that."

She took in another sweet kiss from him before he led her into a small room.

He whispered to her as he knelt down in front of her, stroking her legs. "I love a woman in disguise."

In the nude, Aniyah stood lifeless while he eased his hands down to her ankles. Her body tingled.

"A special gift," he said.

Aniyah felt him click a chain around her left ankle. Her face glowed. "Diamond ankle bracelet?"

"Crystal clear." Brant clicked another chain around her other ankle.

Once the clamp locked, and she could not move her legs, Aniyah snatched the blindfold off.

Brant jumped away from her. "Surprise."

Aniyah stared at her ankles, and then she looked up at him. "Brant Logan, this is not a diamond bracelet."

Aniyah reached down to free herself but had no success. The clamps around her legs were hooked to a long roped chain inside the room. She held out her hand to him. "Give me the key."

Brant laughed. "Not happening."

Being in bondage gave Aniyah a flashback of her prison

days.

She stood erect.

Looking into the home, she noticed the sunlight coming through the numerous windows. It gave the space an open feeling. But what puzzled her most were the black bars that covered a few windows. The home was no comparison to hers. It was the size of a small bedroom. Everything was compact. Near the door sat the tiniest L-shaped kitchen she had ever seen. A full-size, stainless-steel refrigerator sat in the kitchen's corner. It had only twelve feet of granite counter space with a four-burner, stainless-steel stove. The backsplash tile was fiery red. Aniyah turned her head to the right and noticed the twenty-square-foot bathroom, with a compact shower and a composed toilet. She noticed there was no window in it.

"This is where you'll be staying for a while," he revealed.

"Logan, I'm not for this. You really don't know me very well."

Again, she tried to unfasten the chains but had no luck. When wiggling out of the chains didn't work either, she called, "Get these damn things off of me and give me my clothes."

"Not today."

Brant pushed Aniyah further into the room. He locked the wood sliding door.

"Are you crazy? Let me out of this shoebox." She banged on the door.

He opened a small peephole made into the door. "Sometimes you have to appreciate the little things to get to the big things."

Again, Aniyah banged her fist against the door. "Let me out. I want to go home. I have to pick up my son from school."

Brant peeped into the hole. "You won't be seeing your son or husband for a while."

Shocked, Aniyah shouted, "You jerk!"

His phone rang. When he answered it, she put her mouth against the peephole and belted, "Help!"

"Save your breath. This is not your savior on the line."

Aniyah quieted down. She listened to his conversation.

"This chick won't be going anywhere near her husband or child for now. She's in good hands. I'll keep her as long as she needs to be here."

Curiously, she asked, "Are you talking to that old fathead, Papa-in-law of mine? This is his doing. His fake death has been fishy to me. Tell him he won't get away with this. I'll come back strong."

Brant hung up. "Shut up," he hollered.

"How many other lies have you told me?"

He laughed. "I'm not rich. Don't own nothing but this sweet little tiny house of mine."

"It's a shoebox. Nothing compared to the home Jarvis has me in."

Hearing her mention of her husband, Brant unlocked the door and charged at her. He pressed his fingers into her arms, enough for her to feel like he had stopped her blood circulation.

"It's not fancy enough, huh? Start loving it. It's your new home."

To get him to lighten up, she submitted. "You're right. I'm sorry."

Brant let go of her. He pointed his finger in her face. "I'll keep the door open as long as you behave yourself."

"Let's have fun." She devoured his lips.

Putting her pickpocketing skills to use, she eased her hand down in his pocket. Right away, Brant grabbed her hand, checking it to make sure she did not pull the key out of his pocket.

"I see you're going to be difficult." He shoved her into a chair of a small desk.

When he got close to her again, she hollered, "Please keep the door open. I'll be good."

He walked out and gave her, her wish. With caution, Aniyah stood to her feet.

"Stay inside. Or I'll lock it," Brant said.

Aniyah shivered. "It's chilly. I need my clothes."

"Ain't happening. I have something else for you to put on later."

Aniyah cried. "Why are you doing someone else's dirty work? Once my hubby finds out I'm missing, he'll have everyone looking for me."

"No he won't. You'll call and tell him that you've left him."

"He won't believe it. I'll never leave him or our child."

Brant reentered the room. He gripped her arm. "You'll make this call or else?"

Aniyah surrendered. "I'll do it."

"You try anything and I'll cut the call short."

"I need my phone. It's in my bag."

"I have it, over here."

"My phone?"

"No. Your bag," he said, picking it up off the floor near

the loveseat.

Brant had retrieved her bag when he had helped her out of the vehicle. Instead of handing it to Aniyah, he had dumped the contents on the floor. There was no phone. She cried. "I left it at home on the kitchen counter."

"You're lucky. I would have thrown it away, anyway. You'll use the phone I gave you. It's a prepaid one. We'll call him later."

Aniyah, tired of standing, took a seat on the floor nearest the room door. She did not dare go all the way into the room. She hoped Brant would have a change of heart and let her go. The real question was, was her father-in-law the one pulling the strings and pretending to be dead?

"When you speak to Papa Powell, tell him, he'll never win. I've been through worse. Jarvis and I have a strong bond. We love each other."

"So you were using me? You thought I had plenty of money?"

Again, Brant stormed at her, snatching her up off the floor. She swung at him. Brant slid his foot under hers. Aniyah hit the floor in a sitting position. He gripped her chin and squeezed it between his thumb and index finger. Tears flowed from her eyes.

"You're hurting me."

He laughed and let her go. Brant left the room, locking her inside. The peephole remained open.

More tears welled in her eyes. She begged, "Please let me out of here."

Aniyah yearned to get herself out the mess she had created. *No man outsmarts me,* she thought.

.

CHAPTER 19

*J*arvis had finished attending a board meeting. His receptionist greeted him, when he entered the receptionist area.

"Mr. Powell, you have a call on line two."

"Thanks, Terry."

Jarvis walked into his office. His eyes brightened. There stood the bank's staff.

"Happy Anniversary, Mr. Powell," the employees said in unison.

Terry darted past him and picked up a butter-cream cake. She sang, "Happy Anniversary, Boss."

Jarvis showed off his glossy white teeth from happiness. He went around the room shaking hands, hugging, and kissing the cheeks of female employees to show his gratitude.

"Mr. Powell, we tried this morning to call your wife to invite her, but we never could get in touch with her," Terry said disappointedly.

"That's not like Aniyah to not answer her cell phone. I'll tell her she was wanted here today." He also had tried to contact her earlier.

"She's probably preparing a special night," Terry said.

Jarvis teased by pretending to walk out of the door. "I'm leaving."

Everyone laughed.

Terry pulled on his jacket. "Before you go, Mr. Powell, I have something to say." She turned to the other employees. "Grab your glasses."

With a filled goblet, Terry toasted. "Mr. Powell, you're a true example of what a good boss, father and husband should be. May you and Mrs. Powell be blessed with many more years of happiness. Cheers!"

Terry held her glass up in the air, and then took a sip, along with others. She then handed Jarvis an envelope. He opened it to find a monetary gift from the staff.

"Thanks. I'll give this to Aniyah. She'll love a new pair of shoes."

They laughed.

Once the celebration ended, the staff dispersed for the day, as he too, was eager to get home. Jarvis called his wife again, but there was no answer from the landline phone or her cell phone. He felt a little weary, but not enough to think there was anything major wrong. He left the office to prepare to celebrate his wedding anniversary with his wife.

He first stopped at the jewelry store. Jarvis purchased a diamond bracelet and a matching necklace to dazzle his wife with. From there, he drove to a nearby florist and bought three-dozen red roses. On to the Italian restaurant, he ordered a meal for two: Chicken Parmesan, plenty of garlic bread with an appetizer of spinach dip and a Caesar salad. For their beverage delight, he purchased a bottle of champagne.

His vehicle smelled of a pizzeria with a scent of rose petals. Once he reached home, his eyes sparkled when he eyed Aniyah's car in the driveway. His mind wandered, for a second, to the day they got married in the heat of the moment among the nightlife in Las Vegas.

Jarvis drove into the driveway of the two-story stucco home. With one click of a button over the dashboard, one side of the garage opened. He eased his car inside, hitting the button one more time for the garage door to shut.

For fun, he blew the car horn to get his wife's and kid's attention, but there was no response. Jarvis hopped out of the vehicle. He gathered up as many things as he could for the first go-round into the house. In one hand was the big bag that held the meal and in the other was the bottle of champagne. When he approached the closed door, he set the bottle on the step. Once he opened the door, he picked it up and proceeded inside. "Aniyah," he called to his wife in a melodic tone but got no answer.

From the garage, it led him into the foyer and then inside the kitchen. As he placed the meal and champagne on the island, he immediately noticed Aniyah's phone. He looked at it and saw the unanswered calls that awaited her response. He presumed his wife had made a run with Nellie and forgotten it. Together they would get Jarvis III from preschool.

Jarvis returned to the garage. He got the rest of the things he had purchased and brought them inside. He placed them on the other end of the oversized island counter. Jarvis unpacked. He placed the champagne into the refrigerator to chill.

His cell phone rang. He looked at the unfamiliar number displayed on the screen. "Telemarketers," he grumbled, yet he answered it anyway.

"Hello."

"Jarvis," Aniyah said.

He let out a sigh of relief when he heard his wife's voice. "Aniyah. Where are you? You left your phone here at the house. It's our anniversary. Celebration time. Get home."

Her voice lowered. "Jarvis, I'm not coming home."

"You and Nellie put off your extra errands. Tell her to bring you home."

"I'm not with Nellie."

"Who are you riding with?"

"Jarvis, listen to me. Things aren't the same. Your papa left you broke. I can't live in that house anymore. It's not the real Powell home. You let Milandra steal it from you."

He became baffled. His eyes popped wide open and his cheery smile disappeared. "Are you telling me that you're leaving me on our wedding anniversary?"

She gasped for breath. "Yes, I've found someone else who can give me the life I want to live," she uttered.

Jarvis sat on a barstool. He pleaded, "Aniyah, please come home. I'm not flat-out broke, and our love for our family should be able to get us through this."

"I need more. You can't give it to me."

Jarvis' mind rushed to the property his mother had left him.

He blurted, "We'll be fine." Then he revealed, "I have ownership of my mother's old house and townhouse. No need to worry."

The line was silent for a moment.

"Aniyah," he called to her.

"Jarvis, that's not enough. I can't be with you anymore."

"Damn you, Aniyah. I lost everything. I believed you truly loved me."

"Love isn't enough."

"My God. My dad was right and everyone was so right about you. You're nothing but a money-hungry blood-sucker."

Jarvis found his way to the refrigerator. He pulled out the bottle of champagne. With a corkscrew, he opened it and took a gulp. His mind went to Jarvis III.

"Bring me back my son, or I'll have every officer in the state of South Carolina looking for you."

The next thing Jarvis heard was a dial tone. He attempted to call the number. It just rang. In a daze, he hurried to scope out his home. He headed to the second floor and looked inside his master suite. Aniyah's belongings were in the closet.

"This can't be happening. Aniyah!" he screamed to the top of his lungs. "J.P.!"

He ran to his son's room, still furnished with superheroes and all of his other belongings.

"You're not getting away with taking my son!" Jarvis shouted. He went to dial 9-1-1 when his cell phone rang again. It was his son's preschool.

"Hello?"

"Hello, Mr. Powell. Your son needs to be picked up. Would you be able to come for him?"

A teardrop escaped from his eye. Jarvis III was not with

his mother.

"I'm on my way to get him. If his mother shows up, do not let him go with her."

Jarvis had no time to think. He grabbed his keys and dashed to his vehicle.

Jarvis had apologized to the preschool for his lateness. When he saw little Jarvis, he wiped away the tears that stung his eyes and scooped his son into his arms.

"Hey there, fella. Dad is so happy to see you. I love you, J.P."

"Mama-Mom loves me too?"

Jarvis did not respond. He put his son in the vehicle and took him home.

When Jarvis entered the house with his son by his side, Jarvis III chanted, "I want cereal."

Jarvis took him straight to the kitchen and sat him at the table. He wiped his hands with a wet paper towel. Then, he made Jarvis III a bowl of Honey Nut Cheerios. While his son munched on the cereal, tears came to Jarvis' eyes. He never imagined Aniyah leaving him, much less their baby boy.

Jarvis made a phone call.

"Noelle, my marriage has fallen apart," he cried as he sat on a stool at the kitchen island.

"Aniyah left you?" she assumed.

"Yes," he admitted.

"I'm so sorry. She's evil to take your son away from you."

"She left him, too."

"Because you're hurting, I won't bother to say what I truly want to say."

He wept. "Today is our anniversary."

"Are you sure she's gone for good? Did you check the closets?"

"Yes. Nothing is missing. She left with nothing. She found someone else."

"I bet he has more money."

Tears flowed down his flushed face. "This is my dad and Milandra's fault. Aniyah always wanted to live in Lake Murray at the family's main home."

Jarvis got up out of the seat. Walking like a drunken man, he staggered, got a tissue out of a box and wiped his face.

"Do not make excuses for her. She should love you for you, not what you have or had. Sid and I are on our way to your home. We're here for you."

In a rage, he picked up Aniyah's cell phone and flung it across the kitchen. He shattered the bottle of champagne in the sink and pounded his hand into the door of the refrigerator. He called his wife's name.

"Aniyah, Aniyah. I thought you loved me as much as I loved you."

He fell to the floor. Jarvis III, startled, ran to him.

Jarvis wiped his eyes to give him a clear vision of his son, who was crying too. He realized he had scared him with his unruly behavior.

"I'm sorry." He patted his son on his back. "Go eat the rest of your cereal."

With swollen eyes, Jarvis picked up Aniyah's cell phone

from the floor and made his way to the front door. Noelle and her husband stood in the doorway. Once she stepped inside, Jarvis hugged her.

"I thought my life was perfect. Wife, child, a good job and house. Everything a woman would want from a man. Where did I go wrong?"

"Bro, you have done everything right," Sid said.

"It's her trifling ways," Noelle chimed in.

Jarvis moved away from her. He defended his runaway wife. "Noelle, don't speak of Aniyah in that way."

Sid spoke, "Bro, we know it hurts. The reality is Aniyah left her family."

Noelle went to Jarvis. She showed compassion. She embraced him.

"I know you love her," she said cautiously, not to trigger him again. "The reality is she cares nothing about your feelings."

"Bro, you did nothing wrong. Believe it," Sid said.

Noelle looked around. "Where's J.P.?"

"At his table. He's eating cereal," Jarvis answered.

"I'll get him ready for bed," Noelle volunteered.

Jarvis pointed toward the kitchen.

Jarvis took a seat on the staircase that led to the second floor of the house. Bowing his head, he shed more tears. "Men are not supposed to cry," he said.

"You're human," Sid said. He patted Jarvis on the shoulder.

"The woman I married and love has shamed me. I need another glass of champagne, wine or something."

"You and J.P. need to come home with us. No need in

feeling miserable on your anniversary night."

"Nah, I need to stay here in case Aniyah has a change of heart and comes home."

Sid pulled Jarvis by the arm. "You and J.P. are coming to our place, whether you like it or not. Noelle and I won't let you go through this alone."

"No, not yet. I just thought of someone who might be able to help me sort things out."

Jarvis opened Aniyah's cell phone. Luckily, the Otterbox had protected the screen from shattering.

"Who are you calling?" Sid wondered.

"Nellie. Aniyah's best friend." Jarvis put the phone on speaker. When she answered, Jarvis said, "Hi, Nellie. Have you spoken to or seen Aniyah today?"

"No," she responded. "I called her and left a message. She never got back to me."

Jarvis blurted, "Aniyah has left me and our son."

Nellie was baffled. "She wouldn't do that. She loves ya'll too much."

"Aniyah has this thing of putting material things before family."

"Never would she leave her son. Never, ever," Nellie insisted.

"Has she been seeing another man?" Jarvis was curious of his competition and would her best friend be honest with him.

Nellie paused. "This may not be of importance, but I saw her one day at a restaurant with a man. A fine-looking dude. Aniyah said he was her personal trainer. She was getting more fit for you."

Just hearing Nellie talk about the man, who entertained

his wife, made Jarvis jealous. He flopped back down on the staircase and rested his head in the palm of his right hand.

"She lied to you. He must be the one she ran off with. I'm her bestie and she didn't let me in on her secret."

He wondered how had he allowed another man to capture his wife's heart over his. If true, he would kill him for destroying his family.

"I thought it was odd that she needed a trainer. The love I saw between you guys, I believed her. Did you guys get into a fight?" Nellie wondered.

Jarvis explained to her his phone conversation with Aniyah. Once he hung up, he took Sid up on his offer.

When Noelle finished getting Jarvis III dressed in his pajamas, Jarvis gathered up the cooked food and locked up the house.

CHAPTER 20

*A*t Noelle and Sid's home, Jarvis drank most of the bottle of champagne from their winery, while his son slept in one of the guest rooms. In a slouched position, he sat on a plush sofa. He tried to drink away the stabbing feeling he felt in his heart. In the midst of losing his father, inheritance, and dealing with the devious ways of his father, he had never imagined that his wife would be the one to hurt him the most.

He grumbled, "Aniyah, please come back to me. I love you."

Jarvis picked up the bottle of champagne and brought it to his lips for another sip, but Noelle snatched it out of his hand.

"That's enough."

Jarvis stuttered, "Give it back to me." He attempted to stand to his feet, but fell back onto the sofa.

"You'll have a heck of a headache tomorrow."

"I love my wife," he cried.

"She doesn't feel the same. Face it, she's not loyal to you or anyone."

"Aniyah," he called with slurred speech. "Happy Anniversary."

"You got it bad."

"He's whippy, whip," Sid said, joining them.

Jarvis bragged, "I would work her over and give her another baby."

"Bro, that ain't happening tonight or maybe never again," Sid said.

"She loves me. She'll be back. And I'll give her all of me," Jarvis said. He opened his arms and spread his legs apart. Luckily for Noelle, he was fully dressed.

Noelle pushed his legs closed. "That's enough. You're drunk."

"Save the goods for the next woman in your life," Sid said.

Jarvis, with one eyelid opened, looked up at her. "Noelle, you know where Aniyah is?"

"Me?" She pointed to herself. "I'm the last person to know where and what Aniyah is doing. To not speak bad of her, I'll keep my mouth closed."

"You never thought she was good enough for me," Jarvis said.

He'd had no knowledge of Aniyah's wrongdoing to the Houstons, until later in their relationship. Like him, the Houstons had no knowledge as well of his interaction with Aniyah. With Aniyah already impregnated with his baby, he was too far gone in his love for her and eventually forgave her for her past.

"It has nothing to do with her upbringing. It's the vindictive ways she has," Noelle said.

"You never know where you'll find love," Sid said. He himself had worked for Noelle's family limo service before he'd become involved with her. Now he supervised the drivers.

Noelle kissed her husband on the lips. "You have a good heart and soul."

"I tried not to judge her. After breaking bread with you and Aniyah, I thought she had changed for the good. She proved us all wrong," Sid said. He was eager to say more, but did not want to piss off Jarvis. "Bro, let me get you to bed."

With Sid's help, Jarvis wobbled down the hall to the guest room near the one where his son slept. Not able to stay alert, when his head hit the pillow, Jarvis dozed off.

CHAPTER 21

*O*nce Brant snatched the phone from Aniyah and ended the call, she forgot the chains were on her feet and stormed toward him. He stepped far away from her. Aniyah fell face-forward on the hardwood floor. She wiped her mouth when she saw blood on her lips.

Scrambling to her feet, she belted, "I hate you! You destroyed my marriage on my wedding anniversary." The anguished tone in Jarvis' voice replayed in her mind. "No one hurts my man and gets away with it."

Brant chuckled. "Like you didn't play a part in it. You forgot you were going to give yourself to me over there." He glanced at the loveseat.

Up on her feet, holding on to the wall, Aniyah made her way into the bathroom. In a small sink, no bigger than a mixing bowl, she wet a paper towel and wiped her busted lip.

Brant stood in the doorway of the room door. "You've lost Jarvis Powell." He slammed the door shut.

"No! Don't lock me in here." Aniyah made her way to the door. She fumbled with it, but Brant had secured it. She gazed her eyes on him through the peephole. She banged on the door until her arms grew tired. Aniyah eased down onto the floor bawling in tears.

After a while, she smelled the aroma of bell peppers and onions. Peeping through the hole, she watched him as he stood at the stove, never taking her eyes off him until he finished cooking. When he unlocked the door, she moved backward.

Brant carried a plate of sautéed vegetables over a bed of brown rice with no meat. He handed her the plate. "I don't want to hear a word out of you. Now eat," he ordered.

Aniyah, hungry, scurried to the small desk and took a seat. She ate her food. Brant set a glass of water on the table. She drank the water to quench her thirst. Brant left her and returned in the doorway with the cushions from the loveseat. He tossed them into the room.

"Sleep on these." He locked the door.

When Aniyah finished eating, she lay her naked body on the homemade bed. Her body sunk into it like it was being suctioned.

No one outsmarts me. Not even you, Brant, or Papa Powell, she thought.

A howling dog awakened Aniyah. Another sound besides her kidnapper's voice sounded good. She saw nothing but darkness until Brant, dressed in a pair of button-up pajamas and black boots, slid open the room door. Aniyah looked into the common area, where sunlight beamed through the bars that covered the windows.

He came closer to her. "Beauty, what are you doing up so early?"

She shivered from the coolness in the home. "It's cold. I can't sleep. Please let me go home to my bed, son and husband."

Brant ignored her words. "I've been awake. I milked the cows. Tomorrow you'll learn how to do it."

"I buy milk from the store."

"I don't. And, after tomorrow, you won't either."

Aniyah watched as Brant went into the kitchen, got a bucket and poured milk into canning jars.

"Would you like for me to help in the kitchen?" Aniyah hoped he would release her from the chains.

"Get washed up. There's a toothbrush, washcloth and towel in the bathroom for you."

"Can I at least have a bathrobe?"

Brant went to a hidden space under the loveseat, where he had stored her belongings. He removed her bra and panties. He shoved her underwear under his arms.

"My papa-in-law planned this crap to get me away from Jarvis. Tell that old creep, it won't work."

He returned to her and handed her the bra.

"Is this all I'm supposed to wear?" Aniyah asked, while she put on her bra.

"Shut up. Now put your hands behind your back."

Rolling her eyes, Aniyah did as she was told. Brant slapped a set of handcuffs on her hands. One at a time, he unlocked the chain around each ankle, letting her put her feet through the holes of her panties. He secured the chain on her ankles before he removed the handcuffs from her hands. Aniyah pulled her underwear up to cover her bottom.

***

While she washed her face and brushed her teeth, the aroma of scrambled egg whites with Swiss cheese and blueberry pancakes filled the room. Aniyah came out of the bathroom and walked into the other room. She saw that she was once again locked in.

She peeped through the hole. "I'm finished."

Brant came to her. "Stand back," he ordered.

Aniyah stepped away, and he unlocked the door.

"Have a seat."

Aniyah followed his orders. Brant placed her breakfast on the table with a glass of milk.

"I have to go to the market today." Brant walked out of the room, slammed the door closed and then locked it.

Aniyah jumped up and ran to the door. She banged her fist against it while she peeped through the hole. "You can't leave me here. Please let me go. What will it cost? I'll pay you more than Papa Powell."

Brant laughed as he headed to the front door.

Noticing that he still was dressed in his nightclothes, Aniyah asked, "Aren't you going to wash up and change out of those pajamas?"

"Yes, before I get to the market. The bathroom here is yours for now to use."

He left.

Aniyah worked hard to remove the chains. She tried to wiggle out her foot, but had no success. The aroma from the blueberry pancakes made her give up. She took her seat at the table and ate her breakfast. Throughout the day, she hollered for help. The only response she received was from the howling dog.

***

Inside the room, Aniyah felt like she was losing oxygen. The only light that seeped through the boarded window was from the cracks in between the plywood. She concentrated on her son. It had been one day, and she already missed him dearly. The sound of a key unlocking a door grabbed her attention. Aniyah dashed to the peephole. She watched Brant enter the house with bags in his hands.

"Beauty, I'm home."

She watched Brant drop the bags in the kitchen area, and then he headed to her.

"Stand back," he insisted.

Aniyah did what she was told. Brant unlocked the room door and slid it open.

She took deep breaths to suck in the air.

He pointed to the wooden desk. "Hand me that plate."

Aniyah moved fast, scared he would lock her up again, but he did not.

She handed him the plate.

"You can come out here, as long as you act like you got some sense. Go sit on the stool."

With one foot in front of the other, Aniyah made her way to the front of the tiny house. She took a seat on a low-height barstool. A bag of food sat on top of the narrow counter for her. Before checking inside of it, Aniyah looked back into the home. Above the room, where he kept her captured, she noticed a loft.

Instead of stairs to the loft, a ladder was hooked on to the rail near where the room door closed. She eyed a bed and realized that was where Brant slept. Aniyah searched inside the bag. She discovered four chicken wings and a pecan waffle with maple syrup. While she ate, she watched him unload groceries. He removed a plastic bag of string beans.

"You'll snap these for our meal."

"I buy frozen string beans."

He took the bag and a bowl and set it in front of her. He cuffed his hand under her chin. "I like fresh beans. Snap them or be punished."

Aniyah did not understand what he meant about being punished and did not want to find out. Once she finished eating, she snapped the beans, tossing them into the bowl. At times, she picked some off of the wooden floor. She stared at Brant, while he was busy cooking a small pot of rice and stew chicken on the stove.

I have to win him over to get out of here, she thought. It was time for her to give herself to him on another level. It was for a good cause. Her worries faded.

"Logan."

"What do you want?"

"I've decided you're the man for me."

He chuckled.

"You really are, Brant Logan." Aniyah, with caution, stood and made her way to him. She placed her hands on his shoulders while rotating her hips, dancing to a tune in her head.

He brushed her away. "You're trying to suck me into your world."

Aniyah steadily danced while she grabbed hold of the kitchen counter to keep her balance. She teased, "You want me?"

She watched him walk away from her. He opened the refrigerator and returned to her with a lemon in his hand.

"Pull your panties down," he ordered.

Still dancing, Aniyah let her underwear fall around her ankles.

"Stay still," he said.

Aniyah stopped moving and watched as he loosened her bra strap, releasing her plump breasts. He circled around her.

"Magnificent." He trickled lemon juice on her body. He bragged, "Beauty, you're so sweet. That's why I need lemon to cut the sweetness of your juicy sugar."

He licked the juice off her body. To him, she was a fresh slab of meat, and he was ready to devour her. When his fingers touched the flesh of her inner thigh, Aniyah's knees buckled.

He chuckled. "You don't want me. You're nervous and cold as ice."

"I do," she cried.

"Time will tell."

She watched as he reached inside a hidden storage compartment, under the loveseat, and pulled out a small packet. He pushed the packet into his pocket. Her eyes widened when he charged at her, scooping her up with her underwear still dangling at her ankles. He carried her into her room.

"Please, don't lock me up," she begged.

He didn't. Instead, he carried her through the room into the bathroom. He put her down to let her stand. Aniyah saw that moment as the perfect time for her to take charge. She eased her way into the narrow shower, pulling his dressed body inside. She rested her back against the shower wall. She kissed him with passion, while she eased her hand down near his pants pocket. As soon as she felt the keys to set her free, Brant gripped her by the wrist.

"Don't try it."

Aniyah jerked her hand away. "It's not what you think." She traveled her fingers down his right earlobe.

Brant brushed her off. He stepped out of the shower. Then he reached inside the shower and turned on the faucet knob.

She stared down at her ankles. "My panties are getting wet."

"They'll dry soon enough."

The cold water made goose bumps form on her skin. They soon disappeared once the water became warmer.

Brant tossed her a bar of organic rose petal soap and said, "Suds up."

Resting on the wall of the tiny shower, she lathered soap on her body.

Once Brant's member perked up, the aroma of burnt food tickled his nose. He turned the water off and tossed her a towel. Brant dashed for the stove, cutting the eyes off to discover he had burned the stew.

Aniyah walked out into the opening. "I need to get out of these wet panties. Get a break from these chains, also."

Brant returned to her. He pulled her into his arms; she felt the tight excruciating grip that he had around her waist.

"Nothing has changed. My rule stands."

She felt a sting in her hips after he slapped her across her behind. Brant plastered her lips with his. Once he came up for air, he pushed her back into the room and clipped the lock.

Aniyah banged on the door. "This is not fair."

He smiled. "Get used to it."

Through the peephole, she watched him toss a condom onto the counter. Disgustedly, she sat down on the cushion. It would take more time for her to hook him in her web.

.

CHAPTER 22

*M*ilandra strutted into the seafood restaurant to meet up with her sisters. They met at least once a month to have lunch. When she got settled at a table, she took it upon herself to order glasses of iced water and a bottle of wine.

Noelle was the second to arrive, wearing a soft-pink, sleeveless dress. "Hello, Milandra."

The sisters embraced with a kiss on each cheek.

"Where's Kenley?" Noelle questioned. She took her seat, picking up the menu to study it.

"I have no idea. You never can tell with our bratty sister."

"I hear you talking about me," Kenley said.

Turning their heads, the sisters eyed their baby sister.

Milandra looked at her watch. "One more minute and you'd be late."

Kenley gave her oldest sister a kiss on the cheek. "I love you too." She followed by giving Noelle a kiss on the cheek.

"I'm so hungry," Kenley said. Like her sisters, she browsed the menu.

The waitress returned, and they placed their orders.

Milandra ordered mahi-mahi with a side of roasted red potatoes and broccoli. Noelle ordered a whole fried rainbow trout with a side of turmeric rice and green beans. Kenley decided on a plate of shrimp and grits. The sisters chatted while awaiting their food.

"Milandra, I knew sooner or later, you'd run Nolan off," Kenley teased.

"He's a good man," Noelle voiced her opinion.

Milandra took a sip of the wine. "I owe no man any explanation as to what I do with my heritage money."

"You stole Jarvis' coins," Kenley said.

"Hush, Kenley, with your inappropriate ways of communicating. I purchased it fair and square."

"Speaking of Jarvis, have you heard the news?" Noelle asked.

"I hope Aniyah is not having another baby," Kenley said.

Noelle wiggled her finger in disagreement. "She left Jarvis. Didn't tell him she was leaving him to his face. Would you believe she told him over the phone?"

Milandra raised her glass. "Cheers. That ruthless thing was after the Powell family's fortune. I salute Mr. Powell Sr., for leaving Jarvis nothing. That despicable thing would have run through his fortune."

The waitress interrupted their conversation and served them their food. When she left, they resumed chatting.

While Milandra and Noelle dove into their food, Kenley made a phone call.

"Put that phone away," Milandra demanded.

"I have to tell Tessa about her niece, even though they don't speak," Kenley said. She placed the phone on speaker, lowering the volume.

It was news around town that Aniyah and her Aunt Tessa had bad blood between them. Tessa was not fond of her niece's past when it came down to her reputation of preying on men with money, including her own man.

"You've lost your table manners, Kenley Houston."

"Be quiet," Kenley said once she heard Tessa Sanchez-Chavis' voice.

"Hello, Kenley," Tessa said with joy.

"Hi. I'm with my sisters having lunch. Can't talk too long. I called to let you know Aniyah left Jarvis."

In a low tone, Tessa said, "My poor great-nephew will be raised without his father. I hurt for Jarvis."

Noelle jumped in. "Hi, Tessa, this is Noelle. You're on speakerphone."

"Hello, Noelle."

"Aniyah didn't take J.P. He's safe with his father," Noelle said.

Kenley tapped her fork on the charcoal-colored plate. "She must have another dude in her life."

Noelle gossiped. "You guessed right. Jarvis is heartbroken."

A sorrowed Tessa was not surprised of her niece's action. "Thank you for calling me. God bless you, Houston sisters," she said.

"Love you, Tessa," Kenley said.

"Bye," Noelle added.

Milandra did not utter a word until Kenley ended the call.

"It serves Jarvis right. He should've listened to Mr. Powell," Milandra said. She resumed eating the broccoli, garnished with lemon pepper.

"Now maybe you can do the right thing and give him back his inheritance." Noelle looked over at Milandra.

Milandra cleared the food in her mouth. "If it was only a hat, I would return it. Never will I give back property I got legally."

"You're so wrong," Noelle said to Milandra.

"That's your opinion," Milandra replied.

"Big Sis, you'll get your hubby back, if you return it," Kenley said.

"My marriage is not open for discussion," Milandra said.

Kenley teased. "Don't you miss his kisses?"

"Enough. You need to find yourself a more suitable man." Milandra voiced her opinion. "Pete has and is nothing."

Kenley pointed her fork at Milandra. "He's everything to me. Plus, he's hired to work at one of the Houstons' construction sites."

"I wasn't aware of this," Milandra said.

"I had one of the foremen to hire him," Kenley said.

"That's not enough money to take care of your type of lifestyle," Milandra said.

Kenley argued, "It's not always about money."

"Lower your voice," Milandra ordered. She noticed customers in the restaurant had shifted their attention to their table.

"Milandra, if he makes her happy, that's all that matters," Noelle said.

"That boyfriend of Kenley's is living on our family property for free," Milandra said.

"He'll stay living there as long as I live there. If he goes, I go." Kenley pouted.

"No one is going anywhere. He's no trouble, and he works. I vote he can stay living with Kenley on the property," Noelle said.

Kenley raised her hand. "I second it. Milandra, you're overruled."

"You two are acting like the men you're with. Foolish," Milandra said. She held up her right pointer finger to get the waitress' attention. "Check, please."

Milandra was the first to leave. She did not bother to give her sisters a farewell hug.

Through the revolving doors, Milandra entered the bank. She took the elevator up to Jarvis' office. The receptionist announced her presence to him.

"What brings you here?" Jarvis wondered.

She noticed his droopy eyes. She saw he had the signs of a person whose spouse had abandoned him.

"I hear your wife has vanished from you and your son's life."

"That's no business of yours."

Milandra took a seat in front of his desk. She clenched her purse. "You should thank me for saving the Powell fortune from falling into Aniyah's gold-digging hands."

"You, my dad and Aniyah are all the same. Vindictive."

"Please do not degrade me to trash. I have class."

Milandra planted her red bottoms on the floor and stood. She shoved her purse under her arms.

Jarvis slammed his fist on the desk. "Vicious people come in all forms. Leave my office unless you have bank business to discuss."

Milandra came closer to him. She got in his face, almost nose to nose. "You may be right. Aniyah and I have one thing in common. We never let a man outsmart us or rule us."

Jarvis laughed. "So you think."

"Believe it," Milandra said, blowing in his face. With her hair tossed into a French roll-styled bun, she spun around in her turquoise designer linen skirt suit in the door's direction. "Make sure this bank is run A-plus."

When Milandra left his office, a frustrated Jarvis made a call.

"We need to talk," he said to the person on the other end of the line.

Milandra took the last bobby pin out of her French roll, and her hair fell over her shoulders. She slipped on a black silk nightgown before she climbed the bed-stool and got into a high-raised bed. Under the soft lilac coverlet, she rested her head on the memory-foam pillow, covered in a silk lilac pillowcase. She placed an eye mask over her eyes, ready to sleep.

"What an exhausting day," she grumbled.

Milandra sensed a presence in the room, causing her to snatch the eye mask off her face. Standing at the foot of the bed dressed in boxer shorts was Nolan.

She sat upright, turning the night lamp on. "What are you doing here? You're not allowed on the premises."

"I'm still your husband."

"Not for long."

"I want to change that. I want a second chance. I'm sorry."

She chuckled. "You realized how good you had it living off the benefits of a Houston."

Nolan waved his hands up in submission. "I've come to my senses."

She watched him ease into the bed and under the covers. "You played hardball, but you missed me."

Milandra turned away from him. He crept up behind her, cuddling her around her waist. She tried to resist his touch but her body reacted. She was still Mrs. Nolan Rice, giving her free access to be with him. Nolan turned her over on her back. He slipped the thin straps of her nightgown off her shoulders and eased her out of the nightgown. He tossed it onto the carpeted floor.

Milandra lay in a red-laced, bikini-styled panties with her breasts exposed to him. She watched him strip her of her underwear, then he came up to her, smothering her lips, kissing her with passion.

"I missed my wife so much." He stared into her eyes until the sparkle of his eyes hypnotized her. Nolan stroked her inner thighs.

Milandra cooed and said, "You're the boss in bed. I'm the boss out of bed."

"Whatever you say."

They said no other words, caught up in the act until they released their marital duties. Milandra turned over on her side with her back to him. She smiled. *This Houston always gets her way,* she thought.

CHAPTER 23

*J*arvis was living his life as Mr. Mom. He unbuckled the carseat, lifting his son out of it. He snuck a kiss on the cheek, ready to carry him into the house. "Love you, J.P." He reassured his son, he would never abandon him like his mother had done. "It's pizza night."

"Yay," Little Jarvis said.

Halfway to the front door, a vehicle pulled up.

"We have company."

"Mama-Mom?"

"Sorry, son. Your mama-mom ran out on us."

The black Mercedes-Benz was familiar to Jarvis. When Tessa stepped out, Jarvis' eyes widened. He hadn't seen her since Jarvis III was born. She had shunned away from any communication with Aniyah. Jarvis never understood what had happened between them. Like everyone else, Aniyah's past of wrongdoing made people shun away from her.

As Tessa walked up the driveway, she called, "Hello, Jarvis, and my handsome great-nephew. It's so good to see the two of you."

Jarvis put his son down. He met Tessa halfway and gave

her a hug. "Hello, Mrs. Chavis. What brings you here? It's been a while since we saw you."

"It was for the best. Aniyah and I never saw eye to eye on things." Tessa went to Jarvis III. "I miss this little boy. You've grown." She held her hand out to him. Jarvis III jumped into her arms like he had a regular relationship with his great-aunt.

Jarvis watched her cuddle him, placing kisses on his face. Then she put him down.

Jarvis instructed his son, "This is your auntie. Tell her your name?"

"J.P."

"No tell her your real name," Jarvis said.

"Jarvis Powell, the third," the little one said.

Tessa kissed him on the cheek. "Smart boy." She turned to Jarvis. "I'm so sorry for the loss of your papa and your fortune. Also, the bad news that Aniyah has done you terrible."

"Let's go inside the house."

Tessa put Jarvis III down.

Jarvis took him by the hand, leading him into the house. Tessa followed while Jarvis spoke. "I'm numb to the whole situation. I never thought Aniyah would cross me after all I have lost due to her."

Once inside, Jarvis said, "J.P., go play in the backyard. Don't dirty your school clothes." He turned to Tessa. "We can talk in the sunroom where I can keep an eye on him."

They took a seat in two white wicker chairs.

"I've come to help you. If you let me," Tessa said. "My great-nephew is innocent. He shouldn't have to suffer for his mama's doings. Please let me help. I am family."

Jarvis hunched his shoulders. "I do need you. I can get him to school. It'd be great if you could pick him up."

"I can do that. I don't work anymore. No worries. I'll fill his belly with food. J.P. is in good hands."

"Thanks, Mrs. Chavis."

"You need to start calling me, Aunt Tessa."

"Aunt Tessa it is. So, how did you hear about Aniyah leaving us?"

"Kenley Houston called and told me."

"I wanted to contact you myself. I didn't know if you wanted to hear from me."

"Jarvis, you're a good man. I've never had anything against you."

"That's good to hear. Hey, we're having pizza tonight. Would you like to eat with us?"

"I would love to. Show me where my great-nephew's room is. I'll help him change his clothes."

"Let me go get him."

Jarvis looked out of the window. He saw no sign of Jarvis III. Panicky, he ran out and scurried the yard. There was no sight of his son.

Jarvis ran into the house. He called for his son. "J.P.!"

"He's not out back?" Tessa asked.

With teary eyes, Jarvis darted back out to the backyard.

"Boo!" Jarvis III said, lifting a box from over his head.

Jarvis roared, "J.P., when I call, you answer me." He snatched him up into his arms and shook him.

"Jarvis, it's okay," Tessa said. She stood in the doorway.

With watery eyes, Jarvis fell to his knees. "I've lost my father and wife. It felt for a moment like I'd lost my son, too."

Tessa came to him. She patted him on the back before she took Jarvis III out of his arms.

"You need to get rest," she said.

Jarvis III noticed his father's teary eyes. "Don't cry, Papa-Dad," Jarvis III said.

"I'm fine, son." Jarvis could not take the pain of another loss.

"Papa-Dad?" Tessa wondered.

"Yes. It was confusing to him. Aniyah saying Papa and I'm saying Dad. Aniyah changed it to Papa-Dad for him. He even says, Mama-Mom."

"That's cute." Tessa smiled.

Jarvis got up from his knees. "You go with your auntie." He was content that his son would have someone from his wife's side of the family in his life.

Jarvis III found his way to Tessa. She cuddled him. "I'll keep it simple. You can call me, Tia."

Jarvis III repeated, "Tia."

Tessa grabbed her great-nephew by the hand. "Show me where your room is."

Jarvis III looked over at his father. "Papa-Dad coming?"

"No, you go on with your auntie. I mean your Tia," Jarvis said.

While Tessa got his son changed, Jarvis sat on the sofa. He gulped down swallows of champagne. The doorbell rang and he went to it. At the door, the pizza deliveryman handed him his order. Jarvis paid him a five-dollar tip. "Thanks," he said before he closed the door. "Pizza is here," he announced, looking up the staircase to the second floor. Then he went into the living room and set the box on the coffee table.

Jarvis III, with Tessa in tow, ran to him. "Pizza, Papa-Dad."

Jarvis handed his son a small slice. "Sit next to me."

Any other time, his son could not eat in the living room. However, since Aniyah was no longer around, he no longer cared. Jarvis took another gulp out of the champagne bottle.

Tessa kept her eyes on him. "Jarvis Powell, I've never known you to drink so much. And not straight out of the bottle." She ate a slice of the pizza. "No need in getting drunk."

"I can't get through the pain without a drink." His heart felt stomped on. He took another swallow.

"Aniyah had to plan this, like my dad planned to leave me in the cold with his will."

"It's terrible." Tessa placed her hand on his right arm. "It'll get better with time."

She watched Jarvis gulp another swallow out of the bottle.

CHAPTER 24

*A*niyah's eyes opened when she felt the coldness of Brant's hands on her.

"Wake up," he ordered.

When she moved her legs, they felt light. Brant had removed the chains from around her ankles.

He handed her clean panties, her bra, denim overalls, dark-blue croc shoes and a pair of socks. "Put this on. Don't you try anything foolish."

"I don't do farm clothes."

"Wear what I give you or stay locked up."

Aniyah submitted.

He waited until she got dressed, then said, "Place your hands behind you."

Aniyah continued to follow his instructions. With her back to him, Brant locked her wrists with handcuffs. Next, he placed a mask over her eyes. He led her outside.

Aniyah sniffed the early morning dew. "Where are we going?"

"Be quiet."

By her side, Brant helped her to the rear of the house where he fastened a set of chains around her ankles, connected to a long rope chain around a pine tree. He freed her hands and removed the eye mask from her eyes.

Looking up at the sky, Aniyah saw it was a dusty gray. She looked as far as she could, but saw nothing but green pasture. Then she noticed a garden, filled with tomatoes, squash, and green peppers.

Brant handed her a bucket. "Start picking," he ordered.

In panic mode, her voice escalated loud to the top of her lungs. "Help!"

She jumped, when the mystery dog barked. She had awakened him. Turning around, she stared into the eyes of a pit bull. Luckily for her, Brant had the dog tied to the pine tree but on a shorter rope chain.

"Ahh." She panicked and tried to run but fell to the ground.

Brant laughed. "Bayer is the only one who can hear you."

Aniyah stood to her feet. She looked back at the garden and pouted. "I don't know how to pick this stuff."

Brant snatched her by her forearm. "It's time you learned." He shoved her. "Get to work or else back into the room."

Aniyah, happy to feel the fresh air, plucked the ripe tomatoes off its vine. She worked until daylight seeped through the clouds. Brant took the filled basket of tomatoes from her and set it on the ground. Again, he blackened her vision with the eye mask and cuffed her wrists. Gripping her right arm, he pulled on her, causing her to wobble on foot to her next destination.

When he removed her eye mask, Aniyah's eyes lit up, locking eyes with a baby pig in a pigpen. "Hell no! I'm not going in there."

"Oh yes you are." Brant unleashed the chains from her feet and hands. He pushed her inside, causing her to fall into a muddy pile of slop. Aniyah slipped and slid until she could get up on her two feet. Her shoes had fallen off. The mud had soiled her hair and clothing. When the pig came toward her, she belted, "Get me out of here."

Brant laughed.

"This isn't funny."

Brant entered the pen, pulling her out.

She cried. "You're hurting me?"

When he went to handcuff her, Aniyah pulled away from him and fled, hoping to come upon a house or road with traveling vehicles.

Brant went after her. Even with his bad leg, he caught up to her and tackled her to the ground. He covered her eyes with the eye mask. Before he handcuffed her, he stripped her of her clothing. Aniyah shivered from the morning air. He locked her into his arms and pulled her up on her feet. He scooped her up and carried her back into the house.

"Let me go," she ranted.

Thrown into the room, Aniyah said, "You can't treat me this way."

"Raise your hands up."

She barked, "No!"

Brant grabbed her by the hair. Aniyah thought he would hit her. She squinted.

He pierced his eyes at her. In tears, Aniyah held her hands over her head, while he cuffed chains around her ankles. Never did he take his eyes off of her. Once he heard the chains clicked, he removed her handcuffs.

"You stink. Get washed up." He wiped the mud off his hands onto her body.

"You can't treat me this way."

He pushed her into the bathroom. This was the one time she was eager to go inside the miniature shower. She wanted to wash away the pig smell from her body. She felt the mud in her hair dripping down on her. Turning the shower water on, she washed off the foul odor.

During the day, Aniyah's head throbbed. She wanted to lie down on the cushion. Brant, however, had other plans for her.

"Cook us something to eat," he demanded.

"I have a headache."

"Too bad. You're cooking."

Brant went up into the loft, and returned with a pill. "Take this."

Aniyah hesitated to put it in her mouth.

"I'm not going to kill you. It's an Advil."

"I need water."

"Go get it yourself and start cooking," he ordered, giving her permission to come out of the room and roam the tiny house. "Anything you need to dice, I'll cut it. No knives for you."

Aniyah swallowed the pill with a sip of water. She noticed the tomatoes she picked, sat on the counter.

He requested, "I want to eat vegetable lasagna tonight. If you don't know how to make one, here's the recipe." He tossed a recipe card on the counter.

Aniyah watched Brant get comfortable on the loveseat. With a click of a remote, he turned on a Bluetooth radio. The tiny house became alive with the sound of country music.

Aniyah prepared the lasagna noodles with zucchini, yellow crookneck squash, baby bella mushrooms, minced garlic clove, spinach, yellow and red peppers, marinara sauce, ricotta cheese, mozzarella and parmesan cheese. Once she layered the mid-sized dish with the noodles, sautéed vegetables in marinara sauce, and shredded part-skim mozzarella cheese and fat-free ricotta cheese, she tossed it in the hot oven at three hundred-and-fifty degrees. Bent over with her hips in the air, Brant came up behind her, and she panicked.

Jumping up, Aniyah turned to him. Her heart pounding, she wept. "I'm already a nervous wreck. You scare me."

Turning away from him, not wanting him to see a teardrop in her eyes, Aniyah walked over to the sink of dishes.

Brant caught her from behind. "You're doing a good job." He kissed a lock of her hair.

Aniyah froze when he cuddled her into his arms. He stroked her hair. "Leave the dishes. Go back to your room while the food cooks."

She eased away from him and headed into the room where she fell asleep on the cushion.

"Wake up." She heard Brant's voice. "You bet not burn the lasagna. Go check it. I'm ready to eat."

Half drowsy, Aniyah sniffed the aroma of the pasta sauce and cheese mixture. Her head no longer throbbed.

After walking into the kitchen, she lifted the dish out of the oven and set it on the stove. She noticed Brant had washed the dirty dishes and made a tossed salad.

Aniyah set the table with stoneware gold and brown plates and bowls. She filled the bowls with fresh salad— mixed greens, carrots, cucumbers and tomatoes. She filled two glasses with lemon-iced tea. Hot bread with Brant's homemade oil and vinegar salad dressing were on the table.

Once she sat on one of the stools, Brant joined her. In his husky voice, he blessed the food. They uttered no words until the sound of Brant's cell phone broke the stillness in the house. He hurried to answer it, leaving Aniyah to wonder who was contacting him. While she chewed her food, she listened to him speak to the un- known person.

"You picked a fine time to call," Brant said.

Aniyah could not hear the response of the person on the other end of the call.

Again, Brant spoke, "She's fine. I haven't put my hands on her." He chuckled. "That if she wants me to."

In the background, Aniyah argued, "Papa Powell, you'll pay for this. Faking a death and having me kidnapped. My love is only for my husband."

"Shut up!" Brant shouted at her. Then he said to the caller, "Gotta go."

Aniyah belted, "Why are you doing that old fart's dirty work? Let me go!"

Brant gripped her wrist. "Eat your food. Jarvis is histo- ry. I don't want a mouthy wife."

She jerked her arm away from him. "I'm married."

"You'll be a bigamist. You're marrying me." He laughed.

"I'm Mrs. Jarvis Powell," she bragged.

Brant banged on the table. "Mrs. Brant Logan, you'll be."

He raised his hand at her. Aniyah blocked her face with her right hand, but he did not touch her.

"Now shut up."

Aniyah kept her lips sealed.

When they finished eating, he left her to clean the remaining dishes while he lounged on the loveseat.

During the week, Aniyah heard no other words about marriage from Brant until Sunday.

He handed her a white knee-length nightgown. "Put it on. Preacher is coming to marry us today."

"Are you crazy? That can't happen."

Pulling her into his arms, she felt the tight excruciating grip he had around her waist.

"My rule stands." He smothered his lips over hers. Once he came up for air, he smiled. "Beauty, get moving. The pastor is on his way. You bet not say a word to alarm him. If you do, you'll pay dearly for it."

Under her breath, Aniyah uttered every wrong choice word in hostility to him. She slipped on the gown and asked, "Who gets married in front of a preacher in a nightgown?"

Dressed in his pajamas, Brant chuckled. "Trust me. He can't see you."

The doorbell rang, leaving Brant to open the front door. He greeted the pastor. "Hello, Reverend Austin. Come right on in. My future bride and I are ready to get this over with."

"Good day for a marriage ceremony. I got two more to do. My driver is waiting on me," the pastor said, as he entered the home with a walking cane. In the other hand, he carried a Holy Bible written in Braille.

Aniyah saw he was a man of the cloth, dressed in black pants and a shirt with a white collar.

"I'm right there with you, Reverend Austin. That's how we want it, short and to the point," Brant said.

Aniyah stood frozen while Brant hurried and unlocked the shackles from around her ankles. She felt a pinch on the side of her waistline, after he placed his arms around her.

"Reverend Austin, this is my fiancée," Brant said, pulling Aniyah closer to him.

"Nice to meet you, Ma'am," the pastor said, looking straight ahead as he held out his hand.

Aniyah shook his hand. "Hi," she said in a low tone. She felt another painful pinch from Brant. She gritted her teeth.

"Let's get this over with," Brant said.

"No maid of honor or best man?" the pastor wondered.

"Nah. We want to keep it private."

The pastor proceeded with the ceremony, skipping the part—*if anyone has a reason for these two people not to be married*, Aniyah rolled her eyes to the ceiling. When it became her turn to repeat the vows, she spoke in a low tone. She tuned out any words that Brant had to say.

"I now pronounce you, Mr. and Mrs. Brant Logan. You may kiss the bride," the pastor said.

After Brant gave his new bride a peck on the cheek, he balled a few bucks in the pastor's hand. "Thanks for coming, Reverend Austin."

"I need you both to sign the marriage certificate," he said.

Brant and Aniyah scribbled their signatures on the document. The pastor exited the home. Brant kept a grip on her until the driver pulled off. He reached in his pocket and pulled out the eye mask. He blindfolded her, pulling her outside the door.

"A man has to carry his new wife into the house."

"This is some crazy bull," Aniyah said.

Brant scooped her up off of her feet. She held him around his neck not to fall. He carried her back inside and tossed her onto the loveseat. He removed the blindfold from her eyes.

Aniyah watched him come out of his pants and boxers to expose his goods to her. He rolled a condom onto his member. She had taken extra precaution because she was on birth control, which lasted for months. No way would she want to slip up and become pregnant by her kidnapper.

"No kids for me. You may have trapped Jarvis, but you won't make me a daddy," Brant said. He stripped her of her gown and tears flowed from her eyes.

Brant wiped her face. "I know you're happy." He entered her and had his way with her. The sweat from his forehead dripped onto her breasts. He kissed her and exploded, collapsing on top of her.

When he caught his breath, he lifted off of her. "I've been waiting for this moment to have my way with my bride."

Aniyah felt dirty and disgusted with him. She yearned for her real husband. "Are you insane? We're not legally married if I'm still married to Jarvis."

At the mention of her husband's name, Brant snatched her by the hair and dragged her across the floor into the room.

"I'm sorry. Please don't hurt me," Aniyah cried.

Brant saw the agony in her face and let her fall to the floor. He leaped on top of her. Turned on by her feisty ways, he pinned her down with his large hands and forced his tongue into her mouth.

Aniyah blocked out Brant and instead pictured Jarvis on top of her to get through her second marital duties. She came back to reality, once Brant stood up off of her. She lay still. He shackled her ankles. "What man keeps locks on his wife?"

"You have to prove to me that you're ready to be here with me."

"I just took care of you. As your wife, I'll show you love," Aniyah lied. *That'll never happen*, she thought. This was the only way she would survive, not knowing when Brant would snap and hurt her.

CHAPTER 25

At the Houston Estate, Milandra led the way into the spacious kitchen with her sisters trailing behind her. She had invited them to join her for breakfast. The morning aroma of sizzling bacon and sausage tickled their noses.

"Good morning, Elsa," Milandra and Noelle both greeted her.

"You're the one making breakfast for us?" Kenley asked. She ran and gave a hug to the one person that had worked for their family for years.

Elsa no longer managed the staff, yet she still lived on the property. It was their father's gift to her for her long-time loyalty to the Houston family.

"Milandra told me the rest of my favorite girls were coming this morning. I had to be the one to make ya'll a good down-home breakfast."

"It smells delicious in here," Noelle said, hugging Elsa.

"Ya'll have a seat at the table," Elsa insisted.

The sisters followed her instructions. They sat at the table covered in white linen with china plates and sterling silverware on the side. Juice goblets sat in front of the plates. White linen napkins were there for them to clean their hands. Crystal pitchers of orange, apple and cranberry juice sat in the center.

Elsa placed on the table, a big bowl of cheese grits, a platter of bacon, sausage and eggs, and a tray of hot biscuits.

"Elsa, you make the best breakfast in the South," Kenley said.

"That's so sweet of you to say," Elsa said. She waved to the sisters. "I'm going now; you girls enjoy your breakfast. Call me when you're all done."

"Thanks, Elsa," Milandra said. She dotted her eyes at her baby sister, whom had broken a piece of sausage in her mouth. "We haven't said grace yet."

Milandra took charge and blessed the food. Once done, they ate.

"What do we owe this big morning feast?" Noelle wondered.

Milandra announced, "I wanted you two nosy bodies to hear this from me. Nolan and I are back together."

"Really?" Kenley said.

Noelle, however, jumped up. She hugged Milandra around her neck. "Finally you listened to us."

"Give the man some credit. He loves Milandra. And it has nothing to do with material things." Kenley dotted her eyes at her older sister. "You need to lighten up."

"I run this home," Milandra said, once she finished a glass of cranberry juice that she had mixed with orange and apple juice.

"Marriage is a joint thing. At least Sid and I run ours that way," Noelle bragged.

"Now that you got your man back, give Jarvis his house

and business back," Kenley said.

Milandra pointed her fork at her baby sister. "That'll never happen. If you speak of it again, I'll put you out of here."

"You can't do that. I do have some rights to this house. Don't let the fog cloud your brains," Kenley said.

Noelle hit her glass with the spoon. "Time out. We're here to have a nice breakfast. Let's not spoil it. Mother and Father would be furious to see us fighting like animals."

The sisters went back to eating. They turned their heads, when Nolan entered, dressed in his rugged work shirt and jeans.

"I thought I heard my favorite sister-in-laws," he said.

Nolan made his rounds, giving Noelle and Kenley a peck on the cheek. He went to kiss his wife on the lips, but Milandra moved her head. The kiss landed on her nose.

"Milandra doesn't want us to see you kiss her on the lips," Kenley said.

"Hush, Kenley," Noelle said, before she focused her attention to her oldest sister. She wondered. "You didn't tell your husband that we were coming this morning?"

Before Milandra responded, Nolan blurted, "There's no need for my beautiful smart wife to tell me her every move."

Milandra smiled. "See, my husband and I have a great understanding of each other."

Kenley voiced her opinion. "I'm happy someone like Nolan can put up with my self-centered big sister."

"Kenley, sometimes you talk too much," Noelle said.

Then she turned to Nolan. "Join us. There's plenty of food."

"I gotta run," he said. "See you later, Milandra." Nolan placed a kiss on his wife's neck and left.

Milandra bragged, "I have my husband's full attention. I have the last say-so in this house."

"You're a bully, not a wife," Kenley said.

"Watch your nasty mouth," Milandra warned her. She feasted her eyes on her baby sister.

"You have no say-so over me," Kenley struck back.

"Enough, smart mouth. Milandra is the oldest. Give her some respect," Noelle said.

"Thank you, Noelle. At least you understand my position in this family." Milandra wiped her lips of bacon grease with her napkin.

Kenley jumped to her feet. "One day, you'll see you won't always be in control."

Milandra watched her baby sister storm out of the kitchen. Their morning breakfast had turned into a disaster.

Instead of heading to her office at the Houston Commercial Construction Company, Milandra made her way into her other office at the bank. Dressed in a two-piece, three-quarter-sleeved skirt suit, she took her seat at the desk where Jarvis Powell, Sr. once sat.

The office was refurnished with cream-colored furniture. Mr. Powell, Sr.'s portrait, once hung in front of a hidden safe, was replaced with a self-portrait of Milandra.

She fumbled through the computer, scanning the bank's profits and losses. Milandra stopped and signed checks that needed her signature. She looked up when she heard a knock at the door. She wondered why her receptionist had not notified her of any visitors.

"The door is unlocked." Milandra presumed it was her receptionist.

Her eyes lit up when she saw her husband walk in with a handful of red roses.

"Nolan. What brings you here?"

He made his way to her. He kissed her on the lips and gave her the flowers. "I'm here to see my beautiful wife."

She stood. At that moment, Milandra got lost in his arms. She held the flowers up high not to crush them. Nolan took the bouquet from her hands and placed it on the desk. While he kissed her lips, Milandra felt him slip her jacket off.

She pulled away from him. "Nolan Rice, we should handle this at home."

He whispered in her ear, "I want my lady now."

"My assistant is right outside the door."

"She knows how you are. She wouldn't come in here."

Milandra, weakened by his muscular arms around her and his juicy thick lips against hers, hungered for him. "A man should carry his wife where he wants to make love to her," she said.

Nolan scooped Milandra up off her feet. She held him tight around his neck as he carried her to the leather chaise. He sat her down. Unbuttoning her blouse, he stripped her of it, and the rest of her clothing.

Milandra watched her husband expose his ripped muscular body to her. He sat next to her and gave her a passionate kiss. She loved how Nolan caressed her neck while he played with her lips. Forgetting for a moment that she was at her place of business, Milandra traveled her hands down his back. She admired how strong it was from the years of him lifting furniture. She leaned back down on the chaise, pulling him on top of her.

A knock on the door interrupted them. Milandra jumped up and grabbed her clothing.

She panicked. "Do not open the door. Who is it?"

"It's me, Mrs. Houston-Rice. I need your final signature on the contract for Cardon Commercial Cleaning services."

"I thought I signed it already," Milandra responded to her employee.

"I'm sorry, but I had to redo it. I spilled coffee on it by accident."

Nolan kissed Milandra's lips. "Give her the rest of the day off. We need privacy."

Milandra looked at her husband's goods. "One moment."

Once she slipped into her suit jacket, she stormed to the door. Nolan stood on the other side of the room, not to expose himself to the employee. Milandra cracked the door open enough to take the pen from the receptionist.

She fussed, "Another act of foolishness like this and you'll be looking for another job." She scribbled her signature on the document, pushing the clipboard back at her.

"Thank you, Mrs. Houston-Rice. I assure you, it won't happen again."

"Take the rest of the day off," Milandra said.

The receptionist giggled. "Thanks."

Milandra locked the door. "Nolan, she's aware we're in

here not doing bank business."

"Who cares? She got the rest of the day off." Nolan snatched her jacket off her. He led the way to the chaise.

Their bodies became one. They got lost in their lovemaking. She exploded several times before he let out a burst of joy also. Once Nolan stood up off of her, she slipped back on her clothing.

Milandra scolded, "Don't you dare come to my place of business and disturb me again. Our sex life is for the privacy of our bedroom."

He tickled her. "You enjoyed it."

"Better at home. This is not the example I want to show to my employees."

He pulled her into his arms. "Let's go home and have more fun. We'll eat seafood for dinner, then have each other for dessert."

Milandra widened her mouth to show her pearly white teeth. This was the Nolan she loved—nice, thoughtful and obedient.

CHAPTER 26

Six months had passed and Jarvis had not heard another word from Aniyah. He was in a marriage with a wife, whom had disappeared on him with another man. His heart ached. He prayed that one day she would come to her senses and return—if not for him, then for the sake of their son.

Jarvis was thankful for the support of Tessa, Noelle, Sid and Nellie. They were there for him, giving him help with little Jarvis. His social life was non-existent. His nights and weekends consisted of lots of television, sleep, and a social drink of wine. Sometimes he would stroll the streets or drive around, hoping to spot Aniyah. Any beautiful woman with long dark hair, and a shapely body reminded him of her. It was like Aniyah was a tattoo—a permanent mark on him for life.

With his son taken care of by his aunt, Jarvis drowned himself in his work. His last day on a business trip of meetings at a mortgage loan conference, he headed back to his hotel suite. Walking down the corridor, he heard a distinct squeaky voice speaking to him.

"Hello there."

He halted, swerved around, and stood face to face with a petite woman. He admired her auburn, shoulder-length hair and tiny eyes.

"Hi. Have we met before?"

The woman held out her hand. She smiled. "I'm Charlinda. I'm a new hired employee at Powell, well now, Milandra Houston Bank in Columbia."

"Someone dropped the ball. I thought I was the only one attending this conference. I hope you got something out of it."

"Yes I did. I work in the loan department."

"I'm Jarvis Powell, Jr. The son of the former owner of this bank."

She clenched the iPad she held in her hand to her chest. "I recognized you. Sorry I didn't speak to you earlier. I didn't want to bother you. You seem to be all into the conference."

"The bank business is my passion."

"Sorry to hear about your daddy and wife."

"News travels fast around the bank."

Charlinda placed the iPad in front of her lips. "I shouldn't have brought it up."

"It's no problem. I'm learning to live with it."

She batted her eyes. "It's been a long day of meetings for us. How about we have a glass of wine at the hotel bar?"

Jarvis saw no harm in having a casual drink with an employee. "I can use a drink," he said.

Jarvis escorted Charlinda to a small booth instead of sitting at the horseshoe bar counter. The waiter came to them.

Jarvis ordered two glasses of white wine, and then conversed with her. "Tell me more about the news stirring around the bank."

"Mrs. Houston-Rice told me your daddy died, left you nothing and your wife ran out on you."

He lowered his head. "That's Milandra for you, but it's true."

The waiter returned with their drinks.

"I think we'll need a bottle for the table," he told the waiter. Then he raised his glass. "Here's to my chaotic life."

Charlinda held back her glass. "That's not the right toast. Here's to a fulfilling conference."

"If you say so."

They clinked their glasses.

While she took a sip of her drink, Jarvis gulped his down.

Charlinda placed her hands over his. "It'll get better with time."

"So when you get back to town, who's the lucky man that you'll be bringing in the New Year with?"

Charlinda licked the rim of the glass. "You?"

"Me?"

The waiter set the bucket of chilled wine on the table. Jarvis poured himself another glass. He took a swallow.

"You need my company more than any other man. We can at least do dinner."

"You're straightforward." Tempted to say "like Aniyah," but he decided not to mention his wife's name. "I do have a son. If I can get his aunt to babysit, it'd be fun to get out and socialize."

No sooner than Jarvis took another swallow of his drink, she leaned over and whispered, "Make it happen."

They exchanged numbers.

Jarvis took one last sip of his drink. His head felt woozy. "I need to go check on my son. Get some sleep before I hit the road back home. When are you leaving?"

"Early in the morning." Charlinda got up. She walked over to him. She insisted he take a photo with her. They smiled. "Thanks for the drinks." She gave him a peck on the cheekbone.

Jarvis watched her strut in her fitted skirt. It hugged her slender body.

"Real nice, but not like Aniyah," he grumbled.

Traffic was busy heading to Columbia from Charleston. Jarvis had already arranged for Jarvis III to stay with his aunt for another night. He had lied to Tessa, saying he had to stay another day in Charleston. When he reached home, he fell across the bed. He was ready to relax for an evening at home instead of going out with Charlinda. His cell buzzed in his back pants pocket. He reached down and answered it.

"Hello?"

"This is Charlinda. I'm home. Are you?"

"Yes. So, I never asked, what part of town do you live in?"

"I'm in Irmo. What about you?"

"I'm on the other side of town. Elgin."

"It's New Year's Eve. I hope you'll be able to keep our date tonight. I've made reservations for us to go to a nice restaurant in downtown Columbia." She did not let Jarvis get a word in. She blabbed, "I hope that's okay. It's at eight o'clock."

Jarvis heard the joy in Charlinda's voice. To not spoil her New Year's Eve, he decided to go with her and not have another evening sobbing over Aniyah.

"I'll meet you at the restaurant at eight."

Once he gathered the name and location of their date spot, he hung up, but the phone rang again. He saw it was Noelle's husband.

"Hello, Sid."

"Noelle wanted me to check and see what you're doing tonight."

"Staying home. But I told Tessa I was still in Charleston. I want to be alone tonight."

"Man, you need to get out. It's New Year's Eve. Come to our house. Noelle and I want you to."

"No, Sid. Go enjoy your wife. Happy New Year to you both."

All Jarvis wanted was to nap until it was time to go on his date with Charlinda. In reality, he wanted his wife home.

Jarvis felt his neck being licked. He smelled perfume. He became excited. With his eyes still closed, he threw his arms around the mystery woman and kissed her on the lips. All he thought about was, *Aniyah has come home.* He felt his shirt being unbuttoned and her tongue traveling up his chest. Excited his wife had returned, he landed another passionate kiss on her lips before he opened his eyes. He noticed that he was nose to nose with a woman who wore a brunette wig on her head. Realizing that this woman wasn't Aniyah, he pushed her off of him.

"Who in the devil are you?" he asked.

Jarvis watched her dash for the door. He ran after the woman dressed in skimpy attire. When she hit the first floor, he saw Sid standing at the foot of the stairs.

"Who is this? And how did both of you get in my house?"

"Man, I'm sorry. I used the spare key you gave to Noelle. Bro, I thought I'd help you out. You need something different to get your mind off of Aniyah," Sid said.

"Pay me my money," the woman said. She snatched the wig off her head to expose her cornrowed hair.

Jarvis pointed at her. "You hired *this* to seduce me?"

The woman smacked her lips. "You don't know what you're missing."

"Get out of my house!" Jarvis yelled.

Sid paid the woman, and then he said, "Man, I apologize. Please don't tell Noelle I did this. She'll never forgive me." He tossed Jarvis his key.

"This is not like you, Sid. I can't believe you would do something like this."

"It's New Year's Eve. I wanted you to have a little fun. Forget about Aniyah for a moment."

Jarvis saw in his eyes, he was sincere. "Sid, please leave. We'll talk later. Go home and love on your wife. Stop worrying about me."

Once Sid left, Jarvis checked the time. He had another hour before he would meet up with Charlinda.

In the parking lot of the restaurant, Jarvis got out of his

vehicle once he saw Charlinda step out of her sports BMW. With batting eyes, she came over to him and intertwined her arm with his, as if they were a couple. Jarvis went along with her gesture and escorted her inside.

Packed with lovers out on the town, they sat at a table for two with a bottle of champagne that sat inside a stainless-steel ice bucket.

"I want a nice juicy T-bone steak," Charlinda said, not even looking at the menu that was placed in front of her.

"I'll have the same," Jarvis said.

He watched her take out a compact mirror and a makeup brush and buff her face. Her complexion resembled smooth fudge. A waiter came over and she snapped the compact closed, then shoved it into her silver clutch.

"Hi, I'm Roland. I'll be your server. The bottle of champagne on the table is available for purchase if you like, or you're welcome to order something else."

Jarvis gazed at Charlinda. "Champagne?"

"Yes, please," she responded.

The waiter removed the bottle from the bucket and popped it open. He poured them each a half-filled glass.

"Here's to new beginnings," Charlinda said. She clinked her glass with Jarvis'.

"I'm surprised a pretty lady like you has no man in your life."

"My schedule runs men away. I need a man like you who is busy like me."

Jarvis choked on his drink. He cleared his voice. "My schedule does get tied up," he admitted.

The server returned with their meal. He served them T-bone steaks, garlic potatoes, and a vegetable medley.

While they ate, Charlinda shared more about herself. Jarvis learned that she was one of three children, raised in New Jersey, but while visiting with friends in South Carolina, she fell in love with Columbia and made it her home. She was never married, but what he did learn was that she loved to talk. About time they finished dining, his ears could not tune out her squeaky and boisterous voice.

Being a gentleman, he escorted her to her vehicle. "Thank you for a wonderful evening."

Charlinda looked down at the time on her jewel-cased cell phone.

"One hour before the New Year comes in." She threw her arms around his neck, kissing him on the lips.

The vision of Aniyah came to his mind, and he kissed Charlinda back. He pulled her into his arms and held her closely.

They came up for air, and Charlinda said, "I don't live far from here. Let's at least do another toast to bring in the New Year."

Jarvis got in his vehicle and did merely that, following her to a two-bedroom apartment.

"There's wine in the freezer." Charlinda said, pointing to the right toward the kitchen. "I'm going to use the bathroom."

Jarvis felt at home in her kitchen. He poured their drinks. In the living area, he set her glass on the circle-shaped coffee table. He took a sip of his drink.

"Relax. Have a seat," Charlinda said, once she saw him standing with his glass in his hand.

"First, let me use your restroom." Jarvis placed his glass

on the coffee table.

Charlinda directed him to the bathroom. She took a seat on the sofa and swallowed a gulp of her drink.

While Jarvis took a leak, he took a deep breath. He wondered how could Aniyah put him in this position. He zipped his pants up and washed his hands.

"I need help." Charlinda summoned him in a frantic tone of voice.

Jarvis ran into the living room, but he saw no signs of her.

"Help!" she called again.

He followed her siren voice into a master suite. He found her stretched out across a brass-poled, queen-size bed and dressed in a red-laced gown. It barely covered her hips.

She got up and came to him. She stared into his eyes, removing his suit jacket. Then she loosened his tie, pulling it over his head. Next she unbuttoned his shirt and eased it off of his muscular arms. After sipping on so many drinks, including at the restaurant, Jarvis had a buzz. He visualized Aniyah as he took Charlinda into his arms, kissing her with passion. Her lips got lost in his lips. Jarvis slipped out of his shoes, pants and boxers. He watched as Charlinda let her gown fall to the floor, exposing her small breasts to him. His member hardened.

Charlinda handed him a condom, one thing led to another, and they were on the bed with Jarvis riding on top of her. The more he thought of his wife, the faster he rode her.

Charlinda moaned from the pleasure he gave her. She

hollered. "Happy New Year, my new man!"

Jarvis exploded from the thought of making love to Aniyah. He fell on top of Charlinda, and then said, "Happy New Year, Aniyah."

"Aniyah?" Charlinda pushed him off her.

Jarvis moved his hand across his face as if he was wiping it. "I didn't mean to call my wife's name."

He got up and got dress. "I apologize. I loved my wife."

Charlinda looked at him. Never had she saw a man cry for a woman. His watery eyes told it all.

"She's moved on. I can help you to forget her. Give me that chance." Charlinda got up and hugged him.

"I don't know how."

"You'll start tonight."

Charlinda helped him out of his clothes. She led him back into her bed. He rested in her arms, like a child being consoled by their parent. They took another shot at a second round of lovemaking. The vision of Aniyah dominated his mind again. Jarvis was cautious not to blab her name.

From that day on, Charlinda became a part of his life. He never shared his relationship with her to anyone. He kept her away from his family, never bringing her around, using his wife's aunt and son as an excuse to keep Charlinda from his doorsteps. She was the void he needed to put a bandage on his wounded heart.

CHAPTER 27

*I*t was a career day at a local school, giving high school students the opportunity to listen to professionals and people that carried a trade. Each speaker had fifteen minutes to give the students a look into their careers. Afterward, students interested in the careers went to the front and greeted the guests to receive material on their career interest.

Sophomore students filled the auditorium. One after the other, the speakers spoke of their jobs. Being the next to the last speaker, Jarvis took his seat once he finished his speech on life as a banker. He eyed the last speaker who had arrived somewhat late, hurrying up to the podium while walking with a limp.

Unlike him, dressed in a custom-made suit for his body frame, the speaker wore rugged jeans and a T-shirt.

He disregarded the man's clothing and listened to him speak. The man stared into the crowd; not once did he look toward his right, giving Jarvis a side view of him.

"Hello, I'm Brant Logan. I'm a farmer," the speaker announced.

Jarvis listened to the man speak of his duties and the

journey of working lots of time outdoors. Something puzzled him of the familiar tone of the speaker's voice. Jarvis had heard the voice before.

"That can't be *the* Brant Logan. The one I went to college with," he thought out loud.

When the event was over, Jarvis headed toward Brant, whom had met him halfway.

"Hello, Jarvis Powell," Brant said.

Jarvis looked into his face. The two-hundred and something-pound student athlete from college had shed his weight and had bulked up.

"Football player, Brant Logan?"

"That's me."

"You used to be huge."

"Those were the football days."

Brant gave him a manly hug. "I caught the end of your talk. Big Banker man."

"It's a job. But you grow your own vegetables and eating from the earth is awesome. I might grow something with my little boy."

"You have a son?" Brant asked.

"Yes, I do. How about you?"

"No kids. I'm a newlywed."

Jarvis patted Brant on the shoulder. "Congratulations to you."

"I assume you're married?"

"Yes. It's not going well. My wife left me."

"Sometimes women be trippin', man."

The principal interrupted their conversation. "Gentlemen, may we get a photo of you two?"

Jarvis and Brant stood side by side. A teacher snapped

the photo. Brant did not hesitate to get a copy of the photo sent to him via text. He followed behind Jarvis to the floor of the auditorium where the students interested in asking the guests questions waited.

The men interacted with the students, giving them advice. When the line smoothed, Jarvis approached Brant.

"How did you go from football to farming?"

"It's a long story."

Jarvis thought back in time. "Hey, man, I hope it had nothing to do with what happened between us."

"Nah. Things just didn't work out."

"Where can I buy some of your farm products?"

"At the farmers market. Soon, I'll be moving to my next gig. Right now I'm a caregiver for farmers whenever they go on vacations or run into problems. Grow some tomatoes. You can't go wrong with them. Try it."

"Will do."

Jarvis shook his old schoolmate's hand. They left to go their separate ways.

After a morning with high school students for career day, Jarvis got into his vehicle, and sped off to have lunch with the fellas. Parking his vehicle in front of the sandwich shop, he arrived the same time as Sid and Nolan.

"So, how did career day go?" Sid asked, giving Jarvis a manly hug.

"The kids were amazing. I ran into an old classmate. He went from playing football to becoming a farmer."

"That's a big change."

"Hearing him speak to the kids, I say he loves what he does."

They entered the shop, taking a seat, then placed their orders.

Jarvis dined on a pastrami sandwich on wheat bread with plenty of mustard, and Sid and Nolan got the corned beef on rye with mustard and mayonnaise.

"It's good you're keeping busy. You've had a lot of loss. I'm hoping you meet a nice lady," Nolan said.

Jarvis smiled. "My son and job is my love right now."

"That's cool, Nolan, you're back at home," Sid said.

"Happy wife, Happy lockdown life," Nolan said.

"Noelle is the best. Happy she's not stuck up," Sid said.

Jarvis coughed. "Nolan, I think he's calling your wife out."

"Jarvis, don't start any trouble," Sid warned.

"I'm paying you back for 'you know what'," Jarvis said.

Nolan wondered what Jarvis meant. "School me. I'm in the dark."

Jarvis explained to Nolan the incident where Sid had paid a woman to come to his house.

"No you didn't, Sid."

"Hey, I was only trying to get his mind off of Aniyah."

"I've sought help to get over Aniyah," Jarvis admitted but did not tell what kind of help.

"Bro, Aniyah and the crazy things your pops did, soon will turn into a dream for you," Sid said.

"Your life will get better for you and J.P.," Nolan said.

Jarvis' phone buzzed. He had received a text.

"Gotta go to work," he lied.

The men finished their lunch and left.

***

At Charlinda's doorsteps, Jarvis buzzed her doorbell. She came to the door dressed in a bathrobe.

"What's the emergency?" he wondered, after reading her text at the restaurant, interrupting his lunch with the fellas. "I have to get to the bank. Are you sick?" Jarvis watched her limp her way toward the bedroom.

"It's my back," she cried. She placed her hands on the ball of her back. She dropped to the cold wooden floor. Jarvis came to her, helping her up.

"It's that bad? Maybe you need to go see a doctor."

"I did. I got a pulled muscle."

Jarvis helped her to the bedroom.

Charlinda sat on the bed. A sharp pain hit her. It felt like someone had plunged a fork into her. She rested her body on the soft mattress. "Please get in bed with me," she said, wanting Jarvis to be close to her.

Feeling sorry for her, he removed his suit jacket and crawled into the bed next to her. He cuddled her into his arms.

She smiled. "I feel better already. I love you, Jarvis."

Jarvis struggled to say the words, but he did. "I love you, too."

"Sweetheart, it's time we move forward. The first thing is for you to divorce your wife for abandonment."

This was not a subject Jarvis wanted to discuss. It was a decision he had to make when the time was right for him.

"When you feel better, we'll discuss it."

"No, Jarvis. I'll feel better if you tell me you're finished with her mentally, physically and on paper."

He stroked Charlinda's hair. "I'm ready to move forward," he muttered.

"So, this means we can make our relationship public? I need to meet your son."

"We can't do that. Not yet. The bank doesn't allow employees to date other employees."

"You're the head."

"No, I'm not. Milandra Houston is," he corrected her.

Jarvis, eager to leave, stood and pushed his hands in his pants pockets. "I have to meet with a potential client at the bank. I'll check on you later."

He kissed Charlinda on the lips, grabbed his jacket and dashed for the door. Outside, he shook his head. "What have I gotten myself into? The only commitment I want is to my son," he grunted.

CHAPTER 28

*E*very day she woke up, Aniyah wished she could unlock the chains from around her ankles and return home to her husband and son. She missed her family and friendship with Nellie. Any other time she could call her, and Nellie would come to her rescue.

The only communication she had was with Brant who had turned her into a true housewife. He gave her orders of what he wanted her to do.

After months of being with him, she had adapted with the lifestyle of living like a farmer. She was no longer wearing designer clothes or having lunch with her friend, Nellie. Instead, she dressed in overalls and T-shirts. At times she only wore a nightgown.

Her daily life consisted of working early mornings; whether the weather was firing hot or freezing cold, Brant dragged her to do chores. It comprised of a variety of tasks from milking the cows, getting eggs, picking corn or whatever vegetables were in season. The last couple of days were different. He kept her locked up. When she heard footsteps enter the house, Aniyah ran to the peephole. She glued her eyes on Brant.

Banging on the door, she called, "Please let me out of this room."

Brant granted her wish. He unlocked the door. Aniyah, with her hair frizzy on her head, let out a sigh of relief.

Brant tossed her a bag. "Here are some leftover cookies from Career Day at this high school."

She wondered who would ask a madman to come and speak to their students. Aniyah dug into the bag. So hungry, she stuffed two chocolate chips cookies into her mouth.

"I'm thirsty."

"Drink water from the bathroom."

Aniyah paused. It terrified her to go through the room to get to the bathroom; fearful he would lock the door behind her. Her dry mouth caused her to run fast into it, wet her tongue, and rush back out into the open space.

"I got something to show you."

Brant opened his photos on his phone. He turned it to face her. Aniyah stared at it. Tears fell from her eyes when she saw Jarvis standing next to Brant.

"Yeah, your hubby was at Career Day. We had a nice chat. I'd say he's over you."

Aniyah fired at him, "Never! Stay away from Jarvis. He's not hateful like you. I love him and he loves me."

She lifted her foot to kick him, but the metal against her ankle irritated her.

"Put your foot down. Get back into your room."

Alarmed, Aniyah said, "I'm sorry. Remember I'm your wife."

Her words did not help; he pushed her into the room and locked the door. With a flushed face, Aniyah ran into the bathroom. She stood in the mirror. She noticed her eyes were puffy. Her hair, untamed from only being able to wash it with Brant's homemade soap instead of store-bought hair products. Her face was dry from not having moisturizer or the spa treatments Jarvis had gifted her.

She no longer had access to a master closet full of beautiful clothes. In the tiny space, it was a hook in the bathroom to hold her overalls and nightgown. She wiped her tears when she heard the room door slide on its rail. She ran and saw he had reopened it. He came up to her. In a quick instant, she put her hands up to her face presuming he would slap her.

"Are you ready to be a good wife?" he asked.

"Yes, I promise."

"This is your last chance to be sincere to me." He scanned her body with his eyes.

Aniyah was willing to do anything to relieve herself from being a hostage in the small-enclosed space. She placed a kiss on his lips. They spoke no other words. He took her hand and led her out into the open area.

Brant stood at the foot of the ladder. It led to the loft. "It's time you share my bed with me; ladies first."

Shackled with the long chains on her ankles, Aniyah took cautious steps and climbed the ladder. When she reached the top, she could not stand because the ceiling was too low. She crawled her way onto the queen-sized, pillow-topped mattress. Brant followed right behind her.

Before he lay on the bed, he got undressed. Aniyah stared at his buffed body. His eyes mesmerized her, the same way they had the first time she had met him and lured her into his web. At that moment, she again blocked out all of what she used to have with Jarvis.

He pulled her gown over her head, exposing her flesh. She wore no underwear. Brant lay next to her. He pressed his lips against her left breast. Aniyah felt an excruciating pain when he bit her nipple.

"Ouch," she mumbled.

He came up to her lips. Brant shoved his tongue in her mouth, giving her the sloppiest kiss she had ever had. Next, he grabbed her breasts and squeezed them. Aniyah wanted to complain, but was scared that he would throw her into the room. After a while, she got used to it and the feeling became numb to her. To make Brant think she was loyal to him, Aniyah tossed her arms around his neck, kissing him with passion. She channeled her lovemaking with Jarvis, and she joined Brant, giving him a great ride until they both exploded.

Breathing heavily, he fell off of her. "I bet you were thinking of him."

"I wasn't. I promise."

Aniyah placed her arms around his neck and pulled him back to her. She kissed him so he would not be mad at her. With his sweat dripping down on her, and her hair soaked from the heat they had made, Brant caressed her body.

He came up for air. "Beauty, you need to call me your husband."

When Aniyah did not respond, he shoved her. "Go downstairs."

"Husband," she blurted.

He chuckled. "Too late. Go cook. I'm hungry." Brant lay at the foot of the mattress.

Aniyah got dressed. She took her time, not to fall down the ladder in the chains.

While she prepared dinner, she locked eyes with him. As soon as he turned his head, Aniyah took a fork and placed it in her pocket. When Brant came down to the kitchen to eat, she handed him his plate of food, and then jabbed him with the fork. He screamed, when he felt the punch in his left arm, causing the plate of food to splatter on the floor. He swung his other arm around, backslapping her. Aniyah, caught off balance, tumbled down. Brant hit her in her back with his booted foot. Tears flooded her face.

"Crawl to your room," he ordered.

On her hands and knees, Aniyah struggled to move. She felt a knot in her lower back, causing her to fall to the floor.

Brant nurtured his wound with water, stopping the bleeding from his arm. He growled. "Get yourself in there."

Aniyah attempted to lift up on her hands, but the knot in her back was painful. She dropped to the cold floor. She stayed down and moved across the floor like a snake. Once she made it to the entrance of the room door, she took a break and rested. When she felt Brant poke her on her behind with his foot, pain and all, she moved faster than a mouse.

"Husband, I'm sorry."

"I don't believe you."

Brant locked the room door.

Taking deep breaths, Aniyah was thankful he did not kill her.

"I'll be back," he roared.

She heard the front door close. She believed he went to get medical help for his arm. Placing her hands over her eyes, Aniyah's downpour of tears soaked her hands.

"I'm so stupid, thinking I could save Jarvis' inheritance."

When Brant returned, he opened the room door. Aniyah closed her eyes to make him think she had dozed off to sleep. But Brant was not going for that. She felt him take the tip of his foot and stroke her leg.

"Wake up," he said.

Aniyah opened her eyes. She saw his arm was wrapped with gauze.

"You're lucky my injury is minor."

"I wasn't thinking. I'm sorry, Husband."

"Get up. You're coming with me."

"I said, I'm sorry."

"Get up."

Aniyah gritted her teeth. The pain once again hit her up and down her spine. She did not complain. She wobbled to her feet.

"Hold your hands out."

Aniyah did as she was told. He handcuffed her and placed the blindfold over her eyes. Then, he unleashed her ankles from the restraints.

"Please don't hurt me."

Brant didn't say a word. He pulled her to the front of the tiny house, opening the front door and leading her outside into the cool air. Her breasts puckered from the chill. He picked her up and carried her over his shoulder.

Like a rag doll, he tossed her body on the back of his pickup truck. Her fragile back hit the floor. Tears rolled down her face from under the mask. "My back hurts," she said.

"Hush. Don't disturb my dog."

"It hurts bad."

Aniyah nearly fainted when Brant rocked the truck, bouncing her up and down. He did not stop until he saw the agony in her face. Her body felt numb. Brant took an old blanket from the truck and tossed it to her. "I'm finished with you for the night. I'm going in the house. You better be in your room before daybreak. Keep the mask on."

Aniyah yearned to run for her life. She was in no shape and too fearful to leave.

With the blanket over her, she shivered.

Aniyah stayed in the back of the truck until she got enough strength to move. She pulled up in a sitting position, using the blanket around her as if it were a coat. With her thumb, she lifted the blindfold up enough to slide her way to the end of the truck bed. She paused, taking in the pain, before she eased one foot to the ground, then the other.

Taking a deep breath, she strolled with blurred vision from the downpour of tears from her eyes and the blindfold halfway over them. Somehow, she made it into the house. Brant was asleep on the sofa once she entered. She peeked under her blindfold to see where she was going and crept past him, hoping he would not awake.

Aniyah went into the room, got down on the cushion

and snuggled her aching body in the blanket. Her little boy's face appeared in her mind. *Mama will find a way to come home to you,* she thought.

It took days for Aniyah to feel better. Brant kept her hostage in the room. His thick rubber-sole boot tapped her leg. She woke up. This morning, he ordered her to do chores, something she dreaded.

The weather was foggy, but the air was warm. Brant escorted her to the barn. Aniyah, dressed in overalls, absorbed the fresh morning dew. She milked a cow and Brant saw that she carried the milk into the house. She made her way to the chicken coop and got five eggs for their morning breakfast. Once she returned into the house, she changed back into the nightgown and prepared breakfast.

Aniyah sizzled turkey bacon and turkey sausages and scrambled eggs with cheese. She also had a small pot of hot water boiling for grits. Brant sat at the counter in his rugged jeans and no shirt, exposing his muscled body.

"You'll get to stay out of your cubbyhole. I'm not working at the market today."

Aniyah felt relieved. She was grateful to hear that she would not spend another day in the cramped space.

While they ate breakfast, Brant's phone rang. He answered the call, but she only heard his response to the caller.

"Done deal," he said, then ended the call.

"What did the old-fart have to say today?" She presumed it was her father-in-law whom Brant had spoken to. She scooped a spoonful of grits into her mouth.

"You'll be surprised."

"He's coming here?"

"Stop asking questions. I owe you no answers. Finish eating. I need a day with my wife. Can you give me that?"

"Yes."

When they finished eating, she placed the soiled dishes in the sink. While she washed them, Brant came up behind her. He reached around her and got a cup, filling it with the water running from the faucet. Aniyah sighed, when he poured it between her breasts, wetting her gown. He turned the water off and turned her to face him. He pushed her up against the refrigerator, then stripped her of her clothing. Before Aniyah knew it, they were on the floor, having another marital workout.

Brant rolled off of her onto the floor and rested on his back. They both lay in silence until they heard an unfamiliar sound. Aniyah jumped, hoping it was help to get her away from her kidnapper.

Brant stood to his feet. He pulled up his pants and zippered them. He laughed. "That's no one. It's probably a stray cat looking for milk."

Things were different that evening. Brant received several phone calls. He had nothing much to say to his last caller. The only words Aniyah heard were, "Phase two."

She did not understand what it meant. She watched Brant gathered up most of the chains he'd used on her around the house. She wanted to ask questions, but dared not to in fear of being chastised. That night after having a hot cup of tea with him, Aniyah struggled to keep her eyes open. She tried to fight the sudden exhaustion, but it did not take her long to doze off.

CHAPTER 29

*I*nstead of looking up at the ceiling in the tiny house, Aniyah stared at the moon until it faded away. She rubbed her right foot against her left sore ankle. She felt no chain. The cushion had changed into the hardness of the concrete ground. "Am I dreaming?"

She shivered, wrapping a plaid blanket around her, then dozed back off.

Awakened by the morning sun, Aniyah opened her eyes and noticed that she was at the edge of a driveway. She paused, looking around until she saw that there was a mailbox, with her married name *Powell* engraved on it, right next to her. Struggling to her feet, Aniyah stood and stared into the driveway at her vehicle. As water built up in her eyes, she twiddled her fingers while her knees shook. She became nervous when she looked ahead and saw the two-story home she once yearned for Jarvis to move her out of. The house looked the same to her, with mint-green vinyl siding and eggshell shutters and doors.

Taking a deep breath, she took baby steps, dragging the blanket with her up the driveway. Her vision blocked from her sobbing. With a full bladder, she could no longer hold it. Urine trickled down her legs, soiling the gown she wore. She took the blanket and wiped her legs dry. Aniyah studied her surroundings; there were no signs of Brant. It was as if he had never existed in her life.

Aniyah rang the bell with one hand and banged on the door with the other.

Jarvis opened the door. He stood face to face with a fragile woman—his wife. Aniyah no longer had the curvy body, which attracted him to her.

"Aniyah?"

She dropped the blanket when she looked into her husband's face and fainted. Jarvis caught her before she hit the ground. He snatched up the blanket out of the doorway and left it in the foyer. He carried Aniyah into the family room, laying her across the sofa.

"Mama-Mom," Little Jarvis chanted.

"Go play with your toys," Jarvis said to him. He ran and got a cool washcloth, placing it on his wife's forehead. He held her hand. She looked like a worn sleeping beauty. Tears flowed from his eyes. All the anger he thought he would reveal when he saw her, never seeped into his heart. He loved her, the same as he had the day he had met her. He looked down at her ankles and witnessed the bruises.

"Aniyah, where have you been?" he wondered.

Tessa had let herself in with the spare key. She was little Jarvis' ride to preschool.

"Aniyah has returned home," Jarvis announced, once she entered.

"Rosie Aniyah came to her senses," she responded. She

was the only one that identified her niece by her first and middle name. Tessa was hesitant to reunite with Aniyah. She worried Aniyah would reject her.

She followed Jarvis into the family room to care for his wife. Jarvis updated Tessa on her niece's condition.

"She fainted," Jarvis said.

"Where has she been?"

With a cold compress against Aniyah's forehead, Jarvis fanned her with his other hand. "I have no clue. She had a blanket and this nightgown on."

"Please take J.P. to school. I don't want him to be around his mom right now."

Tessa called her great-nephew's name. He came running to her.

"Tia," Jarvis III called.

Tessa picked him up, giving him kisses on the cheek. She called back to Jarvis. "I'll be right back."

Aniyah opened her eyes. She wept. "Jarvis, your poppa is alive. He had someone kidnap me."

Removing the cloth off her forehead, Jarvis brushed away her flowing tears, and said, "Dad is dead."

"No, he isn't. The old fart is alive," she cried.

"Aniyah, relax. Have you taken any kind of drug?" He gripped her shoulders. "Let's get you out of this wet gown, into the bathroom so you can clean up."

Hearing his words, Aniyah leaped to her feet. "You can't lock me up in there!"

Astounded, Jarvis assured her, "I wouldn't do that. You'll bathe and then you'll go to bed."

Aniyah threw her arms around his neck. "I love you, Jarvis. I always loved you."

Jarvis pressed his lips against hers. Then he carried her to their master suite.

"I want my son."

"You'll have plenty time with him when he comes home from school."

When Jarvis put her down, she said, "I don't deserve to come into this bedroom."

"Aniyah, it's okay." He held out his hand to her.

In a daze, she let go of his hands and her feet sunk into the deep blue carpet as she strolled over to the bed. Aniyah pressed her fingers into the soft mattress before she headed into the master closet. Her eyes sparkled when she saw her clothes. *No more overalls*, she thought.

"You didn't throw my things away?"

"No, I didn't." Jarvis watched her wobble, holding on to the wall. "You need to take a bath and rest. We have plenty of time to talk."

"Jarvis, since the day we said, 'I do,' you've always pampered and protected me. It makes me feel good."

"You can sleep in here. I'll take the guest room until we sort things out."

"You lost your love for me. Are you feeling pity for me?"

"I've loved you from the day we got married."

Aniyah fell into his arms. "This bed is more than big enough for me and my man." She pressed her lips against his.

Jarvis yearned to have his way with her, but he let go of her. "I need to make a call to the bank."

Aniyah went into the bathroom, leaving the door wide open.

Jarvis went into his son's room to check his cell phone. He missed a call and a text message. It was from Charlinda. She wanted him to call her. He contacted her.

"Hi," he whispered, once she had answered the phone.

"You miss me?"

"Yes. How are things going?" He made small talk not to get her suspicious.

"Nice day here in Chicago. I'll see you sooner than you think. My trip was cut short."

Jarvis panicked. "When?"

"I'm boarding the plane." She spoke in the tone of someone cheering at a football game. "Meet me at the airport. And bring your baby boy. It's time I meet him."

"He's at school. Another day," Jarvis said.

He thought, *that's not about to happen. Aniyah is home.*

Jarvis listened to Charlinda run down her flight information.

"Text it to me."

"Lots of love. Bring my future stepson with you. It's time I meet him."

Jarvis heard Charlinda blow kisses in the phone. Her joyful spirit attracted Jarvis. She helped him cope with a broken heart.

Tessa returned fast. She was eager to get an update on her niece.

"How is Rosie Aniyah?" her aunt asked Jarvis.

"She's taking a bath. She has this crazy idea that my dad had her kidnapped."

"Mr. Powell?"

"I assured her, dad is dead. The strange thing is, Aniyah

would never be caught looking the way that she does. She smelled like urine." He showed Tessa the plaid blanket. "She had this too. It smells."

"One can never tell with my niece. Throw it away."

"I'll put it in the trash on the way out." Jarvis checked his watch. "I need to leave. I know you two have had your troubles, but can you please stay here with her?"

"That's what I'm here for, to help out."

Jarvis caressed her hand. "You're the best."

CHAPTER 30

*O*pening the car door, Jarvis tossed his suit jacket across the driver's seat and hopped in. When he started the engine, he synced his phone to the car and made a call. After three rings, his party answered.

"What's up?" Sid asked.

"Where are you?"

"Home."

"Is Noelle home?"

"Yes. What's going on?"

"Aniyah came home."

"Bro, say what?"

"You and Noelle stay put. I'm headed to your house."

Jarvis drove forty minutes to Lake Murray. He parked in front of the Houston Villa.

Before Jarvis could get through the screen door, Sid rushed to him.

"I'm happy for you and J.P."

"There's something strange going on with her. She returned wearing a nightgown. Her body is thin," Jarvis said.

Sid rested his hand on his shoulder. "Did she explain why she left?"

"Not yet. The way she looks, Aniyah is in need of rest."

"Milandra and Nolan are here. They're in the den with Noelle," Sid said.

Jarvis followed Sid into the family room.

Once he eyed Milandra, she voiced her opinion right away. "Aniyah had the audacity to return to you after she vanished for months? She must have realized the roses on the other side had lots of thorns." Milandra chuckled. "When will you ever learn? You're married to an unstable woman."

Noelle scolded her sister. "Stop it. Jarvis didn't come here for you to beat up on him."

Nolan defended his wife. "Milandra has a right to voice her opinion."

Jarvis watched Milandra take her husband by the hand, showing unison with him.

"I have enough going on in my life. Don't badger me." Jarvis checked his watch. "I can't stay. I got another stop before I head back home."

"You should go home. Aniyah might have returned to steal J.P.," Milandra said.

"J.P. is at school. Her Aunt Tessa is at the house with her," Jarvis said.

"I thought she no longer spoke to Aniyah," Milandra said.

"Mrs. Chavis loves her family. She'll never give up on her niece," Noelle said.

"Tessa is not like my dad. He didn't have faith in my choices," Jarvis admitted.

"He had common sense not to let Aniyah get her paws on his fortune. It's a good thing he turned things over to me," Milandra bragged.

When Jarvis cut his eyes at Nolan, Nolan pulled Milandra closer to him, placing his arms around her waist.

"I'll see my way out," Jarvis said.

When Jarvis darted out of the room, Noelle moved to go after him, however, Sid pulled her by the arm.

"We men will go," he said, eyeing Nolan.

"You go ahead," Nolan said, never leaving his wife's side.

Sid ran after Jarvis, catching him in the front yard.

"Hold up, Bro," Sid called.

Jarvis stopped in front of a pink azalea bush.

"Sorry, man. When you called, Milandra and Nolan weren't here. I had no idea they were coming over."

"I got other things to worry about besides Milandra's sarcastic ways."

Sid laughed. "I see she has Nolan on lockdown."

Jarvis had no choice but to chuckle.

"Hey, I made you laugh."

Jarvis' smile vanished when his cell phone rang. He had forgotten to put it on vibrate mode. He pretended like he did not hear it, but Sid's keen ears did.

"Bro, answer your phone."

Jarvis eased the phone out of his pocket. He saw it was a call he did not want to deal with but answered anyway.

"I'll call you back." He ended it.

"Dang, that was cold." Sid noticed his abrupt conversation.

Before Jarvis could put the phone on vibrate, it rang

again. He moved a few steps from Sid. He took the call. Charlinda's loud voice blasted through the speaker.

"You bet not be late," she said.

"Is that a female?" Sid asked, being nosey.

Briskly moving his hand across his neck, as to ignore Sid, Jarvis continued his conversation with her. "I'll be there to get you."

Right away, Sid questioned Jarvis. "Explain who the squeaky-talking female on the phone is."

Jarvis had kept Charlinda a secret. He was not sure what the outcome would be with them. He turned to Sid. "This information is between you and me. Not you, me and Noelle."

"A man thing. I got you."

Jarvis lowered his voice. "I must confess, I'm seeing another woman. Her name is Charlinda. She's the help whom I'm been seeking to get over Aniyah."

"Are you confused about which one you want to be with?"

"I've always been in love with my wife."

"Then you have to come clean with Charlinda. She knows you're a married man. And it was a chance Aniyah would come back."

"She won't like it."

"It's a whole new ballgame. She should understand that."

"I'm on my way to get Charlinda from the airport. I'll have to let her down gently."

"Bro, you deserve happiness. You've been through a lot."

"Thanks, Man."

***

Jarvis spotted Charlinda as she strutted through the airport with a tote bag on her arm. She wore her auburn hair in a ponytail. Her mineral makeup looked freshly done on her tiny face.

Jarvis did not have to say a word; Charlinda always made herself known in a room with her boisterous ways.

"You're late," she belted, broadcasting to travelers making their way through the airport.

"Lower your voice." Her mouth was his least favorite thing about her.

Even though she complained, she went on and plastered his lips with her burgundy lipstick, and then paraded ahead of him as if she knew where he was parked.

"I bet you like what you see from behind," she teased him, switching her narrow hips in the penciled skirt.

He spoke what she wanted to hear. "Every bit of it."

Once they got in his vehicle and drove off, she argued. "I called you specifically this morning, so you'd be here on time. Was she that important for you to be late picking me up?"

"Running behind time doesn't mean I'm with another female."

"I see it that way," Charlinda said. She pulled down the overhead mirror and checked her lipstick. When she flipped the mirror closed, Charlinda noticed Jarvis drove toward her home. "I want to stay the night at your house. Drive me there."

"First, we'll check on things at your place." This would give him time to break the news to her.

Charlinda rolled her eyes at him. "You're not getting out

of it, Jarvis. It's time I meet your son."

While Charlinda put her belongings away, Jarvis poured himself a chilled glass of wine and poured her a glass. He set the glasses on the coffee table, and then took a seat on the plush gray sofa.

Charlinda returned with an overnight bag tossed over her shoulder. "Let's go!" she demanded, leaning on one hip.

"Not before we have a drink." He held the glass up that he had poured for her.

Charlinda removed the bag off her shoulder, took the glass out of his right hand and sat down beside him.

They took sips of the wine.

"I say my man needs an appetizer." She placed her glass on the table and then nibbled on his neck.

"I think we should talk."

"When we get to your place." She licked his ear with her tongue and made a trail to his lips.

Resting his back against the cushion of the seat, Jarvis repeated, "I think we should talk."

Charlinda ignored his words. She crawled onto his lap, sitting on him like she were on a bike. She smothered his lips.

Jarvis pulled her away, smacking his lips. "I need to tell you something."

"It can wait. I want my man." Charlinda tussled with his belt buckle and pants zipper.

He grabbed her hands. "My wife came home," he belted.

"Say what?" Charlinda pounded him on his chest. At the

top of her squeaky voice, she hollered, "So that's the reason you were late? You were taking care of business with your runaway wife?"

Jarvis took hold of her arms. "No. Aniyah is not in a good place."

"How long has she been back?" Charlinda jerked away from him. She got her another drink.

Jarvis explained in details his dilemma.

Charlinda poked him in the chest. "Get over her. Get your divorce papers in order, pay your child support as a good father, and move on—marry me. You owe me that."

"I better go," he said, heading to the door.

"I'm still coming with you. She needs to know today, I'm the new lady in your life."

Jarvis turned to her. "Please, Charlinda, don't be like this. Give me time to explain things to Aniyah."

"I don't play second to anyone." She walked closer to him. "Take this home with you." Charlinda smacked a juicy kiss on his lips.

Jarvis pulled away from her. He exited her apartment.

CHAPTER 31

*A*niyah crawled under the bedcovers. She relaxed her body on the plush mattress. Tears seeped through her eyes. She wiped them away. When she rolled onto her side, she heard footsteps. "Jarvis?"

"It's me."

Aniyah heard the familiar Spanish-accented voice. She locked eyes with her aunt, whom she had not seen in a long while. Her vindictiveness toward her aunt had caused them to keep their distance from each other.

"Aunt Tessa?" Aniyah studied the floral skirt. Her aunt had considered it fashionable ever since Aniyah was a teenager.

"Hello, Rosie Aniyah," Tessa said, as she stood holding a tray. She set it in front of her niece.

"Why are you here?"

Aniyah propped herself up on a pillow. She felt her aunt was always more loyal to her former employer, the Houston family, and her lawyer husband, Baron Chavis, than to her own flesh and blood.

"Not for you. I'm only here for my great-nephew and his father. They needed me. Remember, you weren't here for them."

"It wasn't by choice. I was kidnapped," Aniyah confessed. She blessed her food. She ate the Mexican omelet, cooked with red and yellow peppers, onions, sprigs of cilantro and Monterey Jack shredded cheese.

Tessa challenged her. "You got away. I see you yet to call the police."

"I want to, but I can't. They'll think I'm crazy since that old fart, Mr. Powell, is supposed to be dead. He had me kidnapped to get me away from Jarvis."

Tessa, sitting at the foot of the bed, responded, "Yes, they would think you've lost it. Mr. Powell is dead. His ashes are gone."

Aniyah stopped eating. "Really? Did you see them fry him in the fire? I'm not crazy. He's alive. I'll find him and prove it."

"Well, did you see Mr. Powell with your own eyes?"

"No. I believe he's the one who hired a farmer from the marketplace, here in town, to kidnap me and keep me in a small house on a large farm. I couldn't hear the person on the other line talking to Logan. That's the name the farmer used to identify himself. He followed the caller's orders." Aniyah waved her hand at her aunt. "Stop asking me questions. I owe you no answers about my life. I'll handle the old fart. He'll pay for these bruises on my ankles."

Aniyah swung her legs from under the covers.

Tessa did not seem bothered when she looked at the black, blue and purple marks on Aniyah's ankle. She flung the covers back over her niece's legs and turned her head. "You've given others more scars than that."

"Get out of my room. Leave my home!"

Tessa snatched the tray from Aniyah, since she had finished eating the omelet. She set it on the floor, away from the bed.

When her aunt came back to her, she gripped Aniyah by her wrists. "I'm not going anywhere. You may not like it, but I will be in J.P.'s life. He needs his family, including his Tia."

"He doesn't need you. Jarvis and I are his family."

"You didn't think about him when you got in that truck with the farmer. He had enough of you and threw you out."

Aniyah jumped to her feet. She shoved her aunt. "How do you know he had a truck?" Then she yelled, "It was you! You had Brant Logan kidnap me."

Tessa shoved her hands away, pushing Aniyah back down on the bed. She chattered. "Yes it was me. It was your fault Jarvis lost everything. You had to go."

"I'm having you arrested." Aniyah ran toward the phone.

"Go ahead and you'll lose Jarvis. I bet you were a slut and slept with him."

"I did not."

Tessa called her bluff. "Rosie Aniyah, I know you better than you know yourself. You gave yourself to him. I have proof."

"I had no choice."

"You should thank me for having the farmer to let you go. Being with J.P. and seeing the hurt in Jarvis' eyes is the only reason you're here."

Aniyah rested the cordless phone on the cradle.

Tessa snickered. "I thought you would change your mind. Get your butt in bed."

Aniyah had never seen her aunt act in such an ugly way. Never did she think her righteous aunt would strike back at her.

"I thought old man Powell was alive." She cried. "I went after Brant Logan for his money. He told me he was wealthy and owned the Powell Estate. I wanted to get it back for Jarvis."

"You took the wrong road to get your way. You can't use people."

"I hated being locked up in that small room for hours."

"You needed the time to see that family is more important than money. Your husband has stuck by you through your craziness."

"So, now what do you want from me, dear Aunt Tessa?"

"This will only be our secret, if you be a great mother and wife. Raise your son to be a good man and love your husband if he's willing to forgive you. For now you don't have to like me, but in due time, we can renew our relationship."

Aniyah cut her eyes at her aunt. "Really?"

"Yes. You tell Jarvis you felt guilty about everything he lost from being with you. You thought it was better for him to have ya'll son. But you had a change of heart. I don't have to tell you, you're a pro at alluring men."

"Where's the farmer?"

"Far gone."

Aniyah fell onto the pillow. "I want to be alone." All she wanted was to have the marriage with Brant annulled before anyone found out, especially her husband. She was thankful that Brant had not mentioned it to her aunt.

"I'll leave you to yourself." Tessa took hold of the tray. She carried it away.

With her hands clashed to her body, Aniyah awakened from sleeping a long period of time in the comfort of being in her own bed. She looked around, happy she was no longer hostage in the small home with shackles on her ankles.

"God, I thank you," she uttered.

Her eyes brightened when she heard her son, chanting.

"Mama-Mom, Mama-Mom."

His voice echoed as he ran into the master suite.

Aniyah hopped out of bed. She picked her son up in her arms. Tears flooded her face. "I missed you so much. I love you, J.P. You're my heart."

She placed kisses on his face.

"Love you, Mama-Mom," he cried.

"Spend time with your son. Your meal is cooked. I'm headed home," Tessa said. She gave her great-nephew a kiss on his forehead. Then she patted Aniyah on the forearm.

Aniyah lightened up. "Thanks."

After playing with her son, Aniyah headed downstairs to the kitchen for dinner.

While Jarvis III ate his beans and rice off his plate, Aniyah contacted Jarvis.

"Hi. This is Aniyah."

Hearing his wife's gentle voice soothed him. He smiled.

"You sound a lot better."

"I'm with my baby boy. He's eating."

"I'll be home soon. Tightening up some loose ends here at the bank."

"I have a lot of explaining to do."

Listening to Aniyah, Jarvis felt she was on the verge of shedding more tears.

"We'll talk later on tonight when J.P. goes to bed."

CHAPTER 32

*A*t the office, his cell phone rang and Jarvis answered the incoming call.

Before he could say hello, Charlinda's voice was like an alarm going off in his ears. "Nothing should change with us."

"I need time to think."

"I'm lonely." She went into a whiny voice. "Come to me."

"I made a detour. I'm at work." He explained his time period since he had last seen her.

Charlinda chattered. "I'll come to your office."

"Please don't do that," he begged.

"I told you, Jarvis Powell, I don't play second to anyone. Take me to lunch tomorrow."

"I'll call you later." He ended the conversation.

He looked up and Milandra, escorted on the arm of her husband, strolled inside his office.

"What do you want, Milandra?"

"I have come to warn you, and Nolan agrees with me. If you rekindled your marriage with Aniyah, you'll have to find another bank to work for. Mr. Powell wanted me to at least let you keep your job, but I won't have Aniyah set foot in a Milandra Houston Bank."

"You have the nerve to speak ill of Aniyah. Nolan, I don't know how you put up with a bossy wife," Jarvis said.

"I've warned you," Milandra said.

Nolan cut his eyes at Jarvis, as if to say don't mess with my wife. He and Milandra held hands, leaving the office.

Jarvis scratched his head. He grabbed his suit jacket, slipped it on and left for the day.

When Jarvis arrived home, the first floor was quiet. Aniyah and his son had made their way upstairs. He tiptoed into the kitchen. His covered plate of food was prepared for him on the stove. With a lack of appetite, he took two scoops of the beans and rice and left the rest. Turning off the lights, he made his way to the second floor. As he passed by his son's bedroom, he heard cartoons. He peeked inside to find that Jarvis III had fallen asleep. Jarvis turned the television off.

When he reached the master suite, he saw Aniyah coming out of the master bath. He admired her wrapped in a light-blue bathrobe. Her long hair was pushed away from her face and up into a ponytail, showing off her dark-brown eyes.

"It's been a long day." He unbuttoned his shirt. "How are you feeling?"

"A little exhausted but better." She turned from him, removing her robe.

He eyed the low-cut of the short, light-blue gown, exposing her smooth back. He still could not get over how thin she had gotten. Aniyah got into the king-sized bed. He went into the bathroom and showered.

Jarvis returned, dressed in drawstring pajama pants and a sleeve-less T-shirt. The muscles in his arms and chest bulged out, those being results of his consistency in going to the gym. "I need to know what happened before I join you in bed."

Aniyah burst into tears. "I'm sorry. I felt responsible for you losing your fortune. That's why I left. I wanted you to believe I ran off with someone else. You and our son deserved better."

He sat on the side of the bed next to her. He calmed her with a stroke on top of her head. "Where did you go?"

"I went to visit an old friend. I became so depressed. That's why I've lost weight. I missed you and J.P. so much. I couldn't take it and came back home. I didn't even realize I hadn't gotten dressed."

He wondered. "The bruises on your legs."

"I tied a rope around my ankles and would pull it so tight until it hurt. I wanted to feel pain from hurting your life."

"Aniyah, I loved you for you."

He melted like warmed cheese when Aniyah placed her arms around his neck, pressing her lips against his. He helped himself to the delight of the sweetness of her juicy lips.

"Please forgive me. I want my family."

After Jarvis plastered another kiss on her lips, Aniyah lay down. He took his place under the covers, on the opposite side of the bed. He turned off the light. "Good night, Aniyah," he whispered.

"Night, Jarvis."

He turned on his side. After several months of envisioning making love to his wife, when he was intimate with Charlinda, he wondered were the sparks still the same as being with her.

"Jarvis, I'm yours," Aniyah admitted.

Hearing his wife say those words, Jarvis rolled over, pulled her into his arms and passionately kissed her. He threw the bedding off them. Slipping her out of her nightgown, he sniffed the aroma of her flesh, from her head to her toes. Then, he traveled up her legs, licking on her until he reached her right earlobe. "My beautiful wife," he said, finding his way to her lips.

As they kissed, Aniyah spread her legs apart. They moaned as he entered her, moving their bodies as one. It was the fastest he had ever exploded. With dripping sweat, he collapsed on top of her from exhaustion, but was ready for another round as soon as he caught his breath. Aniyah was everything he had envisioned and yearned for since the day she had disappeared.

"I love you so much," he admitted. "You've always been the love of my life."

"You're my soul mate. I'll be a good wife for you, I promise."

"I want you again. Is that too much to ask?"

Aniyah crawled on top of her husband and in return, she gave him the same pleasure he had given her. Jarvis wanted control, and flipped his wife over. He entered the wetness of her inner flesh again. He did not want to explode, but the sensual parts of her body made that impossible.

Lying on top of her, drenched in sweat, Jarvis gave her one last kiss and then said, "Good night."

She caught her breath. "Good night."

With her face resting on his chest, Jarvis cuddled her. In the silent room, they listened to the thumping of their healed hearts.

The landline interrupted their peacefulness when it rang. It frightened Jarvis. Letting go of Aniyah, he crawled to the nightstand and answered it. "Hello," he said.

Charlinda asked, "Why are you out of breath?"

He placed his hand over the mouthpiece. "Sorry, Sid. I'm busy." He ended the call.

Aniyah had turned away from him. He crawled closer behind her, however, his cell phone echoed in the room.

He answered it.

"Jarvis, don't hang up on me again," Charlinda argued.

He lowered his voice. "This can wait until tomorrow."

"I need you to come ASAP," Charlinda demanded.

"Not tonight. I have to work in the morning."

He ended the call again.

He eased closer to Aniyah, who had closed her eyes.

When he wrapped his arms around her, she opened her eyes. "Who is she?"

Jarvis rolled over onto his back. Staring up at the ceiling, he explained, "It devastated me when you left. You vanished out of my life. I needed to ease the pain from losing you. Charlinda was there to comfort me."

Aniyah's eyes watered. "I drove you to another woman?"

Placing his hands behind his head, Jarvis continued to stare up at the ceiling. He massaged his neck to relieve the tension building up in his neck muscles. "Yes. You did."

"I've lost you." Aniyah jumped out of the bed, snatched her gown and slipped it on. She stormed out of the master suite in tears.

Jarvis wobbled to his feet. "Aniyah," he called, while he slipped on his pajama pants. He ran down the stairs and into the kitchen.

When he entered, Aniyah had poured herself a glass of wine. He stared at her swollen eyes and the non-curves that she used to have. He remembered the way she would sashay in front of him, but now that was gone. He picked up the wine bottle, pouring himself a drink.

"This is my dad's doing. He left this earth making you feel guilty for his wrongdoings. He wanted to divide us. It almost happened, but I'm not going to let it. Come here, Tiny."

"I'll gain my weight back in no time."

"Whatever size you decide to be, I'll love you, anyway." He tickled her nose with his fingertip.

He grabbed the bottle of wine and threw his left arm around her shoulder, escorting her back upstairs to the master suite. While Aniyah got comfortable in the bed, he lit two candles and turned off the lamp. As if the call never had happened, he cuddled her into his arms, pressing his lips against the side of her neck. They went another round of lovemaking.

Aniyah took control, showing him she was a better lover than the person who had been on the phone. She rested on top of him and rode him like a stallion. They cried out in ecstasy.

Jarvis' heart awakened with joy. He had never lost her love. "I'm a happy husband."

Aniyah grinned. "I plan to keep it that way, dear husband."

Jarvis brushed his hands through her untamed hair, giving her another kiss. Then he blew out the candles on the nightstand.

"This time, good night for real."

"Night, my love," she said.

Under the covers, in the darkness of their room, they cuddled like college lovers. With a big smile on his face, Jarvis thought, *I choose my wife. A cheerful wife makes a cheerful life.*

CHAPTER 33

*T*essa hummed an unfamiliar tune, while she baked an apple pie at the Powells' home. It felt good to be back into her niece's life and part of her family. The chime of the doorbell interrupted her jolly mood.

"I'll get it, Rosie Aniyah," she called to the second floor of the house. "You just rest."

Tessa walked to the door and peeped out. She eyed a slender woman. Right away, she figured it was Jarvis' lady friend. Aniyah had schooled her of their relationship. She opened the door, walked out and closed it behind her.

"May I help you?"

"You must be the auntie? I'm here to see Jarvis' runaway wife."

"You're right. My niece is not home."

Charlinda pointed at Aniyah's vehicle in the driveway. "Is that her car?"

"I don't have to answer that."

Charlinda stood with her back arched. Snappy, she asked, "Where is she? I don't have time for games."

"Watch your tone of voice and I suggest you leave."

"Charlinda is my name. Tell her I'm Jarvis' new woman. She lost her rights."

Tessa gazed into her eyes. "The only lady who has wife-rights of Jarvis is Mrs. Rosie Aniyah Sanchez-Powell. I'll be sure to inform her, some delusional woman thinks she has more rights than she." Tessa pointed to the driveway. "Leave this property or I'll call the police on her behalf."

"She'll have to face me sooner or later."

Tessa was tickled. "I don't think you want to cross my feisty niece."

Charlinda marched to her vehicle.

Standing her ground, Tessa did not return into the house, until Charlinda got back inside her vehicle. She watched from a distance as Charlinda punched the keys on her cell phone. She presumed she was contacting Jarvis.

Once Charlinda sped off, Tessa went inside.

Up the stairs, she knocked on the master suite door. "Aniyah," she belted.

"Come in, Aunt Tessa." When Aniyah saw her aunt, she asked, "Who was at the door?"

"The woman whom Jarvis has been seeing."

"Charlinda?" Aniyah moved the cold compress off her ankles. "Is she downstairs? I need to tell her to find herself another man."

"I believe you've met your match. She's a piece of work. She doesn't scare easy. It took me a moment to get rid of her."

"She needs to get over Jarvis."

"The woman is a loudmouth. Talks like a parrot."

"I'll speak to Jarvis. If he doesn't handle her, I will."

"Let him deal with her. You work on being a loyal good wife," Tessa said.

"She was a warm body for him. Now that I'm home, her body has gone ice-cold to him. She might as well move on."

"I pray it'll be that simple. The mouthy hell-raiser might not go away that easy."

CHAPTER 34

*W*hen Jarvis arrived at his office, he noticed the empty chair behind the receptionist desk. He wondered where his receptionist was. He headed into his office, ready to call and get an update of her status. When he entered, his ex-girlfriend sat behind his desk.

"Charlinda? What are you doing here? Get out of my office. Go downstairs to your own desk."

She ran to him, unbuttoning his suit jacket. Jarvis squirmed away from her.

"This is not the time for this. Please leave. I need to locate my assistant."

"If you don't want me to make a scene around here, I suggest you stop treating me like I'm suddenly a bother to you."

"What do you want from me?"

"I want you to divorce her."

"Things have changed."

Jarvis took a seat at his cluttered desk.

"Your wife doesn't get to pick and choose when she wants to come in and out of your bed."

Charlinda flopped her narrow bottom on his lap. She put

her lips on his shirt collar and smeared lipstick on it.

"Why did you do that?" Jarvis noticed the deep-chocolate lipstick stain. To get her off of him, he stood up, giving her no choice but to stand to her feet.

"You can take a piece of me home with you," Charlinda confessed. "I went by your house. I wanted to confront your wife. To let her know my feelings about our situation."

"No you didn't speak to Aniyah. Stay away from her."

"Lucky for her, her aunt protected her. I spoke to *that* woman."

Jarvis sighed. "I'm thankful her aunt stopped you."

Charlinda took jabs at him, as if she were a boxer. Her eyes watered. "You're protecting that chick. No way, Jarvis, you'll not treat me like I'm the one who did you wrong." Her voice escalated. "Married or not, I'm your damn woman! She doesn't have the right to come back into your life on a free pass to have you back. I don't want to hear another word about your poor wife. All I want is for us to discuss our future plans."

"Charlinda, I hate to hurt you." He paused. "It's over between us. Aniyah and I are working things out."

"You don't mean it. This is her doing. I see I need to have a meeting with that chick."

"Stay away from my wife," he ordered. "I'm sorry, but this is how it has to be. Please, just go to work."

Charlinda looked at the clock on the wall. She was late for reporting to the loan department. She threatened him. "This isn't over." She smoothed her finger across his lips. "See you later, Sweetie."

Once she left, Jarvis came out of his white shirt. He

tossed it in the trashcan. He went inside a drawer, and pulled out a brand-new white shirt.

When he sat at his desk, he opened another drawer and pulled out a framed photo of him and Charlinda from the conference. They were wearing big smiles on their faces. They looked as if they were a match, made-in-heaven.

He took the back off, removed the photo and tore it into pieces. He tossed the shredded photo into the trashcan. It landed on top of his stained shirt. He placed the empty frame into the desk drawer.

His cell phone chimed.

"Hello," Jarvis grumbled.

"Hey, Bro," Sid said. He heard the nervousness in Jarvis' voice. "What's wrong?"

"Charlinda was in my office when I got here. She wants me to divorce Aniyah, pay child support and marry her."

"She moves fast."

"I broke it off. Aniyah and I want to rebuild our marriage."

"If that's what you want, Bro, I wish you well."

"Thanks, Sid. I got another call coming through. Talk to you later."

Jarvis switched over to the other line. "I hope you got good news to tell me," he said. Jarvis listened carefully. Hearing the caller's words, helped to cheer him up. He smiled. "Just what I wanted to hear."

Ending his conversation, Jarvis reached into the back pants pocket for his wallet. Inside was an old photo of his father with a cigar in his mouth. Jarvis stared at the jolly smile his father displayed. Tears welled in his eyes. "Dad, even in your death, your goal is to continue to control and screw up my life."

He removed the photo from under the plastic shield, tearing it into pieces. He discarded it.

CHAPTER 35

*C*harlinda had driven for two-and-a-half hours to Greenville, South Carolina. She turned off the paved road onto a graveled one. Driving amongst a forest of trees, a house on wheels caught her eye. She parked.

"Why are you here?" Brant asked, greeting her when she stepped out of the vehicle.

"Long time no see, Brother. I've been trying to call you."

"I hope you moved on." Brant scratched the right side of his face.

Charlinda noticed her brother had not groomed himself. He had not shaved his face, giving him a full beard. He looked like an older man to her. His hair had grown out to the point it had curled.

"I'm still in it." Charlinda passed by him. She entered the home. "You let her go too fast. Jarvis has forgiven his wife. He wants her, not me."

Brant fussed, shutting the front door. "Our last phone conversation you told me you had him hooked. He was over Aniyah. One of the reasons why I let her go."

Charlinda, persuaded by Brant, had pursued Jarvis. He

had given her a full report of the life Jarvis was living. She had wanted no part of her brother's obsession with the banker, but it was her opportunity to land a job at the bank, and pursue Jarvis to be in the position to move up the corporate ladder. But what was supposed to be a short-term relationship, had turned into her falling for Jarvis. Plus, the bank was a perfect place for her to work.

Brant took a seat on the loveseat. "I told you to end it once you thought he had fallen deep for you."

"Actually, he's a good guy. I'm in love with him," Charlinda blurted.

Brant balled his hands into tight fists. "No way will you be with Jarvis Powell. He destroyed my life. Stay away from him."

Her brother believed Jarvis was the reason his football career had ended. Enraged, Charlinda said, "Get over it. Forgive him. Jarvis and I are made for each other. You need to come to Columbia and get Aniyah. Keep her for you. You owe me that much."

"I had the hots for Aniyah. I married her."

"You did what?" Charlinda asked, surprised at her brother's words.

Brant laughed. "I had a blind reverend to marry us. I wanted to add more problems for them."

"Go get your wife and let me have my man."

"I don't want you with Jarvis."

"You don't get to say who I can be with."

Brant gripped his sister's arm. "He's off-limits."

"He's the man for me."

"Forget it."

"It's not fair," she whined.

With tears in her eyes, Charlinda stormed out of Brant's house.

Once she felt the outdoor air, Charlinda let out a sigh of relief. She pulled out her cell phone and made her way into her vehicle. She hit the speed dial and called Jarvis, only to get his voicemail. She sent him a text.

While she drove, she never heard her phone buzzing to let her know she had received a text. The long drive made her more furious about how Jarvis had treated her. She reached for her phone, still not seeing the text notification, and called his home.

It rang twice before she heard a female voice answer.

"Whom am I talking to?" Charlinda asked. She wanted to hear Jarvis' wife reveal her name.

"I'm the one and only Mrs. Aniyah Sanchez-Powell, wife of Jarvis Powell, Jr."

The next thing Charlinda heard was a dial tone. She banged her fist against the steering wheel. She pulled over and tried his phone again. When she got his voicemail again, she left a message.

"Call me before the end of this day, or I'll show up at your house screaming my head off."

After reaching Columbia, Charlinda stopped at a grocery store. She had no milk in her refrigerator. Her cell phone buzzed as she was placing the milk inside her vehicle. Her eyes lit up once she saw the message she had left for Jarvis had made him contact her.

She ignored his hello. "Jarvis, it's not over between us. I demand you reconsider things."

"I don't mean to hurt you. There's no future between us. Move on."

"Never," she argued, picking up speed on the highway. She headed home.

"I never intended to hurt you."

"I'm your woman. Tell that Aniyah chick, she better not ever hang up on me again."

"You spoke to Aniyah?" he questioned.

Charlinda explained to him her short conversation with his wife.

"Stop this madness," he demanded.

Tears filled her eyes. Her voice escalated. "I'm not going to say this again, married or not, I'm your damn woman. She has no right to come back into your life on a free pass to have you back."

"You really don't get it, Charlinda. I love my wife."

"No, Jarvis, you don't get it." Charlinda ended the call. She grunted. "I'll let the world know that you're my man."

CHAPTER 36

*M*ilandra and her sisters sat in the kitchen, sipping on a cup of hot mocha coffee. In the family room, their men watched basketball. They cheered their team on.

"They're so loud," Milandra said.

"It's a basketball game," Kenley replied.

"I'm happy to hear Nolan's voice in this house. Thank God you and him worked things out," Noelle said.

"As long as he behaves," Milandra said.

"Nolan isn't a pet," Kenley said.

Milandra cut her eyes at her baby sister.

The landline rang. Milandra took the call. "Yes?" she answered.

"There's a Charlinda Logan to see you," the Houston security guard said.

"What did she say she wanted?"

"She says, it's important that she speaks to you."

"Let her in," Milandra ordered.

"You have a visitor?" Noelle asked.

"One of my employees from the bank," Milandra explained. She took another sip of her drink.

"You made friends with someone who works for the

bank?" Kenley asked. "I need a sip of something harder than this coffee."

Milandra, again, cut her eyes at her baby sister. "No way. It must be bank business that can't wait."

The sisters chatted until Charlinda stormed through the doors.

"Sorry to disturb you and your family," Charlinda said. "May we speak in private?"

"Whatever you have to say, you can say it in front of my sisters," Milandra responded.

"Have a seat," Noelle said to Charlinda.

"She can stand. This won't take long," Milandra said. "What's the urgency?"

"I have a problem. I've been dating a co-worker," Charlinda revealed.

Kenley giggled. "Girl, you don't kiss and tell."

Milandra demanded, "Who is he?"

"Jarvis Powell."

Milandra did not show any signs of surprise. When Aniyah had left home, she had thought it would be the perfect time for Jarvis to find another woman long enough for him to divorce Aniyah.

"You spoke too much of him. That's why I hired you in the loan department. I sent you on the trip to the conference a few months ago in hopes you two would connect," Milandra admitted.

"Milandra, you're wrong for interfering in other people's lives," Noelle said.

"Aniyah won't like this news," Kenley announced. "This is juicy."

"Kenley, be quiet," Noelle said.

Charlinda smiled. "So ya'll know his wife is back?"

"I was afraid that Aniyah would have her fun, then run home to Jarvis. I had hoped he would fall for you long enough to divorce her," Milandra said.

"I've fallen for him," Charlinda blurted.

Milandra balled her hands into a tight fist. "Like Aniyah, you're not for him either. He needs a society woman. That's what his father would have wanted."

"Gosh, Milandra, stay out of Jarvis' romance life," Noelle said.

Kenley teased, "Girl, Aniyah will let you have it."

Enraged, Charlinda bellowed, "I'm not afraid of her! Jarvis is my man. I have my own place and job. I carry myself like a lady like ya'll do. I do agree his wife is not good enough for him. She left him." She poked her chest. "I'm the one for him."

Milandra rose out of her seat. She pulled down on her suit jacket, smoothing out any wrinkles. "Don't you dare come into my home and raise your voice at me or my sisters. Bank policy is, no employee dates other employees. You're on the verge of losing your job."

"I have bills to pay," Charlinda muttered.

With her arms folded, Milandra paced the floor. "However, rules are made to be broken. You can still see Jarvis, if you think you can get him away from Aniyah."

Noelle interjected, "Milandra, you wouldn't want anyone to destroy your marriage."

"They don't have a marriage. It's an arrangement for Aniyah."

Kenley raised her cup. "I put my bet on Aniyah."

"You stay away from Aniyah. You can't handle her,"

Milandra said to Charlinda.

"I'm not scared of his wife. I went to see her. Her aunt answered the door. It was like she was on guard duty for her niece."

"Her aunt will protect her family. You concentrate on getting Jarvis away from Aniyah," Milandra ordered.

They turned their heads when they saw Jarvis in the doorway. Milandra wondered if he had overheard their conversation.

"We're having a private meeting," Milandra said to him.

"I came to say hello. Nolan and Sid invited me over to watch the game with them." His eyes widened when he saw his other woman.

Charlinda, happy to see him, ran to him and threw her arms around his neck. She went for his lips, but Jarvis shoved her to the side.

"Get off me. What are you doing here?" he asked Charlinda.

"Excuse me?" Milandra butted in. "This is my home. You don't question my guest. Please go into the other room with the men."

Noelle went to her sister. "Milandra, you've crossed the line. You don't get to talk to Jarvis any kind of way."

Jarvis held up his hand. "I can take care of myself, Noelle. Thanks." Jarvis darted his eyes from Milandra to Charlinda. "You ladies are up to something."

"It's a private matter," Milandra informed him.

"I wanted our boss to know we're a couple. I love you," Charlinda said.

The sisters watched Charlinda throw herself at Jarvis. Once again, he scrambled from her.

Kenley fell back on the sofa. "Girl, the man doesn't want you."

"Hush, Kenley," Noelle said.

"Your father's wish has always been for you to get rid of Aniyah," Milandra reminded him.

"I'm sick of you and my dad." He pointed first at Milandra, then at Charlinda. "I'm sick of you, too."

"Get out of my house. Go to the bank and pack up your things." Milandra smirked. "Jarvis Powell, Jr., you're fired."

"You're crazy, big Sis," Kenley said.

Noelle added, "That's unnecessary."

Jarvis moved closer to Milandra. She stepped backward when she witnessed the rage in his vicious eyes.

"I help build that bank. You, my dad or no one else will put me out," Jarvis said.

"Nolan," Milandra summoned her husband.

Nolan, along with Sid, made their way into the family room.

"What's going on in here?" Nolan asked.

Milandra shouted, "I'm firing Jarvis. He has one day to gather up his belongings and leave. Turn in his bank ID into Human Resources."

"That's uncalled for," Sid said.

"It is, if my wife says so," Nolan argued.

Jarvis scurried to find his way out of the house.

"Thanks," Milandra said to her spouse. She gave him a peck on the cheek.

Sid ran after Jarvis. Nolan gave the women their privacy.

"I'm leaving," Noelle said, making her way out of the

sight of her older sister.

"Not me. I'm watching the show," Kenley said.

Charlinda had buckled to her knees.

"Girl, get up off the floor," Kenley said.

"She's too wimpy for Jarvis or any man," Milandra said.

Charlinda rose. "I'll get him back."

Milandra chuckled. "Now that Jarvis knows I'm involved, I have no use for you. Pack your things. You're fired."

Charlinda huffed. "I have bills."

Kenley chuckled. "Too late. You told on your own self."

"See your way out," Milandra ordered Charlinda.

Milandra strutted to her seat. She took another sip of her coffee.

Charlinda stood in disbelief.

Milandra noticed she did not move. She threatened, "Leave or I'll have security escort you out of my home."

Charlinda blew a strand of hair off the tip of her nose. "You people with more money than others, think you can treat others any kind of way. I don't think so."

Milandra cut her eyes at Charlinda. "Dismiss yourself."

Kenley burst into laughter waving her hand. "Bye, Bye."

CHAPTER 37

*A*ir was what Jarvis needed to cool down from the frustration he had felt from his encounter with Milandra. If he took his blood pressure, it would be elevated to the max. Furious, he clicked one button on his car key and started the engine. Another button unlocked the doors. He swung the driver's door open and got in. When he put the vehicle in drive, ready to pull off, he spotted Sid running across the yard. Jarvis shifted the gear in park.

Sid held his hand up. "Yo, Bro," he said, "Wait a second."

Jarvis rolled down the driver's window. "I've had it with Milandra. She had the nerve to say I'm fired from a place I help to build."

"I'm glad it's not me. No telling what I'd do to protect my own."

Both men looked up and saw Noelle come out of the house.

"Jarvis," she called.

Seeing her, Jarvis got out of his vehicle. "This isn't right at all," he fussed.

"I don't know what's gotten into Milandra. Please let

her cool off. She doesn't mean it. She needs you to help run the bank."

"She needs to come to her darn senses, and give Jarvis back his stuff," Sid announced.

"She has a thing about having power over others," Jarvis said.

"Sister-in-law is nothing like this woman right here," Sid said, referring to his wife.

Jarvis watched him grab Noelle at the waist. He placed kisses on her neck.

Noelle blushed. "Stop it. You're embarrassing me."

They made Jarvis smile. "It's called love. I have the same feeling for Aniyah."

Jarvis did not expect a response from Noelle, but to his surprise, she spoke, "I see Aniyah makes you happy."

"Look, Bro, back to Milandra. What are you going to do about a job?"

"I already have one. Milandra nor anyone else will throw me out of my company."

"I'm not going back inside. I'll call her when I get home," Noelle said.

"Tell her I'll be in my office at nine o'clock," Jarvis spat. "I'm prepared to handle her."

Jarvis saw Noelle had noticed the threatening look in his eyes.

"Sid and I will come to make sure the conversation goes smooth," Noelle said.

"Jarvis," a squeaky voice called his name.

He, Noelle, and Sid turned toward Charlinda, who was in tears and rushing toward them.

"I didn't mean for you or me to get fired. Baby, I'm sorry."

As she hurried toward Jarvis, Noelle blocked her from getting to him.

"He's off-limits tonight," Noelle said. "Take your butt off this property, or I'll see to it you're hauled off by the police."

"You act like your sister. Nasty."

"Go on now. That's my wife you're talking to." Sid defended Noelle.

Charlinda looked around Noelle at Jarvis. "I'll call you later. Think about how good we can be together."

Jarvis took a deep breath. "I'm so sorry, Charlinda, for hurting you. It never was my intention."

He watched a tearful Charlinda get in her vehicle and drive off. He turned to Sid and Noelle. "Thanks for being here for me." He shook Sid's hand and gave Noelle a hug. "Love you guys."

Jarvis got in his vehicle and drove off.

Instead of going home, Jarvis had made his way to the Lake Murray Dam walkway. The cool breeze from the rippling waters brushed against his face. Glitter of lights sparkled on the waters. He presumed Jarvis Powell, Sr.'s ashes were thrown in the lake. His father loved the water.

Tears watered his eyes. This was his first time after his father's death that he had visited the lake. His anger toward him had kept him away.

Jarvis yelled. "Dad, by any chance are you here?"

He did not expect an answer, but once he saw the waters ripple, it gave him a sense that the answer was yes. Jarvis felt his father's presence. He wiped a tear from his face.

"Dad, you did me wrong. You died on me, then had Milandra to give me the news of your death. You dismissed me as if I never existed in your life. I was and am your son. You named me after you, Jarvis Powell, Jr. What father raises a son, names him after himself and treats him like mud, all because of your disdain for my wife? I love Aniyah. Do you hear me, Dad? I love her. You nor anyone else will take that away from me."

Jarvis looked around. A late-night jogger stopped to speak to him.

"Are you okay, Sir?" the guy asked.

Jarvis chuckled. "I'm fine. Having a private conversation with my deceased dad. I'm not crazy. It's therapeutic for me."

The man patted him on the upper arm. "I talk to my dead wife sometimes, too. Be safe."

"You do the same," Jarvis said.

He waited until the man made it far away from him before he spoke to his father again.

"Milandra fired me. I bet you got word of that from the angels. I'm not going anywhere. You hear me, Dad? I'm Powell Bank."

Jarvis picked up a nearby pebble and threw it in the water.

"Bye, Dad. I'm going home to Aniyah."

When he walked away, Jarvis left in peace. He had vented his feelings to his father, whether or not Powell's ashes were dissolved in the waters.

The house was quiet when he entered. Jarvis hurried up the staircase. "Aniyah," he called.

She greeted him at the doorway of their master suite.

"Honey, you're home early. That was a quick game."

Jarvis slipped the straps of her nightgown off her shoulders, letting it drop to the floor. He scooped her up into his arms. Instead of taking her into the bedroom, he carried her down the hall into a spare guest room.

"You came home because you wanted me?" Aniyah stroked the ball of his head.

"You're the only one who can help me escape the thoughts of my problems."

"Is there something wrong?"

Jarvis gave her a kiss. "Take care of me."

He laid her on top of a striped gray and blue quilt. Stripping out of his clothes, he crawled on top of her. Jarvis went straight for what he needed from his wife. Making love to Aniyah was the perfect way for him to release his frustrations. It did not take long before he exploded. He fell on the bed beside her.

"You were like a wild horse. Why?"

"Milandra fired me."

Aniyah sat up in the bed. "It's time she hears from me."

Jarvis pulled his wife by the arm. "Take it easy."

Aniyah eased down and rested her head on his sweaty chest. "What are you going to do?"

"I'm headed right to the office in the morning. I got a word or two for her."

Aniyah stroked his chest with her fingertips. "That's right, Hubby, don't let her get away with it."

"I want you there by my side."

"That'll make her mad. Miss Uppity don't like me."

Jarvis squeezed her nose. "She'll just have to deal with

it."

CHAPTER 38

*T*he next morning, while her son slept in bed, Aniyah wrapped in her robe, scrambled around the kitchen to serve her husband a hot breakfast. She prepared a pot of grits, sausage, bacon and eggs.

"It smells good in here," Jarvis said, entering the kitchen.

"I couldn't let you go to the bank on an empty stomach." She kissed him on his lips. "I made you coffee. Two spoons of sugar and extra cream."

"That's how I like it." Dressed in his suit and tie, Jarvis took his seat at the table.

"A woman who loves her man never forgets."

Aniyah placed the hot cup of Colombian coffee in front of him. The morning pot of coffee brew stimulated his nostrils.

Jarvis dived into his food. He chewed his bacon. "This is the best breakfast I had in a long time."

In recent months, his routine to work was a stop at a donut shop for a to-go meal, a chicken and egg biscuit and a cup of coffee.

"I'm leaving a little earlier for work. You don't mind

driving yourself?"

"No," she said. Aniyah took a seat at the table and began to eat.

"Please be there by nine. I want you by my side. It'll feel good to see the look on Milandra's face when she sees you."

Aniyah chuckled. "With her nose up in the air."

Jarvis joined in on the laughter. It did not take long before they had finished eating. While Jarvis headed out the door, she blew kisses at him.

"See you soon." She waved bye to him.

Returning into the kitchen, Aniyah cleared the table of dishes. Then the doorbell rang. Aniyah rushed to the door presuming Jarvis had left something important behind that he needed for work. She opened it. In front of her stood a woman, wearing smoke-gray pants and a purple blouse. She was petite and looked like she wore nothing more than a size zero.

Startled by her early presence at her doorstep, Aniyah said, "Yes, may I help you?"

She continued to stare at the woman's hair, hanging straight below her shoulders, and her lips painted with hot-pink lipstick.

"I'm Charlinda... Jarvis' girlfriend." She did not beat around the bush.

Hearing the woman's voice, Aniyah recognized she was the caller whom had phoned her. She held her head up and spoke. "In case you can't hear well, I'll repeat this one last time to you. I'm the one and only Mrs. Aniyah Sanchez-Powell, wife of Jarvis Powell, Jr."

"About to be ex-wife."

"What the hell do you want, Trick?"

The women had a stare down, neither one showing any signs of being threatened.

"We need to talk," Charlinda said. She forced her way inside, brushing past the opened door.

Aniyah snatched her by the arm, pulling on her. "Excuse yourself out of my house."

Charlinda jerked away from Aniyah. She pointed her finger at her. "You think that after all these months, you can just move me out of the way and take my man from me?"

Aniyah giggled. "I can't help it if my husband has an everlasting love for me."

Charlinda moved closer in on Aniyah. That move made Aniyah tense up. She was ready to throw down if need be.

"This is how I see it," Charlinda said, posing, and swinging her hair. "Give Jarvis a divorce. You and your brat pack up and give him his space with me."

Aniyah gave her a stern look. "You got mental issues." She then pointed at Charlinda. "I'm warning you, you better not say another word about my son." Aniyah made a move. "I'm calling the police."

Charlinda caught the back of her bathrobe, pulling on her.

Aniyah retaliated. She snatched a clip-on piece of hair from Charlinda's head, dropping it on the floor.

Charlinda did not let go until she tackled Aniyah onto the floor. She shouted in her squeaky voice, "I'll tell Jarvis the truth. You left him to be with Logan."

Hearing her words stopped Aniyah right in her tracks.

She let go, and so did Charlinda.

"You know Brant Logan?"

"I hit a nerve?" Charlinda smirked. She picked up the clip-on hairpiece from the floor and reattached it to her natural hair. "It's time Jarvis knows you thought the sex was much better at the next house."

"Logan kidnapped me," Aniyah said. She had gotten off the floor.

"That's what you say. He says different."

"How do you know him?"

Charlinda laughed. "Well, wouldn't you like to know?"

Aniyah snatched the open door handle. "He's lying. He's a con artist and you're a trick. Get your tail out of my house."

Aniyah waited for answers, but Charlinda revealed no more information.

"At least I don't go marrying another man when I'm already married. So, who are you really? Mrs. Jarvis Powell or Mrs. Brant Logan?"

"I had no choice in marrying that maniac," Aniyah retorted. She adjusted her bathrobe. It had come loose, exposing her breasts.

"Jarvis won't see it that way," Charlinda said, rolling her eyes, but noticed Aniyah had a little more to offer Jarvis.

"It was a big mistake," Aniyah explained in detail of her good intentions for her husband.

"Not my problem."

"Look, I get it that you were there for Jarvis. But, you knew it was a chance I could make my way back to him. So please, for my son's sake, don't destroy our happiness."

Charlinda continued to laugh. "Jarvis isn't a bargain chip. I don't play second. And, once I tell him the truth, he'll come running to me—his real love."

"Go ahead, tell him. I don't care. Let's see whom he sticks by. Now, get the hell out! I have a son to tend to."

"This isn't over. Give him a divorce," Charlinda insisted.

Aniyah watched her unwelcomed guest strut her way out of the door. She slammed it closed behind her. Aniyah collapsed down on her knees and wept. With a throbbing headache, all she wanted was a painkiller.

Aniyah popped a pill into her mouth and swallowed it after taking a gulp of water. Still rattled by what she had learned from Charlinda, she made a call to her aunt.

"Hi, Aniyah."

"Aunt Tessa, I need you to come quick."

"Is there something wrong? Where is Jarvis?"

"He's gone to work."

"Do you want me to call him and have him come home right away?" her aunt asked, concerned for her niece's safety.

"No, I have to join him at work. Can you come and take J.P. to school for me?"

"I'm on my way."

When Tessa arrived, Aniyah fell into her arms. Jarvis III followed suit and hugged his aunt around her leg. Tessa consoled them until Aniyah let go of her. She picked up her great-nephew. "What's wrong with you?" she questioned Aniyah.

Aniyah paced the floor. "I can't lose my husband." She took a seat on the sofa, rocking back and forth, with her hands balled up so tight, that her palms became sweaty. In a humbled voice, she pleaded, "Lord, please forgive me. I'll be a good wife to Jarvis. Please, give me another chance. I do love him."

"Mama-Mom cry baby." Jarvis III pointed his tiny finger at his mother.

The doorbell rang. With her great-nephew in her arms, Tessa went to answer it. It was Nellie.

"I heard Aniyah is home," Nellie said. I've been out of town."

"Yes. She's in the living room," Tessa confirmed.

The ladies went to Aniyah.

Nellie smiled. "Hi, Aniyah. I got your message. I was on a cruise ship."

Aniyah looked up at her friend. She gave her a hug. "It's so good to see you."

"Wow, you've lost weight. What size are you now?" Nellie questioned.

Aniyah turned her nose up at her friend, and then said, "Nellie, do me a favor. Take J.P. into the kitchen. Give him a bowl of cereal."

"Is everything okay?" Nellie said.

"I need to finish speaking to my aunt."

Holding him by the hand, Nellie escorted Jarvis III into the kitchen.

"Aniyah, what happened?" Tessa wondered.

"Jarvis will leave me."

"What makes you think that?"

"I didn't tell him the truth," she cried. "How could I be

so stupid?"

"Quiet down, Aniyah," Tessa said, "keep your mouth shut."

"Damn that woman. She wants me out of his life. She'll tell Jarvis about me and Brant Logan."

"Charlinda?"

"Yes."

"How did she find out?"

"That crazy heffa knows him."

"Oh my Lord."

"She busted in the door," Aniyah explained. "I told her not to come back here." Aniyah stood on her feet. "What am I going to do, if she tells Jarvis the truth? Aunt Tessa, you hired him. You never heard of her?"

"Absolutely not."

"I should tell Jarvis the truth."

"You, of all people, want to be honest for once? I can't believe my niece is acting her age."

"I love my husband and child." Aniyah looked at the time on the clock. She had twenty minutes to be at the bank to join Jarvis. "I got to go. My man needs me by his side at his job. Tell Nellie I'll catch up with her later."

"I'll get J.P. to school and lock your door.

CHAPTER 39

*O*n the arm of her husband, Milandra made her way to the eighth floor of the bank. She had five minutes to be at her desk before Jarvis would join her in her office. Noelle had insisted she meet with him.

Off the elevator, she heard voices. When she entered the lobby, she witnessed her sisters, Sid and her attorney having a conversation.

"What's going on here?" she asked.

"Good morning, Mrs. Houston-Rice," Baron, her attorney, greeted her. He shook her hand. "My secretary told me you wanted to meet with me this morning."

"Nonsense. I never scheduled for you to be here." Milandra focused her attention on her family. "What's your excuse for being here, sisters? And you, Sid?"

"We're here on behalf of Jarvis," Noelle said.

Kenley added, "We need to voice our opinion on you rehiring him. Big sister, you're wrong and you know you're wrong."

Milandra scolded them. "This has nothing to do with our construction company, where you two should be at the moment. This is my bank. I handle it the way I see fit." Milandra flung her hands at her attorney. "You can leave."

"Milandra, maybe Mr. Chavis should stay. This meeting might turn nasty; you may need legal advice," Nolan said.

Milandra patted her husband on his face. "At least someone is on my side."

The loud popping of gum made Milandra and her company turn around. It was none other than Aniyah.

"This is ridiculous." Milandra frowned.

Aniyah blew another bubble, this time, in Milandra's face. When it popped, she said, "I'm back, deal with it."

Kenley came toward Aniyah. "Girl, get away from my sister."

Baron stood between them. He turned up his nose at Aniyah. "When you think a bug is long gone, it comes right back."

"Good seeing you, too, Uncle Baron. My Aunt Tessa is happy to have me back in her life."

"Trust me, Aniyah, it has nothing to do with you," he announced.

"Where's the Raid bug spray? It won't take much to blow her away," Kenley said.

Like her sister, Milandra noticed Aniyah had shed pounds off her hips. "Jarvis made a big mistake asking you to be here on this matter. This is to be handled between him and I."

Noelle looked toward the doorway. "Aniyah, where's Jarvis?"

"Yes, where is he?" Milandra asked. "I don't have all day."

Aniyah wondered as well. "I thought he was here. Jarvis

left home early. He's probably on his way up from his office. My hubby is the brainy one around here."

Milandra ignored her words. With her sisters working at the Houston Commercial Construction Company, it gave her plenty of time to oversee the bank. She was thankful. Before Powell, Sr. had passed away, he had groomed her on the ins and outs of running a bank.

"I'm going into my office," Milandra said with Nolan escorting her inside. The rest of them followed her.

All eyes darted at the desk, when the person sitting behind it swiveled around to confront them.

"Good morning. I've been waiting on everyone."

With a flushed look on her face, Milandra hollered, "How dare you, Jarvis Powell, sneak into my office and park your rear in my chair? That's it! No one in this room can convince me to keep you on."

She turned to her attorney.

"After today, I want a lawsuit filed against Jarvis if he fails to refrain from entering this bank."

Aniyah yelled, "Watch your mouth. That's my husband you're speaking of. Stay in that chair if you want to, Honey. Milandra, sit your tail on the floor."

"Why don't you shut up and let Jarvis and Milandra work things out," Kenley said. She directed her comment to Aniyah.

"Everyone, be quiet," Baron interjected. "Can one person school me in on what's happening here?"

Just then, another gentleman entered the office. Milandra recognized him and so did Jarvis and the others. She saw the man dressed in a burgundy suit was the attorney who had handled Jarvis Powell, Sr.'s paperwork before Powell had died.

"Mr. Bloomberg is representing me," Jarvis announced.

"It's not clever to use the same lawyer whom your father had used to leave you nothing. Get out of my chair," Milandra said.

Milandra saw that Jarvis did not budge. She tapped her husband. "Remove him from my chair."

Noelle blabbed, "Don't do it, Nolan. It'll start a fight between you and Jarvis."

"My husband will do as I say," Milandra said. She watched Nolan hurry toward the desk.

Baron caught Nolan by the arm. "Noelle is right. It won't solve anything with you trying to remove Jarvis from the seat."

"It's okay," Nolan said, easing away from Baron Chavis. He walked over to the desk. "Are you comfortable, Jarvis?"

"Yes I am," Jarvis responded.

"Sorry, Milandra. Jarvis wins." Nolan shrugged.

Milandra's eyes blossomed. She stabbed her pen into the desk. "Remove him, Nolan."

Noelle hollered, "Jarvis, please give Milandra her seat. You're making it worse. Don't you want to keep your job?"

"Milandra won't have the honor of sitting here anymore," Jarvis revealed.

Milandra chuckled. "Remember, I own this bank."

Nolan jumped in. "No, wife, you don't. I signed it over to Jarvis."

Milandra tossed the pen on the desk. "You don't have

authority to sell it."

"You gave me power of attorney to handle your affairs," Nolan said.

Enraged, Milandra screamed. "Never would I do such a thing!"

Aniyah ran to her husband. "We got the house and bank back?"

"Yes," Jarvis said.

Aniyah kissed her man right in front of everyone.

Jarvis turned his attention back to the group. "Bye, Milandra. Your services are no longer needed here."

Jarvis handed Nolan a folder, who was ready to hand it to Milandra, but she snatched it from him. She studied the document.

"It's your signature," Nolan said.

"Your attorney can look at it," Jarvis added.

She handed it to Baron. Everyone watched him read over the durable power of attorney.

"Milandra, you granted Nolan the rights to handle any aspect of your businesses."

Milandra beat her husband on the chest. "Why would you do this to me?"

Nolan argued, "I told you from the beginning to give Jarvis his inheritance. You bought it behind my back and I sold it behind yours. We're even."

"Sis, you got played." Kenley shook her head. She walked toward the door, waving her hand. "I'm out of here. Houston Commercial Construction Company is where I belong. So do ya'll, Milandra and Noelle."

Milandra felt her sister pull her by the arm. "Let it go. You can now give your full attention to our company,"

Noelle said.

Milandra jerked her arm away from Noelle. "You can leave. You came here on Jarvis' behalf, not mine."

Jarvis' attorney spoke on his behalf. "Jarvis purchased it in good faith. All documents are intact." He handed the folder to Baron, who scanned through more pages of the document.

Milandra waited for his words.

Baron spoke, "Milandra, Nolan had the power to sell, not only the bank, but the Powell home as well."

Milandra charged at Nolan. She punched him in the chest. "You tricked me into giving you power of attorney to sell the personal things I owned."

"I did not." Nolan pushed her away from him. "You signed the papers willingly. Your assistant was your witness. Her signature is on here. We can call her into this office and ask her."

Jarvis had already summoned for the receptionist. She walked into the crowded office.

"Yes, may I help you?" the receptionist said. All eyes were on her.

Milandra disgusted, said, "Did someone pay you to witness to a power of attorney between my husband and me?"

"Mrs. Houston-Rice, you had me to be a witness to the papers," the receptionist said.

"When did I do such a thing?" Milandra asked.

"The last time your husband visited you in your office."

Milandra shouted, "You're a pathetic liar!"

"I witnessed it. That's what you asked me to do. I'm not a liar. I'm leaving," the receptionist announced.

Jarvis chimed in. "No, you're not going anywhere. Milandra is the one who is leaving out of this building. Nolan, do me a favor and take that photo of Milandra off the wall. She can take that with her too."

Milandra watched her husband unhook the framed portrait of her. She ran and took it from him. "You're no longer welcome at the Houston Estate." She looked over at her attorney. "I want to file for divorce." Looking back at Nolan, she said, "You won't get a penny of the Houstons' fortune.

Nolan stood with pride. "I'm a hardworking man with my own business. I don't want anything from you. If I did, I would've cleaned you out."

"Nolan has no worries," Jarvis said.

"Honey, please carry the picture for my sister," Noelle said to her husband.

Sid had stood quiet through the big reveal. He attempted to take the portrait from Milandra. She hurried and handed it to Baron. "I don't need you or Noelle's help," she said.

"Sis, you got issues," Sid said to Milandra.

"Let's leave." Noelle reached for Sid's hand.

Jarvis waved his hands at them. "Thanks for coming."

Before Milandra exited the door, Jarvis blasted to her, "I forgot to tell you… you're fired!"

Milandra looked into his and her husband's face. She witnessed the sparkle in their eyes. They had swindled the property from her legally. They high-fived. *Jarvis Powell, Sr. would choke me* if *he were alive*, she thought.

When Milandra left the office, Jarvis rose from his seat.

He shook Nolan's hand.

"Thanks, man, for all you've done for me. I hate for your marriage to be over with."

"My marriage has ended long before I agreed to help you. Milandra is a controlling woman."

"It's the way her dad raised her," Jarvis said.

"She thinks she's better than everyone," Aniyah said. "Uppity."

She hugged Nolan's neck and thanked him. Then she left him and kissed her husband on the lips. "I'm so happy for you."

"Happy for us," Jarvis said. "We must celebrate soon. Invite Nolan, Noelle and Sid."

A teardrop ran down Jarvis' face. He studied his new office and announced, "The bank's new name might be, Jarvis Bank. I never want to see Houston or Powell on it again. I want to start a new tradition for my son."

"He'll be a banker like his daddy," Aniyah said.

"Our son has plenty of time to decide his career path. It'll be his choice," Jarvis said.

CHAPTER 40

*W*ith the good news of her husband getting his business and property back, Aniyah worried. Would Charlinda reveal her truth to Jarvis and ruin her marriage? To ease the tension built up inside her, Aniyah stopped at the nearest nail salon. It had been a long time since she had pampered herself. She got a pedicure, manicure and her eyebrows waxed. Once done, she headed to a local dollar store. There she purchased ten candles, set in heart-shaped glass dishes. She grabbed the bag, thanked the cashier and dashed out of the store.

When she arrived home, she contacted her aunt.

Tessa answered. "How are things? You didn't say a word to Jarvis, did you?"

"Aunt Tessa, I feel so guilty. I need to tell him the truth before she does."

"Rosie Aniyah Sanchez-Powell, keep your mouth shut. Continue to love your husband and your son. It'd be your word against hers."

Aniyah thought what her aunt said was true. If Charlinda had evidence, she would have revealed it to him already.

In a perky voice, she said, "Aunt Tessa, will you pick up J.P. and take him home with you for the night? I want to show my husband a good time."

"I would love to."

"Jarvis has the bank and the Powell home back."

"I heard. Baron called me right after the meeting. It's sad Milandra's marriage has ended. Nolan and her make a good couple."

Aniyah smacked her lips. "I don't feel sorry for Mrs. Uppity. Nolan is fine without her. He'll get him a down-to-earth woman. Not one who acts stink."

"It's never good when a marriage falls apart."

Aniyah became annoyed. "Bye, Aunt Tessa."

It was getting near time for Jarvis to come home from work. Aniyah placed lavender-scented candles throughout the master suite, including the bathroom. With her hair pulled up in a clip, in a short royal-blue nighty, and her flesh exposed through the lace bodice, she slipped on a long matching royal-blue satin bathrobe.

The doorbell rang.

The timing was perfect for the delivery of the dinner she had ordered for her and Jarvis. They would dine on Chicken Egg Foo Young and for appetizers, spring rolls and California sushi rolls. When she opened the door, the money in her hand fell to the floor. Her eyes widened as she stared into the face of Brant, dressed in a suit and tie, as if he was her date. His eyes, as always were mesmerizing, but through the dreamy eyes, she envisioned the flashing warning sign, that reminded her of his disturbed ways.

Aniyah went to slam the door, but Brant wedged his black leather shoe in the doorway to stop her from closing it.

"You're supposed to be long gone," she said.

Brant pushed his way into the house. He demanded, "Get your things and let's go."

"Please leave. Jarvis is on his way home."

Brant caught her by the arm. "Then we should get going."

Aniyah ran toward the kitchen but Brant caught her. With the back of his hand, he lashed out at her, slapping her across her face so hard, Aniyah landed on the hardwood floor. She felt her body being dragged toward the door. Somehow she worked her way from his grasp.

"I love Jarvis!"

He shouted, "You're my wife!"

Tears flooded her eyes as she crawled backward on the floor to get away from him.

"You'll come and stay with me again. You'll pay for the debt."

Aniyah had no clue what he was speaking of. She wondered had her Aunt Tessa not paid him in full.

"I'll give you money. How much does my Aunt Tessa owe you?"

In a rage, he said, "I don't know your doggone aunt."

"She hired you to kidnap me," Aniyah said.

"Tell your auntie thanks for taking the rap. Have no clue who she is. Now, shut up and let's go."

Aniyah attempted to run again. He caught her and gave her another slap across her face.

"You don't mean a thing to me," he said.

"Then why do you want me to go with you?" she questioned him, as blood oozed from her lips.

"You'll pay me for the pain I went through."

"You got it twisted. I'm the one who was held hostage."

"Broad, you have no idea." He grabbed her around her waist and forced her toward the door.

Exhausted from playing tug-of-war with him, Aniyah found herself outside. She looked around. The road and the acreage between the homes showed no one in sight to help her.

Brant carried her to his pickup truck. He shoved her in the passenger seat and slammed the door closed.

As soon as he entered the driver's side, Aniyah opened the door and jumped out. Barefooted, she ran straight up the driveway into the house. She attempted to lock the door behind her, but his manly power overthrew her. He shoved her against the wall as she fell to the floor. For a man who walked with a limp, he was fast on his feet.

"Ahh." Aniyah's lower back throbbed with pain.

"Wait until I get you back at the house. You'll pay." He snatched her back up off her feet. This time, he carried her over his shoulder.

"Let me down," she cried, kicking and beating him on the back.

"Aniyah." She heard a familiar voice call her name. Jarvis had entered the house.

Stunned by the sight of another man with his wife in his arms, Jarvis said, "Brant Logan, put my wife down."

The men locked eyes.

By the authority in her husband's voice, Aniyah sensed he was acquainted with Brant and not only from their time spent together during Career Day.

Brant stood his ground. "Move out of my way. It's long overdue you got what's coming to you."

With fiery eyes, Jarvis loosened his tie. Then he removed his suit jacket, tossing it on the floor. "Put my wife down or else. Whatever issues you have with me, leave Aniyah out of it."

"Let me down." She beat Brant on his upper back.

As if Brant held a football in his hand, he charged toward Jarvis. Jarvis slugged him in the stomach, causing Brant to buckle to his knees and let go of Aniyah. She landed on her feet.

"Call the police!" Jarvis yelled.

Instead, Aniyah stood frozen. She watched her husband and Brant battle it out.

During the men's senior year of college, the star player on the football field, Brant Logan, had introduced Jarvis to weightlifting. The training section had turned into a disaster when Jarvis accidentally had dropped the heavy weights on Brant's right knee, causing damage. Brant had been the number one pick for the draft to go pro. Despite the injury, Brant had played in his championship game. In the fourth quarter and two minutes left on the clock, with the score tied, Brant had run the ball for his team to make a touchdown. However, halfway into the end zone, a player from the other team had tackled him, crashing into his knees. Brant had swerved and twisted his leg, falling to the ground in agony.

The fans had gasped when they learned that he could not stand to his feet. That day, it would mark the end of Brant's chances of playing professional football. Jarvis tried to visit him afterward, but Brant would not hear of it. Jarvis had sent Brant a heartfelt letter of apology, but his letter was returned to him. He never heard from Brant again until he saw him on Career Day.

Brant, now on his feet, punched Jarvis in the mouth. "That's for you screwing up my life."

"Man, I thought you had forgiven me. It was an accident," Jarvis said. "Besides, I heard you played again and got hurt on the field."

"You messed up my knee first. My legs were my future. You took that away from me. I'll never forgive you," Brant said.

Jarvis sucker-punched him. "I won't forgive you for messing with my wife."

While bent over, Brant fought back with words. "Your wife? She's my wife."

Jarvis darted his eyes at Aniyah. "What is he talking about?"

Aniyah wept. "I can explain. The truth is, Brant kidnapped me. He forced me to marry him."

Enraged, Jarvis grabbed Brant by his collar, but Brant pushed his hands away. Regaining strength, he slugged Jarvis.

"That's for breaking my sister's heart."

"Sister? Who, Charlinda?" Jarvis wondered.

"Yeap. I took your wife and had my sister to screw you over."

"You and your sister set me up?" Jarvis slugged Brant two more times before Brant fell to the floor.

Brant wiped his bloody lip. "Charlinda was dumb to fall in love with you."

With clarity of Charlinda's connection to Brant, Aniyah contacted the authorities. At the door, she watched Jarvis pull Brant to his feet. Before he tossed him outside, Jarvis sucker-punched him one last time.

"That one is for me," he announced.

Brant hollered in agony as his own blood stained his suit jacket. The police and the deliveryman arrived at the same time. While Aniyah gave the officer her story, Jarvis paid for the food she had ordered.

Brant in handcuffs staggered to the patrol vehicle. He was placed in the backseat.

Aniyah joined her husband. With Jarvis' left arm around her waist, they watched as the patrol vehicle drove away. The whole time, Brant stared at them through the rear window.

The police had Brant's pickup truck towed.

Inside the house, Aniyah had to come clean with her husband.

"I'm so sorry I lied to you. I thought you wouldn't believe me if I told you I was kidnapped. I thought you would react like others and think that I threw myself at him."

"You should've trusted that I would believe you."

Aniyah got a wet paper towel and dabbed her husband's wound.

She sobbed. "I'm sorry. I've disappointed you again. I thought Brant was long gone. I wanted to put that behind me."

"You're also married to that jerk?"

"I'd planned to find a lawyer and get it annulled."

"I'm the one at fault for all this. I helped mess up his life. I wish I'd never gone to the gym with him that day. My clumsy hands dropped the bars on his knee."

Aniyah placed a bandage below his lip. "You didn't mean to do it. Brant should have forgiven you. They were out to destroy our family. It was cruel of him and his sister." Tears poured down her face. "I was no better when I did wrong to the Houston family years ago. Being on the other side, I understand why the Houston sisters dislike me now."

Drawn into her husband's arms, Jarvis kissed her on the lips. "We learn from our mistakes and move forward. I'll make sure the marriage is annulled immediately. You're my wife."

"I do love you, Jarvis Powell."

Aniyah pulled him by the arm, leading him upstairs into their master suite. "Get comfortable. I want this evening to be romantic for us."

"Not yet, I have a phone call to make."

Jarvis left her in the bedroom. Aniyah lit the candles throughout the room. Like her husband, she made a quick call.

"Aunt Tessa," she whispered.

"What can I do for you?"

"You lied to me. You didn't hire Brant Logan. Why did you tell that?"

"You wanted me gone. So I said and did what I needed to do to stay in my great-nephew's life. I beg you not to now shut me out of his life."

Aniyah heard the love her aunt had for her son. "J.P.

loves you. I won't do that. We want you to stay in our lives."

"Thank you, Lord."

Aniyah bid her aunt a good night and ended the call.

When Jarvis did not return to her, Aniyah came out of the master suite. She called his name but got no answer. She made her way downstairs.

Again she called, "Jarvis?"

She peeped through the window blinds. Jarvis vehicle was gone. She contacted him. "Where are you going?"

"I have some unfinished business to take care of."

"Where and with whom?"

"No concern of yours."

"Hurry home. I need you here with me."

She hung up. Back upstairs in the house, Aniyah blew out the candles and sat up awaiting the return of her husband.

CHAPTER 41

*J*arvis eyed Sid through the passenger window. He unlocked the door. As Sid hopped in, Jarvis placed his right index finger to his lips. He was in the middle of a telephone conversation with Charlinda through the car speakers. Sid sat quiet. On his way to get him, Jarvis had updated him on his latest dilemma. Jarvis continued his conversation with Charlinda.

"I've thought about what you told me. And I've come to my senses. You're right; you're the only woman I want to be with. May I please come over?"

Charlinda giggled in her high-pitched voice. "You don't have to ask for permission to come and see me. Get your butt here to your future wife."

"I'm headed your way."

When he ended the call, Sid said, "Bro, do you really want to do this?"

"Man, I'm tired of people playing me. Yes, I do. I want to make sure she gets the message to stay away from me and Aniyah."

On arrival to Charlinda's residence, Jarvis said, "Sid, I

want you to wait in the hallway. Be ready to hit the record button on your phone."

"She'll call the cops on you."

"She wouldn't do that. She'd be arrested for conspiracy."

They took the staircase, and stopped on the floor where Charlinda lived. Sid sat on the ledge of a windowsill, overlooking a swimming pool, while Jarvis headed down the hallway to her door. Once he rang the bell, Charlinda came to the door, dressed in a short, satin white gown. She invited him inside.

"Hey, Baby, let's play." She grabbed him by the collar. Jarvis allowed her to lead the way.

Jarvis wanted to choke her, but instead, he allowed her to unbuckle his pants. She pulled out the tail of his crisp white shirt. She giggled as she experimented with him. Charlinda pulled down his zipper, and lowered his pants to his knees. She noticed how Jarvis just stood there.

"You're not touching me?"

"Right now, I want you to have fun."

Charlinda unbuttoned his shirt, easing her hands down his chest, feeling his muscles. Then, she licked on him. Jarvis had to admit the way she caressed him, made him feel tempted to shove her onto the nearby sofa and have his way with her, but he held tight.

He stared at her as she moved away from him, removing the thin straps of her gown off her shoulders to let it fall to the floor, leaving her in the flesh. "Jarvis, don't have me playing by myself. Let's have fun together," she begged.

Jarvis came to her, kissing her on her forehead. He

stroked the side of her face. He gazed into her eyes. "I want you so bad, Aniyah."

"Aniyah?" Charlinda asked, turning red.

He gripped her by the cheeks. "That's right. Mrs. Aniyah Powell. The woman I love and will forever love. Not you."

"Let go of me," she threatened. "Or, I'll have you arrested for assault."

"You and your brother took advantage of me and wife."

Charlinda belted, "It was Brant's idea. I started out helping him, but stopped a long time ago. I fell in love with you."

"You and him preyed on me and my family. But you both are the ones who got played. Your brother is in jail right now. And for you, every time I ever made out with you, it was nothing but Aniyah's face that got me through it."

"You're lying." She beat him on the chest.

Jarvis did not flinch. "It's the truth."

"This wouldn't have happened if you hadn't ruined my brother's career."

"It was an accident. He shouldn't have ever gone back to play so soon after the injury to get hurt again. I hated his career ended. But it was nothing I could do to change that."

Jarvis let go of her. He buttoned his shirt. "Stay away from me and my wife, or you'll join your brother in jail. Never step foot in the bank again."

He headed to the front door. In the nude, she ran after him, pulling on his shirt.

Turning to face her, Jarvis pushed her off of him. "All it

takes is one phone call."

Charlinda shed tears. "I love you."

"I don't and never will love you."

Jarvis opened the door, and Sid stood outside. He got a clear view of Charlinda's naked body.

"Damn, she's a stick. Bro, the honey I set you up with was better than this broomstick," he teased, holding his phone toward her to video her.

When Charlinda noticed that he was filming her, she ran inside her home, slamming the door shut.

"Cut it off, Sid. What the heck, delete it." Jarvis pulled Sid by the shirtsleeve to leave.

Sid tapped a button and the recording disappeared. "Yes, you're right. I don't need Noelle finding no naked woman on my phone."

The men chuckled.

"I say we go home to our beautiful wives," Jarvis said.

CHAPTER 42

*A*niyah stuffed her mouth with Chinese food to curve the jitters in her stomach. If Jarvis had not come in the house when he had, she would have eaten his share of the meal. She dropped the fork on the plate when she heard his voice.

"Aniyah?" he called.

She ran to him. "Jarvis, where did you go?"

"I went to see Charlinda."

"Really?"

"I had to let her know that I knew the truth about her and Brant. I told her that if she ever came near us again, she'll join him in jail."

"I hope she doesn't call the police on you." Aniyah listened as Jarvis explained how Sid had accompanied him. She let out a sigh of relief.

"You have to be hungry."

"I don't have an appetite. All I want is you, Mrs. Jarvis Powell." He pulled her into his arms.

Aniyah kissed him, then pulled away from him. She danced her way toward the stairs. She let her bathrobe drop at the foot of stairs and continued removing her clothing every step of the way. By the time she reached the top of the staircase, she had slipped out of her nightie, giving her hubby a full view of her goodies. Jarvis followed suit, removing his shirt.

When they reached the entrance to the suite, he caught her by the arm. Aniyah pulled away. Up and down the hallway she danced, swaying her hips to her own tune. She returned to him, easing her hands across his chest with her fingertips. Jarvis had unbuckled his pants and slipped out of them. When she placed her hands around his neck, he pressed against her letting her feel his bulge. They rocked from side to side. Aniyah held her head back as Jarvis took in the delight of her erect nipples.

Once they made it to the suite, she whispered, "Lay down on the bed."

Jarvis rested on the mattress. Aniyah climbed on top of her husband. She had her way with him. Jarvis groaned. He held her breasts in the palm of his hands, while she galloped on top of him. Her screams of pleasure echoed throughout their home. Jarvis flipped her over and took charge. He moved in full speed until they both climaxed together. They rested on the bed, both breathing heavy and feeling exhausted.

"These have been some crazy months."

Caressing her cheekbone, Jarvis said, "Brant is a charmer."

"And, I was hit with a brick by his charisma at the farmers market. He told me he also helped people to start a garden. I let him come to our house to give me help and he kidnaps me," Aniyah lied.

"He used you to get back at me."

"And, he succeeded. You can't say you weren't hurt when you thought I left you on my own free will," she sobbed.

"I'm happy we can soon put it all behind us."

"Like my annulment from Brant Logan."

"Definitely," Jarvis agreed. "You're only supposed to be married to one man."

Aniyah rolled over on him. She stroked the scar on his face, then kissed it. "I'm the only Mrs. Jarvis Powell, Jr."

"I now have everything I want. My wife, my son, my business and my family home."

Aniyah laughed. "Did you see the look on Milandra's face? I bet she thought Nolan didn't have the balls to pull one over on her."

"He only did it because she belittled him. He insisted on helping me out."

Aniyah put another mushy kiss on her husband's lips. "We'll do something very nice for him."

Jarvis tapped on her nose. "I have the perfect idea. I say we let Nolan live here," he suggested. "And we start a new beginning somewhere else."

"I thought you loved this house."

"We'll move in the family home. That's what you always wanted."

With tears in her eyes, Aniyah said, "It no longer matters to me where I live. As long as it's with my man and our son."

"Will you marry me again? This time we'll have a wedding."

Staring into her husband's eyes, Aniyah kissed him and said yes. Jarvis reached for the chilled champagne that

Aniyah had brought up earlier, and poured some for the both of them. They toasted one another and sipped their drink. They spent the rest of the night making love.

CHAPTER 43

*I*t could not be true. She had let her guard down, allowing Nolan back into her bed to manipulate her into giving him rights to sell her possessions. Husband or not, this should not have happened to her. She was born a Houston.

With her portrait in her hands, Milandra carried it into the office that once belonged to her father, Rupert. He had worked numerous hours at the Houston Commercial Construction Company. She placed the portrait against the painted white wall. She had changed the office furniture from mahogany to white. The chairs in front of the desk were a soft blue.

In memory of her father, his portrait still hung on the wall over a hidden safe. It reminded her of him and his hard work to provide a future for his family. Before she took a seat at her desk, she locked her handbag in a special cabinet that she had built. Milandra dropped her head down on the desk. She had failed as a Houston and dishonored her father. She crumbled papers into balls and then tossed them across the room. She hated that Aniyah, someone who had come from nothing, would have ownership of another family's fortune.

Feeling overwhelmed with emotions, she tried to hold back the tears. When she heard her sister's voices, she wiped her eyes. She hurried to pick up the balled-up papers from the floor, but they arrived sooner than she had expected.

"Are you playing office basketball?" Kenley said.

"Never mind what I'm doing; what do you and Noelle want? Go back to work."

"You're not our boss. We own equal shares in this business," Kenley said.

Milandra never could forget it. Her baby sister reminded her plenty times.

"We're not against you, Milandra," Noelle said.

"Then act the way Father would want you both to act. Be loyal to a Houston." Milandra pointed to herself. She marched to her desk and took a seat.

"I'm not proud of what Nolan did to you. You should've given Jarvis his property and business to him on your own," Noelle said.

"That's not how business goes. For the one-hundredth time. I got it legit," Milandra said.

Noelle flopped into a seat. "You knew Mr. Powell sold it to you to spite Jarvis. Kenley and I wanted no parts of his revenge and hatred for Aniyah."

"Milandra like being messy just like Aniyah," Kenley said.

"The more you talk, the more garbage I hear." Milandra scolded her baby sister.

"Enough, Kenley. Have respect for your older sister," Noelle said.

"I'm out." Kenley headed to leave. Noelle ran after her and pulled her by the arm. "You're not going anywhere. We need to come to a peaceful place with our sister-hood."

Kenley rolled her eyes. She scrolled to a chair and slouched down in it. Noelle sat next to her in the other one.

"Let's forget what has happened. Milandra, you're back here where you belong. There's plenty of work to keep you busy. We have shopping centers being developed around town that need our undivided attention."

Milandra barked, "I endured a big loss. I'm not focused on anything else right now but that."

"Losing Nolan is your biggest loss. He's fine and kind. You blew it," Kenley said.

Milandra raised her eyebrows. "That's a mistake that I'll correct. I can't wait to sign those divorce papers."

"You're cold as snow," Kenley said.

"Let's not start again," Noelle interjected. "Milandra, stop it. You love Nolan. Forgive him and move forward with your marriage."

Kenley faced Noelle. "Nolan doesn't want Milandra. He'll find him a woman who he can be the King of the house and have lots of fun with."

Milandra watched Kenley wiggle her hips.

"You can dance all you want. I don't care what Nolan does, or about whom he does it with. I want my life as a Houston woman," Milandra said.

"Before you make a hasty move, you should think about it," Noelle said.

"The man betrayed me. He's a goner." Milandra stood

her ground.

When her cell phone rang, Milandra flagged her hand at her sisters. "Go to work. My life is no longer up for discussion."

While she answered the caller, Noelle came and gave her sister a hug. "Love you," she said.

"Bye, mean sister," Kenley said, storming out the door.

"Kenley," Noelle called. "I don't know what we're going to do with your smart mouth."

When they closed the door behind them, Milandra hurried and said, "Hello?"

"Hi, this is Attorney Marion Bloomberg."

"I recognized your voice. What do you want?"

"I need to see you."

"For what? Your client got his business and property."

"There's unfinished business with you and me."

Milandra could not possibly know why the attorney would have any more dealings with her.

"I'm here at Houston Commercial Construction Company. You're welcome to come to my office."

"This is a private matter. Meet me in the parking lot in one hour."

When Milandra ended the call, she wondered what this attorney, for the Powells, wanted with her. She thought, would he double-cross his client and help her win back the Powells' estate?

Exactly one hour later, Milandra went to the parking lot. She strolled down a row of parked vehicles looking for any sign of Attorney Bloomberg. Her phone rang.

"I see you. Walk to the next aisle toward the back. I'm

in a brown Lexus," Bloomberg said.

Milandra strutted down the next aisle. She spotted his vehicle.

The attorney rolled down the window. "Get in."

Milandra stood at the passenger door. "This is not lady-like."

The attorney got out of his vehicle. He opened the door for her. "Does this make you feel better, Mrs. Houston-Rice?"

"Call me Miss Houston."

Milandra took a seat on the plush, black leather-seat cushions.

As soon as he got back in the vehicle, she said, "Now tell me what's urgent that you need to see me in my company's parking lot?"

The attorney reached into the backseat and retrieved a large black tote bag.

He set the bag in her lap. "Look inside."

Milandra opened the bag. Her eyes widened when she saw a stack of bills.

"Why are you showing me this bag of money? I suggest you put it in a bank. Just not a Powell Bank."

He smiled. "It's yours. Mr. Powell had this money reserved, in the event his son got his family assets back from you. He didn't want your money, nor could he take it to his grave. He took it from you, to give you a sense of buying power."

Milandra nodded. "He understood Houstons don't like handouts."

"This secret is between us," the attorney said.

"Thank you for keeping Mr. Powell's wishes. You

could've kept it for yourself."

"Mr. Powell did right by me. No need for me to take what's yours."

Milandra zipped the bag. "I failed him," she said, holding back her tears.

Attorney Bloomberg patted her on the hand. "No you didn't. He left this world believing he got revenge on his son and daughter-in-law."

"If I didn't have an attorney already, I'd hire you to represent me in my divorce."

"I've been retained by your husband," the attorney admitted.

"Are you going to betray me and tell him about this money?"

"I get paid too much money to reveal my other client's business."

"Thanks again. The sooner your client signs the divorce papers, the better. I want Nolan out of my life."

Attorney Bloomberg reached and grabbed Milandra's hand. He licked his lips. "It's sad. He was willing to give you up to help Jarvis."

Milandra eased her hand away from him. "Everyone has their own priorities."

Attorney Bloomberg, again, stroked her hand. "You're beautiful."

"Mr. Bloomberg, are you coming on to me?"

He pulled his hand away from her. "I'm attracted to a beautiful, powerful woman."

Milandra looked at the man who was at least twenty years older than her, but a businessman he was.

She grabbed his hand. "You speed up the divorce papers. Maybe then, you can take me to a fine restaurant."

"It'll be quick, since your husband only wants his freedom. It's weird, but that's all he wants."

"It's smart on his part. He's not getting a dime of the Houston fortune." She looked at the handle on the passenger door. "Please open the door for me, so I can leave."

Attorney Bloomberg followed her instruction. Once he opened the door, Milandra got out. She strutted to her vehicle, tossed the bag in the trunk and went back into the building.

With Nolan's vehicle parked in front of their home, Milandra left the bag of money secured in the trunk. Exhausted from a day of work, inside, she caught him packing the last of his belongings in wardrobe-sized moving boxes.

She picked up a coat hanger and hit him with it. "You're despicable. What man turns on his wife?"

"A man who has a wife with no heart or compassion for another human being." Nolan tossed a shirt on the coat hanger. "I suggest you not throw things at me. I'm getting my stuff and leaving. You can have your precious stuffy house to yourself. Grow old right here by yourself. See how happy that'll make you feel."

"It'll feel marvelous. I've been in this home all my life. My father made this happen for my sisters and I. Get over it."

Nolan chuckled. He lifted one box and carried it to his moving truck. Milandra kept her eyes on him, in fear he would take one of her family's possessions.

When he returned, she badgered him. "To think I thought you could be a loyal husband. You, Sid, and that piece of trash, Pete, should never have been allowed to conquer my or my sisters' hearts."

"Speak for yourself. Noelle and Kenley are satisfied with the men in their lives. They're not pitiful like you."

"Hurry up, and get out of my house, or I'll have security throw you out."

Before Nolan grabbed his last box, he snatched Milandra by the arm, gripping it tight. "I can't wait to meet a real woman, not no bougie bitter one."

Milandra pulled away from him. "I only want one thing from you: your signature on the divorce papers."

He cut his eyes at her. "The feeling is mutual."

When Nolan reached the door, Kenley appeared. "No, you can't go."

"Kenley, leave right along with him," Milandra said.

"I'm not. Not until Nolan stays and hears what I have to say."

"Kenley, we can talk outside," he said.

"No," Kenley pleaded. She grabbed hold of the box that he held. "Put it down."

Nolan dropped the box on the floor.

"You two love each other," Kenley said.

"Sometimes, that's not enough," he said.

Milandra folded her arms. "I agree with you on that."

"Milandra, you let Mr. Powell put your marriage in jeopardy," Kenley said.

"He succeeded," Nolan added.

"First strike is on you, Sis. You buy Mr. Powell's assets without telling your husband. I say that's shady," Kenley said.

"What are you getting at?" Milandra wondered.

"You're the reason your marriage is being ruined. You started it," Kenley replied.

"Yep, and I've finished it," Nolan said.

"None of you are winners in this situation," Kenley said.

"What's done is done," he said.

Milandra stared at her husband. "It's over between us. Once someone crosses a Houston, we've nothing else to do with him or her. You can leave now." Milandra dismissed him.

"You're hateful," Kenley said to her sister. "I give up."

Before Nolan exited the house, Kenley said, "I wish you the best. Find yourself a hot sexy woman. No stiff collar, like my sister." Kenley pointed at Milandra. She stuck her tongue out at her, running out the door behind Nolan.

Milandra yelled out the door, "You have a lot of mouth, Kenley."

Back in the house, Milandra peeped through the window and waited until her soon-to-be ex-husband drove off. When the coast was clear, she ran and took the bag out of the trunk and brought it into the house. She tossed the bag of money into her closet. In case Nolan had a change of heart to go after her money, she would wait until the divorce was finalized before she deposited the money into her account.

Falling onto the bed, she grumbled, "The next man in my life has to have the mindset of a powerful person."

CHAPTER 44

*W*ith ownership of the Powell domain, Aniyah joined her husband to visit the home he grew up in. When they reached the gates, a new staff of security had replaced the old ones. During the time Milandra had owned it, she had kept the grounds well, the same way his father had maintained it.

When they parked in front of the brick mansion, Jarvis turned to his wife. "I want to go in alone first. Wait here. I'll come back and get you."

Aniyah leaned over and gave him a peck on the cheek. "I'll be right here waiting for you."

She watched her husband march up to the door. She admired his clean-cut look. He strutted with a bop, dressed in a smoke-gray suit.

Her cell phone rang. She saw it was her friend.

"This is not a good time for me to talk."

Nellie's sniffling voice escalated. "Roy and I have broken up."

"Seriously?" Aniyah asked. Since the day she'd met Nellie, she and Roy had been together.

Nellie sobbed. "He cheated on me."

Aniyah paused. She had no room to blast Roy. She had been in the situation before. "Give it time to forgive him."

"More than once. It's over."

"You win. You know what's best for you."

"Are you at home?"

"No. I'm at the Powell estate. I'm going inside the house."

"You got your wish?"

Aniyah explained in detail how Jarvis had secured possession of the property and business.

When his black and gray leather derby shoes touched the wood floor, Jarvis stared up at the top of the long staircase to the second floor. He visualized his father, standing there wrapped in his royal-blue bathrobe with a cigar dangling from his mouth. As if it were yesterday, he sniffed the imaginary aroma of smoke. The thought of the smell sickened his stomach. His father had understood he disliked his bad habit. Powell Sr. would puff in his son's face to irritate him.

A teardrop escaped from his right eye. The roar of his father's voice echoed in his ear. "Get rid of her. She's nothing but a distraction. You got an empire to run."

Jarvis whined, "Sorry, Dad. No, I'm not sorry. My wife goes where I go. Together we'll live here."

Jarvis went out the front door. He locked eyes with Aniyah. Once she saw him, she hopped out of the vehicle.

Dressed in a pair of sandals and Capri pants, with a sleeveless blouse, Aniyah joined her husband. She followed him into the dining area. She noticed the room was empty. It was the place where Jarvis ate plenty of meals on a long dining table. He and his father would sit vertically across from each other.

"What did Milandra do with the furniture?"

"She and Dad got rid of it."

"Let's check out the upstairs."

They found their way to the second floor. Inside, Powell's former suite was an empty shell. It reminded Aniyah of the last time she had visited her father-in-law. Powell, Sr. tried his best to get rid of her. Her eyes brightened. It was her time to be the first woman of the house. They headed to Jarvis' old suite. It resembled a ghost town.

"The house looks like someone has robbed it."

"Many tangible memories have vanished."

"Time for new beginnings. We'll bedazzle this place with new furniture. Happy colors of paint for the walls," Aniyah said. She smiled. "I'll decorate it."

"This is a lot of house to handle. I'll hire a designer to work with you."

"No. Nellie can help me. She has plenty of free time. She broke up with her boyfriend. This will help keep her mind off of it. It'll be fun."

Aniyah followed her husband back downstairs. They made their way into the basement. The bar still existed, but Milandra had depleted the liquor. It was the place where Powell, Sr. used to enjoy having drinks and listening to his music.

"The whole house has been wiped out." He sighed. "New beginnings."

"We'll give this house life."

He chuckled. "Wait until J.P. get in here."

Aniyah turned to her husband. "Baby, I love you so much." She threw her arms around his neck. She lifted her face to his and kissed him. They got lost in passion and christened the house.

"My dad would kill us if he knew we'd made love on top of his bar."

Aniyah giggled. "Just the thought of me, he's puffing plenty of cigars in heaven."

Jarvis helped her down off the counter. They slipped on their clothes.

Aniyah played with her wild hair to put it back in place. "I can't wait for us to move in."

"It'll be in no time."

"Milandra needs to pay for the trouble she has caused you."

"I got what I wanted."

"Still, she should pay. I'll take care of that."

"No paybacks. It's time we move forward with a peaceful life."

Aniyah fluttered her eyes. "You're right."

"Once we get settled in, I want to invite Nolan over for drinks."

"I'll invite Nellie."

Jarvis cut his eye at his wife. "Oh no you won't do that. No matchmaking."

She kissed him on his scar. "Oops. A slip of the tongue."

CHAPTER 45

*A*niyah had turned the entertainment room in her home into a Sip 'N Dip room. She garnished the bar counter with trays of finger foods. On a round bar-height table that seated six people, bottles of wine chilled on ice in a stainless-steel ice bucket.

When her husband entered, he said, "Isn't this a bit much? We're not having a party. Nolan's only coming for drinks."

"I'm showing you your wife can be classy, too."

Jarvis pulled her into his arms. "I love you as you are. No need to getting snobby on me."

Aniyah spanked him on his rear. "I'm not that kind of lady."

The doorbell interrupted them. Aniyah hurried to answer. It was Nolan.

"Hi." She embraced him with a hug. "We're happy you could come hang with us."

"Thanks for the invite," Nolan said.

Aniyah led him into her entertainment room.

"Hey man." Jarvis greeted him with a brotherly handshake. "How are things going?"

"Things are good. Business is better than ever. My divorce is almost final."

"I hate that things ended the way they did between you two. I wish Milandra appreciated what she had. You're a great man," Jarvis said.

"One woman's loss is another woman's surprise gift," Aniyah said.

"No dating for me. I'm focused on my business."

"Want a glass of wine? Aniyah has a tray of hot wings and veggies with ranch dip for us."

"I'll take a beer."

"I got you covered." Aniyah got him a cold one from a compact refrigerator behind the bar; she opened it, and then handed it to Nolan. She watched him take a swallow of the drink.

"Let us all have a drink. We need to make a toast to Nolan," Jarvis said.

"That's not needed." Nolan took a seat on one of the swivel chairs at the table. He set his beer on it.

"Yes, it is," Aniyah said. She waited until Jarvis poured them both a glass of wine.

With his glass raised, Jarvis spoke, "Thanks to you, I have the Powell family business and my family's home. To show our appreciation, we want you to live in this home, rent free, for as long as you want."

Surprised by this news, Nolan asked, "Are you serious? I've been looking for an apartment."

"Yeah man, I am," Jarvis said.

"Say yes, so we can get our drink on." Aniyah was eager to take a swallow of the wine.

Nolan chuckled. "Yes. I'll take good care of it."

"Cheers." Aniyah celebrated. They clinked glasses. Aniyah took a gulp of her drink.

Nolan stood up and embraced them. The doorbell rang again.

Aniyah set her glass on the table. "I'll get it."

"Who could that be?" Jarvis wondered. "We're not expecting any more company."

"Yes we are. This night will be exciting," Aniyah said, before disappearing.

As she approached the door, she saw her friend, Nellie, standing on the porch, dressed in a pair of skinny jeans and a fitted black, off-the-shoulder top, with her hair pulled back into a ponytail.

Aniyah studied her friend's attire. "Is this the new you? Showing a little flesh."

"I'm working on getting a new look. I'm single again."

"Girl, I thought you weren't coming."

"I needed to get out of the house. So I decided to come."

When Nellie walked past Aniyah, Aniyah pulled at the band around her ponytail. "This, you need to get rid of. Let your hair hang."

"Ponytails are sexy-looking," Nellie said.

"Not tonight. Trust me. You'll thank me later."

Aniyah fluffed her friend's hair.

Nellie moved away from her. "Get out of my hair. What are you up to?"

Aniyah pulled her by the arm until they reached the entertainment room.

"Look who showed up at the door, Jarvis. It's my bestie."

"Hi, Nellie," he said, but gave his wife the side-eye.

"Hi," Nellie greeted them.

Aniyah directed her attention to Nolan. "This is my good friend, Nellie."

Aniyah watched the glow in Nolan's face as he stared and shook her friend's hand.

"Nice to meet you," Nolan said to Nellie.

Nellie responded, "You're married to Milandra Houston."

Aniyah spilled his business. "He's about to be officially divorced from her. And you broke up with your live-in boyfriend."

"Love, you're talking too much," Jarvis said.

"It's the truth." Aniyah shrugged.

"Nellie, would you like a drink?" Jarvis asked.

"I'll get her a drink," Nolan offered. "What will you have?"

"I'll have what you're having," Nellie said, eyeing his drink.

"I got you." Nolan went to grab a beer for Nellie.

"Have a seat next to Nolan," Aniyah suggested.

Jarvis moved closer to his wife. He whispered in her ear. "We'll talk later."

Aniyah giggled. "I love you, too." She smacked lips with Jarvis.

While they carried on several conversations, Aniyah brought up the plans she and Jarvis had made to celebrate their love. "Jarvis and I are renewing our vows. We've never had a wedding ceremony with family and friends. Nellie, I want you to be my maid of honor."

"Of course." Nellie beamed with excitement and

hugged Aniyah.

"I say, Nolan, you're the man I want to be my best man. How about it?" Jarvis asked.

"With pleasure," Nolan agreed.

"More drinks to celebrate this great evening," Aniyah said.

Aniyah handed her guest another bottle of beer. She noticed the more Nolan drank, the cozier he got with her friend. She watched Nellie blush every time Nolan spoke.

Aniyah grabbed Jarvis by the hand. "Excuse us," she said to their guests.

"What's up?" Jarvis asked, feeling a buzz.

Aniyah pulled her husband into the hallway.

"They need privacy."

"Aniyah Powell."

She pushed her husband up against the wall. She covered his lips with hers, giving him a sultry kiss.

When she backed away, she said, "Let's give them thirty minutes of alone time. Conversation never hurts. They're in the same boat."

"They need to find their own way."

"A little bit of help never hurts."

"You want revenge on Milandra."

"Milandra, who?"

Aniyah pecked her husband on his lips once again. They left their company to get more acquainted with one another.

CHAPTER 46

*I*n a year's time, Aniyah and Jarvis had never heard from Charlinda again. Brant stayed locked up in prison. Aniyah had gotten her illegal marriage to Brant annulled. The day had come for Aniyah and Jarvis to renew their vows and move into the renovated Powell family property. In the estate's ballroom their wedding planner had decorated it with red and white roses. The centerpieces on the row of tables, on each side of the ballroom, displayed tall crystal fluted vases. They had built an arch for the wedding ceremony out of white roses. The couple would hold the reception in the same space.

It would be an intimate event. At the request of Jarvis, the Houston sisters were invited. He held no grudges against Milandra. The ballroom filled up with all of their family and friends. Noelle, in a soft-pink linen dress with her hair scooped to one side, arrived on the arm of her husband, Sid. Her sister, Kenley, wearing a sassy polka-dot dress, arrived holding hands with her boyfriend, Pete. Milandra had yet to arrive. Even with the invite, no one expected her to attend.

Inside a small room, Aniyah was receiving the final

touches on her makeup. She teared up when she thought of herself walking down the aisle without being on the arm of her father.

Nellie, dressed in a fitted long gown, noticed her. "You look sad."

"I can't do this. A papa is supposed to walk his daughter down the aisle. I have none."

Nellie hugged her friend. "You'll feel better, once you're in Jarvis' arms."

With a tissue, Aniyah wiped the dripping mascara from her face. "Beat these eyes again."

The makeup artist cleaned up her client's face.

"Nellie, these are moments that I yearn to know my father."

"You're blessed with two awesome guys. Your son and your hubby."

Aniyah smiled. "You're right. I'm thankful for them."

The ladies turned their heads when Tessa entered the room wearing a red gown. Aniyah favored the color.

Aniyah studied her aunt. "You look so much better in a solid color."

Tessa posed with her hands on her hip. "We Sanchezes look pretty in plain colors."

The ladies giggled.

Nellie tapped Aniyah on the shoulder. "You need something blue."

Aniyah pouted. "I already have that. I'm feeling somewhat blue."

"Where is this pity-party coming from?" Tessa asked.

"I don't have my papa to escort me down the aisle." Aniyah's eyes watered once again.

"I have a surprise."

Aniyah stood to her feet. "You found my papa?"

Tessa shook her head. "I wish I could give you that one gift."

Aniyah wiped her eyes. "I wish you could, too."

Her aunt announced, "There's someone here, who'd love to escort you."

Aniyah rolled her eyes at her aunt. "Heck no. Not your husband."

"Never. It's Dr. Guess. He's here to do you the honors. Only if you want him to," Tessa said.

Aniyah had never forgotten the doctor who had delivered her baby. He had never passed judgment on her.

"You invited him? Where is he?"

Tessa went to the door and opened it. Dr. Guess entered.

"It's been a long time." He smiled at Aniyah.

"It's so good to see you," Aniyah said, making her way to the doctor. She embraced him. "It'd be awesome to have you walk me down the aisle."

"My pleasure," Dr. Guess said as he pranced around in his black suit.

Aniyah admired the handsome attire. She marveled over his silky grayish hair. "You can have on a pair of shorts and you'll still look good," she said. "Now, I won't need my little one to walk with me."

"I saw your boy. He's a fast mover, not letting that suit stop him from running around." He laughed. "I'll be right outside whenever you're ready."

With her mascara smeared around her eyes again, Aniyah kissed him on the cheek. She hurried to her seat. "Get this face beat one last time."

Nellie joyfully said, "Girl, you don't need too much makeup."

Milandra had gotten over the ordeal with Jarvis, since her money was back in her bank account. On the arm of Attorney Bloomberg, she strutted into the ballroom with her hair styled up in a French roll. Pearl studs dazzled her earlobe, to include a set of cultured fresh-water pearls around her bare neckline. She was dressed in an A-line, linen turquoise, three-quarter- sleeved skirt suit. Her outfit complimented her small frame.

Milandra made eye contact with her ex-husband, who stood beside Jarvis, next to the wedding ceremony arch. Nolan cut his eyes in another direction. She smirked, hoping he felt bad about what he had lost. She took her seat, once her date pulled out a chair covered in white seat covers with a red satin sash for her. Her sisters had taken their seats at the same table.

Noelle, sitting to her right, whispered in Milandra's ear. "You're here with your husband's divorce lawyer? Isn't the man old enough to be your father?"

Milandra whispered back, "The divorce is settled. Nolan and I agreed on everything. This man is smarter and much wiser. I've moved forward to better things."

Kenley blurted, "Nolan looks fine in his white tuxedo. That red cummerbund is sexy around his waist."

Milandra grabbed the red linen napkin off the table. She swapped Kenley with it. "You have no manners. I have no interest in Nolan's dress attire."

"Ouch!" Kenley said and then darted her eyes at Attorney Bloomberg. She snapped back at Milandra. "I see you're doing old school now." Kenley took a sip of water. Noelle fused the situation. "Let's enjoy the wedding."

The upbeat melody of Shalamar's "The Second Time Around" blasted throughout the room.

"Who plays this type of song to get married to?" Milandra wondered. "No class."

"I can get with it," Kenley said. She bounced to the music.

"This is true Aniyah. Jarvis is letting her have her day the way she wants it." Noelle voiced her opinion.

Sid, at the table next to his wife, interjected, "A man would do anything for the love of his woman."

Milandra watched him give Noelle a peck on her lips. She pouted. "I'll be glad when this trashy wedding is over with."

The wedding started. Tessa and her husband entered the ballroom with little Jarvis III walking alongside them. Baron didn't want to be there, but for the sake of his wife, he escorted her. The wedding party had no bridesmaids or groomsmen. Nellie, the maid of honor, walked to the front of the ballroom.

While the music played, Aniyah, in a fitted, red backless Mermaid gown with long sleeves, showing off her curves escorted on the arms of Dr. Guess, danced down the aisle, between the tables where her guests stood near their seats. She scanned the room. She noticed most of the guests in attendance were there for Jarvis.

"Go home," she mumbled under her breath when she caught eye of the Houston sisters. These are the words she wanted to yell. Instead, she let them feast their eyes on her sparkling white teeth.

Little Jarvis sat on Tessa's lap. When he saw Aniyah coming their way, he reached out to her. He whined, "Mama-Mom."

Aniyah let go of Dr. Guess' arm. She went to her son. Lifting her veil, she kissed him. "Be a good boy for Tia," she whispered.

Tessa placed a sugar-free gummy bear in little Jarvis' mouth. Aniyah joined Jarvis at the ceremony arch. Dr. Guess turned her over to her groom and sat down. With the pastor presiding, Nolan stood at Jarvis' right and Nellie stood to the left of Aniyah. They renewed their vows in front of family and his friends.

Once they were pronounced man and wife for a second time, Jarvis lifted Aniyah's veil and kissed her.

"Save some for later," Nolan teased.

The newlyweds came up for air. They turned to the crowd.

Everyone applauded.

Dancing halfway through the aisle, between the tables, a deliveryman wielded a package wrapped in silver metallic paper. He interrupted them. Startled, the newlyweds stopped dancing and their smiley faces turned sour.

Jarvis spoke before Aniyah could utter a word. "Is this some kind of joke our friends are playing on us? Who makes a delivery, to the bride and groom, during their ceremony?"

"I do," the deliveryman said. "This package is for Aniyah Sanchez."

"I'm Aniyah Sanchez-Powell," she corrected the deliveryman. "You can put the present over there." Aniyah pointed to the gift table.

"Not this one," the deliveryman said. "I have specific orders to ensure this package enters your hands."

Aniyah turned around, handing her bouquet of red and white roses to her maid of honor, who stood behind her. She then took hold of the package. "Now leave."

"Wait," Jarvis said to the deliveryman. "Who sent this?" Jarvis noticed the deliveryman had no company name on his jacket.

"No clue. Enjoy the rest of your wedding." The deliveryman exited just as quickly as he'd arrived.

"Can someone please take this from my wife and put it with the other wedding gifts?"

"No," Aniyah said. "Whoever sent this, wanted me to open it now."

Everyone watched as Aniyah unveiled the package. When she saw the gift was an arrangement, made out of three layers of candy cigars in a cigar box, she let it fall to the floor.

Jarvis knelt down and picked up the gift card. He read the typed card out loud: "Aniyah, never will I claim you."

With teary eyes, Aniyah shivered. "I told you that your papa is alive. He's said these same words before to me."

"Dad is dead. He's not alive. Who would stoop this low to upset you on your wedding day?" Jarvis wondered.

"I know who," Aniyah said. She dashed to the table where the Houston sisters sat, and spoke to the oldest one. "Milandra, you uppity trick. You did this."

Milandra's eyes widened. "You're the bona-fide criminal, not me." Milandra held her groomed hands out in front of Aniyah. "I keep these clean with paraffin wax and manicures. So go blame someone else."

Aniyah pushed her hands away. "If I find out it was you, you'll have hell to pay."

Milandra turned to her date. "Attorney Bloomberg, I believe the bride is threatening me."

Jarvis joined his wife. He looked at Milandra. "No one will do harm to you. Tell me you didn't do this?"

Milandra stood to her feet. She stared into Jarvis' eyes. "I handle business deals not petty things." She turned to her date. "Take me home."

Jarvis stopped her, not wanting to offend any of his guests, including Milandra. "I'm sorry. Please, stay."

While Milandra eased back down in her seat, with her legs crossed, Kenley shouted, "I believe my sister."

"That's not Milandra's character. I believe her," Noelle said, defending her sister.

"Of course you would, ya'll cover for each other," Aniyah said.

"That's not true," Noelle said. "If Milandra is guilty, I would not condone this type of behavior."

"Girl, the man is dead. He's haunting you from his grave," Kenley said.

"Hush, Kenley." Noelle's voice echoed among the quiet guests.

Nellie came to her friend's aid. "Aniyah, don't let Mr. Powell or whoever did this, win. It's your wedding day. Throw that awful thing in the garbage and let's have fun."

Thoughts went through Jarvis' head. With attorneys involved, his father had to be dead.

"She's right," Jarvis agreed, but still wondered who was

behind the delivery. After all, he never identified his father's dead body.

Tessa threw the delivery package in the trash.

"Turn the music on, so that my groom and I can have our first dance," Aniyah said. She skipped the bridal party announcement. Locked inside Jarvis' arms, she leaned her head on his chest. They moved from side to side. Jarvis kept to the beat. "I see someone has been taking dance lessons."

He chuckled. "I'm getting there."

"Could your papa be alive?"

"Not another word about my dad. I'm into you today and forever."

Jarvis kissed her on the lips. Then he turned his attention to their guests. "Come on lovers, join us on the floor."

Before Aniyah knew it, other couples surrounded them. Her Aunt Tessa locked in the arms of her husband. Noelle and Sid glided across the floor as one. Kenley and Pete acted like they were making out, as they ground on each other.

Aniyah darted her eyes at Milandra, when Nolan pulled Nellie on the dance floor, kissing her in front of his ex-wife.

She watched Milandra pull away from her date. "I have to use the restroom."

Attorney Bloomberg took a seat as Milandra scurried away.

Aniyah whispered to Jarvis. "I have to use the potty. I'll be back."

She tapped Nellie on the shoulder. "Sorry, Nolan. I need my maid of honor to help me. It'll be a second."

Standing over the sink, Aniyah spoke loud, while she checked to make sure her makeup was still flawless.

"You and Nolan are chummy. Have you given him any loving yet?"

Nellie blushed. "That's personal."

"Aren't we besties?"

Nellie giggled. "Yes, girl. I thought after Roy, I'd be without a man for a while."

"Who knows, maybe soon you and Nolan will say, 'I do.'" Aniyah smiled.

"He wants to re-marry again."

"You're the perfect woman for him. You're not an uppity snob."

The bathroom stall door opened, and Milandra appeared.

Nellie, flustered, said, "I'm sorry. I wasn't aware you were in here."

"Girl, he's your man now. You owe her no apologies," Aniyah said.

Milandra smirked, heading to the sink. "I'm on the arms of a real man. A big-time attorney. And yes, to you, Aniyah, we've had great sex," she lied.

Aniyah flipped her hair. "You're jealous. Another woman who is not high and mighty as you, got her hooks on your ex."

"We should leave," Nellie said. She pulled Aniyah by the arm, leading toward the door.

While Nellie held the door open, Aniyah yelled at

Milandra. "You can thank me for finding Nolan a woman who can satisfy him in bed."

"No class," Milandra said, while she washed her hands.

Back on the dance floor, the women joined their men and danced. Milandra returned to the ballroom and beckoned her date to leave.

CHAPTER 47

*T*he guests had gone home and Tessa had agreed to babysit Jarvis III.

When Aniyah and Jarvis left the ballroom, they left Nolan and Nellie to oversee the cleanup crew.

Jarvis carried Aniyah up the long staircase to the remodeled, master suite. Jarvis put her down once they came to the door. He turned the knob to open it.

He scooped her back up and carried her into the dark room, resting her on the bed.

Aniyah felt something unfamiliar in the bed. She reached down and touched what she guessed to be crumbs. The strong stench of tobacco invaded her nostrils and she jumped up.

"Turn the lights on."

"What's wrong?" Jarvis asked, while he did as he was told.

When the room brightened, Aniyah saw the layers of crumbled cigar tobacco spread over the bed. She screamed. "Look at the bed!"

Jarvis eyes widened. "This can't be happening, again."

Aniyah looked over at the side of the bed, where she

would sleep. She saw on the nightstand a photo of Jarvis Powell, Sr. with a big grin on his face. A note was attached to it.

With trembling hands, Aniyah pointed at the photo. "Look over there. It's your papa's picture."

Jarvis went over to the photo and picked it up. He read the typed note out loud. "Get out of my house, Tramp."

"I'm telling you, your papa is alive. He's playing mind games with me."

Jarvis tossed the note back on the nightstand. He went to his sobbing wife.

"Aniyah, relax. I'll call the police and find out who is harassing you."

"There's no need in calling them. It's your old fart papa."

"As much as I want to believe he's still alive, he's not." Jarvis let go of her. "You have a seat while I clean this mess off the bed."

"I'm not staying in here tonight or any other night."

"We remodeled this place for us to make this our home."

Aniyah headed toward the door. "This house is not worth it. Your papa never welcomed me into your family, much less his home. He's still alive, or Milandra is his puppet."

"We can find out who's really doing this and put a stop to it."

She shook her balled fist. "It doesn't matter. All I want is for us to raise our son in a loving and welcoming place. This isn't it."

Jarvis pulled his wife into his arms. "I'm so sorry. We'll

get a room at a hotel for tonight. I'll leave the rest of this mess for the housekeepers." He escorted his bride out of the house.

CHAPTER 48

*M*onths passed and they'd never discovered the mystery behind the cigars and packages. Once Aniyah left the Powell domain, no other signs of Jarvis Powell, Sr.'s hatred for her surfaced. Jarvis placed their possessions in storage. He put his father's home on the market for rent. Understanding their situation, Nolan gave them back their home. Since Jarvis' other properties were rented, Nolan moved in the guest room until he and Nellie found an apartment.

Soon, Jarvis and Aniyah would find land and build a home in Lake Murray. The name on the banks no longer carried the Powell name. Instead, Jarvis changed it to Jarvis Bank. He was very selective of what conferences he attended, and made sure at times, Aniyah joined him with her aunt accessible to care for their son.

Sitting on the deck of their home, Jarvis fired up the grill. While he cooked, Aniyah sat at a white wrought-iron table, sipping on a glass of red wine. "I may no longer have my mama, nor my papa, but I do have you, our son and even Aunt Tessa in my life."

"We're fortunate to have you, too."

Jarvis closed the lid on the grill. He came to his wife, pulling her up out of his seat. He snuggled her into his arms. The doorbell rang. They let up.

"That must be Aunt Tessa."

Aniyah opened the storm door, and Jarvis III called for her. "Mama-Mom."

She scooped him up, gave him a kiss on the cheek, and then put him down. "Go see your papa. He's in the backyard."

Jarvis III called, "Papa-Dad." He ran toward the rear of the house.

Tessa scolded him. "Slow down before you fall. No boo-boos."

"Hello, Aunt Tessa," Aniyah said.

Tessa hugged her. To Aniyah's surprise, her husband was with her.

"Baron?"

"Don't even ask," he said. "I'm here."

"I won't question it." Her aunt's husband had no love for her. "Thank you for coming."

"I'll head to the backyard to join Jarvis."

When he left, Aniyah turned to her aunt. "How did you get him to come?"

"New beginnings have to start somewhere and someday. Why not today?"

Aniyah threw her arms around her aunt's neck. "I do love you."

"Love you, too, Aniyah. I prayed many of days that you'd show the good side of you."

A tear came to Aniyah's eyes. "I've made major mistakes."

"Do you have a lighter or match?"

"Yes. It's in the kitchen. What do you need it for?"

"Hurry, go get it," her aunt said, ignoring her question.

Aniyah did as Tessa told her and returned with the cigarette lighter. She followed her aunt into the family room. Tessa walked over to the fireplace. She opened the screen. Aniyah watched her pull a sheet of paper out of her pocket.

"What are you about to burn?"

"This is a list of all the things I think you have done wrong."

"You wrote it down."

"I prayed for the day that you'd release yourself from evil. Do you want to read it?"

Aniyah shook her head. "Heck no. I don't want to relive none of it."

"Take it and burn it. I've forgiven you. Now you forgive yourself, and we'll never speak of it again. Only good times from here on out."

With tears in her eyes, Aniyah tossed the paper in the fireplace. She squat down and lit it, letting the paper burn to a crisp. When she stood, she ran into her aunt's arms. Together they cried for the love of each other.

Again, the doorbell rang.

Aniyah wiped her eyes. "It's probably Nellie and Nolan."

"Are Sid and Noelle coming, too?"

"Yes."

"How about Milandra and Kenley?"

"They hate me. Kenley doesn't want any part of our crowd. And Milandra will always be an uppity snob."

"I'm happy Noelle has accepted you."

"She tolerates me because of Sid. I'll take that for now."

The doorbell rang again. Aniyah went to greet her guests.

CHAPTER 49

*M*ilandra returned to the Houston Estate after secretly marrying the old man attorney. She had him sign a prenup to secure the Houston fortune. Milandra kissed her groom on the lips once they entered the master suite. She wiped the traces of her lipstick from his lips.

"Ever since you gave me back my money, you've been the one for me. You could have kept it."

"I was doing my job," Bloomberg said.

He pulled the zipper down on her dress, easing it off her shoulders, until the dress fell to her ankles. Milandra stood in her yellow lace undergarments that matched her dress color. She loosened his tie. Bloomberg unbuttoned his shirt. Before long, they stripped off their clothing. Her new husband did not have the body of Nolan. Bloomberg's bulging belly stood out. That came from too many bottles of beer. Milandra eased under the covers, and her new husband joined her.

Again they kissed. He flopped himself on top of her. No longer than when he entered her, overexcited to be with her, it was two to three pumps before he breathed heavy and exploded. He rested his sweaty body down on her. It wasn't what she was used to, but she could live with it.

"Roll over." Milandra could not take his heavy weight on top of her fragile body.

"It's been a while," Bloomberg said.

"We do have an equipped home gym."

Bloomberg patted his belly. "I can use it."

While she rested in his arms, she heard her name called.

"Milandra?"

Bloomberg hid his naked body under the covers. Bursting into the room was none other than Kenley.

"Knock before you enter." Milandra held the sheet to hide her breasts.

Kenley darted her eyes at Bloomberg. "Dating is one thing, but to sleep with this dude is another."

"Kenley Houston, watch your mouth. Respect your new brother-in-law."

Kenley threw her hands up in the air. "You and Noelle are flipping out. She's at a cookout with Jarvis and Aniyah. And now you're married to this old dude?"

"I don't care what Noelle, or you, do. You've lost your way as a Houston."

"And you haven't? Look at whom you're with. Pops."

"Hey, watch your mouth. You can't speak this way about me," Bloomberg said. "I may be way older than your sister, but I'm not a bad catch."

"In my eyes you are. Bye," Kenley said and exited the room.

"That girl gives me a headache," Milandra said.

Bloomberg cuddled his new wife in his arms. He puckered his lips. They kissed.

***

Two months later

Driving to the boat dock, Bloomberg called Milandra.

"Lovely, it's a late night tonight. I have a very important case. I need to have ready for tomorrow for court."

"See you when you get home. Be careful; there's supposed to be a storm."

Bloomberg made it to his destination. He hopped on his boat and sailed into the rippling waters of Lake Murray. Beaming lights glowed from homes surrounding the waters. He turned the engine off when he got to where he could view the Powells' family home. Inside a compartment, he pulled out a gold urn.

With the wind blowing, he did not open it. Instead, he stared at the urn and spoke. "Mr. Powell, your daughter-in-law is not living in your home. I've followed every instruction you left behind. I made your daughter-in-law think that you were still alive. I sent her the present made of cigars. The day your son and daughter-in-law moved into the house, I placed cigar tobacco all over their honeymoon bed. Sir, that was a lot of work. I heard it scared the devil out of her. She never stayed one night in your house." Bloomberg laughed. "It's one thing that I couldn't follow, and that's getting revenge on Milandra for losing your property and bank. I've always had a thing for her. I felt sorry for her and gave her the cash you instructed me to hold on to, to give your son, in case he ever divorced Aniyah. I think it's time, Mr. Powell. It's been a journey. I'm letting your daughter-in-law be free of you haunting her. Let her and your son enjoy life with their kid."

Attorney Bloomberg checked his surroundings. When

he saw the coast was clear of boaters, he opened the urn, sprinkling the ashes into the water. "Rest in Peace, Mr. Powell."

The waves picked up.

"Calm down, Powell."

Rain poured from the sky. Lightning flickered over his head.

Bloomberg raised his voice and repeated, "Calm down, Mr. Powell."

When Bloomberg turned the engine on, a bright fiery light came down on him, striking him until he fell to the boat's floor, hitting his head. Blood gushed from his skull.

It did not take long before someone found Bloomberg dead in his boat. It horrified Milandra about the loss of her husband. She retrieved the empty urn from the boat. She assumed her husband had gone out on the waters to disperse Mr. Powell's remains. She checked the compartment and discovered the bill of sale from the delivery of the cigar arrangement.

Milandra was overwhelmed. "It was you scaring Aniyah."

Milandra never revealed her findings to anyone.

The Houston sisters went on to live their lives. Kenley never married. She continued to live with her boyfriend, Pete. Noelle and Sid's love was forever. They never had children. Elsa, the longtime housekeeper, passed away in her sleep.

Tessa stayed happily married to her attorney husband,

Baron Chavis. Nellie and Nolan finally got married with Aniyah as her matron of honor and Jarvis as Nolan's best man.

Aniyah never looked back on her downfalls. Instead she found the happiness she always wanted with her son, husband and Aunt Tessa. She continued to show the world that she was a better person.

ABOUT THE AUTHOR

Christine Young-Robinson is a wife, mother of two children, and grandmother of two grandchildren. She resides in South Carolina. When she isn't penning new sizzling reads, she's putting her years of creativity to use as the Co-Chairperson of the Eleuthera Book Club. Please do not hesitate to email her at miraclewriter4u@aol.com and share your thoughts and views. Follow her on social media. On Facebook and Twitter: @christineyr, and Instagram: christineyoungrobinson